HER COLORADO FIREFIGHTER

ELIZA D. COLLINS

ISBN-13: 978-1-335-46045-5

Her Colorado Firefighter

For questions and comments about the quality of this book, please contact us at CustomerService@Harlequin.com.

Harlequin Enterprises ULC
22 Adelaide St. West, 41st Floor
Toronto, Ontario M5H 4E3, Canada
www.Harlequin.com

HarperCollins Publishers
Macken House, 39/40 Mayor Street
Dublin 1, D01 C9W8, Ireland
www.HarperCollins.com

Printed in U.S.A.

“I see why they wanted this spot for the wedding,” Sienna said, taking in the views.

Blanca towered majestically behind the cabin and a hundred-mile stretch of the Sangre de Cristo range wound away to the north.

Troy leaned against a post on the porch and watched Sienna as she walked into the field, wandering to both sides of the cabin as she mapped the wedding in her head and pointed out the possible locations for the various elements. She moved with the grace of a mountain lion through the tall grass. He guessed she could be as fierce as one, too.

“It really is beautiful,” she said, turning back to him, looking impressed.

Framed against the grass around her and the mountain range behind, her dark hair drifting in the light breeze and a smile lighting up her face, he could say the same about her. *Beautiful* might not even be a strong enough word. *Stunning.* She hypnotized him so he couldn’t look away.

Dear Reader,

Welcome back to Tillacos Creek Ranch!

While Burgess and Tillacos Creek Ranch are fictional places, many towns and landmarks in this series are not. Alamosa is real, though many elements of the town are fictionalized—for instance, that the town has three fire stations with full-time, paid firefighters working twenty-four-hour shifts. In fact, Alamosa, like many small towns, has an entirely volunteer department, with no wildland firefighting team and only two stations for approximately 10,000 residents.

In my distant youth, I worked a number of years as a paramedic for a private San Diego ambulance company that stationed their units in the city fire stations. I've worked shoulder to shoulder with firefighters and, in Colorado, hiked the Storm King Memorial Trail where fourteen wildland firefighters lost their lives in the South Canyon Fire. I understand firsthand the importance of paid fire departments and ambulance crews. If you ever have the chance to support your local first responders through funding measures, I hope you will. They're all heroes.

Best,

Eliza

Award-winning author **Eliza D. Collins** writes heartfelt and heartwarming romance with characters you'll want to fall in love with. She shares plenty in common with her Tillacos Creek Ranch characters, living in rural southern Colorado with her West Texas cowboy husband and their menagerie of horses, dogs, chickens and various strays who adopt them. Look for news of her Tillacos Ranch Romance series on Instagram @elizadcollins or sign up for her newsletter at her website, elizadcollins.com.

Books by Eliza D. Collins

Harlequin Heartwarming

A Tillacos Ranch Romance

Her Colorado Cowboy

Visit the Author Profile page at Harlequin.com.

To dispatchers and first responders everywhere,
thank you.

Acknowledgments

Many thanks to my fellow year-one RAMP group for their continued support and camaraderie, and especially to fellow authors Caragh Leon, Evie Jacobs and Victoria Logan for their help and feedback during the writing of this book. Thank you again to my agent, Stephany Evans, and a big thanks to my editor, Dana Grimaldi, for all you do

CHAPTER ONE

Thursday, July 23rd

SIENNA HUNG UP her phone, extracted the needle-sharp claws from the calf of her jeans and lifted the mewing black-and-gray-striped bundle of energy. "Sorry, baby. Looks like my mom's latest crisis means no booster shots for you today."

She hustled into the bathroom with Tiger and plopped him on his favorite fuzzy blanket where she'd set up the space between the toilet and the bathtub with toys, food, water and a litterbox. The kitten swiped at her hair, catching a claw full, and tried to put it in his mouth. Bent double, she pried herself loose.

"Why? Why did I bring one more thing into my life that I need to be responsible for?" Tiger stared back at her with large green eyes. She gave him a soft nose boop. "Because you're so darn cute. That's why."

That, and because her best friend Kelli Hinton guilted her into taking the kitten when one of her veterinary clients found it alone and dehydrated under their front porch. Sienna placed a kiss on his head and closed the bathroom door.

Moving at a trot, she grabbed her purse from its place by the mail bowl near the front door. A sigh escaped her at the sight of Tiger's carrying crate at the ready on the floor. It felt like the whole day had stumbled and caught its balance a bit to the left of where it should have been. She couldn't help it. An aversion to last-minute changes was in her DNA, engraved on her nerves, just like her dad. Sienna had built her life on a concrete foundation of organization and planning, and her mother was the wrecking-ball driver doing donuts in the parking lot for fun.

She speed-dialed the vet clinic and hurried out to her car. Kelli's vet tech and sole employee answered. "San Luis Valley Veterinary."

"Hi, Rikki, it's Sienna. Is Kelli available?"

"She is. Just a minute."

"Hey, Sienna," Kelli said a moment later. "Everything okay?"

"No. Definitely not okay. I need to reschedule Tiger. My mom broke down somewhere on the way to Alamosa."

"Did she run out of gas again?"

"No. I think her engine might be on fire. At least, that's how she made it sound. I asked her if the oil had been changed since Uncle Marco did it for her when he visited more than a year ago, and she had no idea. Hold on a sec…" Sienna started her car and set her phone in the dash cradle, waiting for the Bluetooth to connect. "Anyway, I told her to call 911 to get the fire department and state patrol on the way. I'm taking off now to pick her up and help her get the car towed."

"Seriously? How do you forget that your car needs oil?"

"Why ask why? This is my mom we're talking about. I swear, I don't even understand how she navigates through life." She shifted into reverse and backed out of her driveway.

"Because she has you."

"I guess. No wonder my brothers stayed in New Mexico. At least her latest crisis happened on my day off."

"Well," Kelli said, "I was going to tell you my big news when you got here, but I guess I'll have to tell you over the phone."

"What big news?" She'd driven three blocks through town and now turned left onto the nearly empty two-lane highway.

"Cole and I decided to move the wedding up."

"It did seem a bit close to Christmas. What's the new date?"

An uncomfortable pause followed, then a hesitant, "August 15th."

Sienna nearly slammed on the brakes in reflex. “What? That’s like three weeks from now.” Her mind spun with the logistics involved. “What… Why?”

“Buttons is ready for you,” came a voice in the background of Kelli’s phone. “Annual physical.”

Kelli murmured, “I’ll fill you in later.”

This didn’t have the sound of exciting news. “Is everything okay?”

“Yes and no.”

Sienna furrowed her brow. “That’s not much to go on.”

“I know. But Mrs. Duma’s dachshund is waiting for me, so I’ll talk to you tonight.”

“I hope Buttons appreciates the fact that I’m playing second fiddle to a dachshund,” Sienna said, resigned to the fact that she wouldn’t be getting any more information until Kelli’s workday ended. “All right. I’m calling you at five o’clock sharp.”

“Good luck with your mom,” Kelli said.

“Thanks, I’ll need it.”

TEN MILES DOWN Colorado Highway 160, almost exactly halfway between her tiny town of Burgess and the marginally larger town of Alamosa, Sienna spotted her mom’s fifteen-year-old Hyundai on the shoulder of the road. A sporty red convertible parked in front of it, top down, pulled onto the highway just before Sienna reached them. Strands of flame-red hair fluttered over the passenger seat headrest.

"What the what…" Sienna muttered.

She parked where the sports car had been. The Hyundai's hood stood propped open and puffs of light gray smoke drifted from the engine like mini smoke signals for help. She dialed her mom's cell number.

"…just going to call you," her mother said, already talking when the call connected. The wind from the open convertible nearly obscured her words. "I hope you haven't left home yet. Dan has taken care of everything."

Well of course she'd already left home. Her mom said she was stranded on the highway with her car on fire. Sienna had been on her way in three minutes flat.

"Who in the world is Dan?"

"My knight in shining armor. He pulled over to help right after you hung up. He already called a tow truck, and he's taking me to brunch downtown while the shop checks out the car. He said he'll drop me at work if it isn't ready when we're done."

"Mama, is this someone you know?"

"Well, I do now, don't I?" Sienna could almost hear her mother wink at *Dan*. "And he told me his *ex*-wife used to forget to change the oil in her car too."

She said the last bit like she was speaking in secret code, but the only thing Sienna keyed in on was that her mom had the emphasis on the wrong word in the sentence.

"I think you mean to say he *told* you he has an ex-wife. Meaning he wants you to believe he's divorced. Meaning—"

"You sound like your father, dear. We'll have to work on that cynicism. Then maybe you'll finally meet your own knight in shining armor."

Sienna sighed. There was no way to win an argument with someone who thought "common sense" was a monetary denomination. Besides, Sienna hated it when her mother compared her to her hypercritical, detail-obsessed father. Okay, she took after her dad more than her mom, but only in that she and her dad were both sensible and logical. And organized. And, yes, detail oriented, but that went with being organized. "Where are you going to lunch?"

"So you can join us and check him out? Don't worry, sweetie. I'm fine. If it makes you feel better, he's the financial aid director at the college."

"What about your car? Do I need to do anything? Remember, I start my three, twelve-hour shifts tomorrow. I won't be able to help you again until Monday."

"Dan looked at the engine, and he thinks it's going to be okay. I thought it was on fire, but he says it was only smoke and probably just needs an oil change and checkup. He knows the repair shop owner and thinks I'll have it back in a couple of hours. You just go on and do what you had planned today."

Too late for that.

"Call me when you get to work, okay?"

"Yes, dear," her mother said in an exaggerated manner before signing off.

Just to be sure, Sienna pulled up the main number for Adams State College and asked the operator for the financial aid department. When the receptionist answered, Sienna requested to speak with "Dan, the financial aid director." She was told he'd called in a few minutes earlier to say he'd been delayed and wouldn't be in until after lunch. Only slightly less worried, Sienna flipped on her indicator, made a U-turn and headed back toward Burgess.

Trying to power wash the whole exchange with her mother from her brain, she focused on her other disaster today. *Three weeks until the wedding.*

With Kelli's and Cole's work schedules, Sienna was going to have to step up big time, because there was no way she was letting her best friend's wedding day be anything less than perfect. She'd made a solemn pinky swear to that effect back in junior high when she and Kelli had promised to be each other's maids of honor. Sienna had taken it a step further, vowing to plan the best wedding *ever* for her friend. Yes, it had been a promise made when she was eleven, but she intended to keep it. To be honest, she'd looked forward to this for years. Planning had always been her forte, and besides, Kelli was far too busy and humble to aim for spectacular on her own behalf. But now, with only three weeks to pull this off, she was going to need more than just Kelli and Cole to take care of the things only the bride and groom could do—she was going to need the best man to step up as well.

She'd need to call Cole's brother as soon as she got home so they could start planning. Based on her one and only encounter with Troy last month, the thought of needing his help would have been worrying even with months to prepare. Working with him under a tight timeline might prove more challenging than trying to get her mother to schedule routine car maintenance. Some people just weren't great at adulting.

They'd only met in person once, even though she kinda-sorta worked with Troy—if a 911 dispatcher talking to a firefighter over the radio counted as working together. But he'd been less than impressive on the day they'd both helped

Kelli move the large-animal portion of her practice to Cole's ranch. Charming, yes. Attractive, definitely. Helpful, not so much.

When Troy had actually worked, he'd been great, but the memories that stood out were the other ones. First, he'd flirted with her when she arrived instead of unloading her car—something Sienna had overlooked longer than she should have due to him being a tall fireman with a killer mischievous grin—and a few minutes later she'd overheard him on the phone with his girlfriend. Nice. Nothing made one feel "oh, so special" like the cute guy chatting you up turning out to be a player. After that, instead of taking twenty or thirty minutes to pick up the pizza they'd ordered for lunch, he'd been gone an hour and a half. Meanwhile, the rest of them got progressively hungrier and moved the majority of the boxes and heavy equipment without him.

She chewed her lip and told herself it would be fine, and it wasn't like she'd fall for his flirty act again. Besides, he'd worked seven years for the Alamosa Fire Department; he had to be at least somewhat responsible, right?

Right?

CHAPTER TWO

Saturday, July 25th

TROY POURED HIS sixth cup of ink-black fire station coffee into his oversize Hello Kitty mug and lifted the cup to his lips. His cell phone rang. He glanced at the screen, hit ignore and slid the phone back into its case at his belt.

His shift captain, "Mac" MacLoughlin, looked up from his paperwork spread across the long kitchen table. He lifted one thick eyebrow. "Sienna again?"

"Yep."

There ought to be a manual for best men, Troy thought. Maybe after the wedding he'd write one and make a fortune helping other hapless men navigate matrimonial minefields. He'd be sure to devote an entire chapter to the horrors of working with the maid of honor.

Cole and Kelli's wedding was still nearly a month away. In the past twenty-four hours, he'd received four calls from Sienna about them getting together to plan everything from seating charts to decorations. It might as well have been a list of everything he knew jack-all about and he'd let each call go to voice mail. And besides, someone telling him what to do and how to do it meant they were sure to be disappointed with him no matter what he did. He'd learned long ago that trying to live up to other people's expectations only made everyone miserable. He should just be called the worst man. If the field at the wedding site caught on fire, he'd be all over it. Short of that, his little brother and the bride-to-be would just have to accept that wedding planning wasn't his forte.

The nonemergency landline rang in the front office.

"Better get that by the third ring, Bouncer," Troy said, walking through the kitchen arch to the bullpen, the station's communal living room.

The trainee had already been in motion when Troy prodded him, but it was fun having a probationary firefighter to needle now and then. After all—like firefighters everywhere—Troy had endured his own rites of passage his first year on the job.

Bouncer made it from the bullpen to the front office in time to catch the phone on the second ring. "Station 2, firefighter trainee Singh speaking."

Troy sat in one of the recliners with his coffee in one hand and the magazine Bouncer had been reading in the other. The overhead PA crackled. Bouncer's voice blared through the station. "Troy Tyler, personal phone call from Sienna Herrera on line one. She needs to talk to you about wedding arrangements but says she's been trying since yesterday and you won't answer your cell phone."

Bouncer found his own ways to get back—like his joke gift of the Hello Kitty mug after an emergency call that Troy would never live down. It was all part of the game.

Troy hurried into the office and grabbed the phone from the grinning plebe's hand. "Thank you," he said, deadpan. He lifted the receiver to his ear. "Hey, Sienna, what's up?"

She skipped the pleasantries. "Why haven't you returned my calls? I got your text Thursday that you were working, but the incident logs show you had plenty of downtime. You texted yesterday that you were too busy on your day off and you'd give me a call in the evening, but you never did. Instead, I got another text promising me you'd call me at noon today, when I could talk on my lunch break."

"Yeah, sorry about that. I was helping Cole on the ranch yesterday and today has kept us hopping."

"You do know I can see your engine has sat in the station since ten forty-nine, right? Three hours straight. Right over my lunch break."

Just his luck, she must be working fire dispatch today. It had been a light bulb moment for him when he'd first met her and made the connection between the 911 dispatcher's voice he heard over the radio and Kelli's stunning best friend—a tall, dark-haired, dark-eyed beauty.

Dispatch for police and fire was housed in the police department's admin building, inside a security-code-locked office. In all his years with the Alamosa Fire Department, Troy had only been inside dispatch once, back during his orientation tour, three years before she'd started working there. He hadn't put two and two together until the day they'd both helped Kelli move her livestock hospital to the ranch.

"Oh, right," he said, trying to come up with an excuse on the spot. "It was my turn to cook for the crew today, and I guess I got busy and forgot." He sounded lame even to himself.

Bouncer leaned back in the office chair, grinning up at him, fingers clasped across his stomach. He didn't even pretend not to listen.

Sienna sighed and continued in an overly reasonable voice. "Personal phones aren't allowed to be on in the dispatch room. I have exactly one minute left for my break and then it's off till seven. My best friend is marrying your brother three weeks from today. They've got enough to do without having to shoulder the things we can help with. Seriously, Troy, I need to get together with you in person and make a plan."

"Yes, ma'am," he said, putting on his best country-boy manners. "Tell you what, my six days off start tomorrow. You name the night, and I'll take you out for dinner so we can talk."

He heard the clicks of a numerical door lock, followed by the murmurings of multiple dispatchers and radio transmissions.

"All right," she said, resignation replacing the frustration in her voice. "Tomorrow, then. I'll be coming from work, so let's say 7:15 p.m. Do you know where…" She gave an exasperated huff. "Denise is pointing to my phone. She's forwarding a call to me. I've got to go. I'll text you later." The call disconnected.

Troy scowled at Bouncer, still grinning up at him.

The station's alarm blared three long tones from the overhead speakers. Sienna's voice came over the PA, professional now and smooth as silk. "Engine 2, respond to a man down, possible cardiac arrest. One-seven-one…"

Troy's own heart skipped a beat at the words "cardiac arrest," and he realized he'd missed part of the address that had followed. Pulling a notepad from his shirt pocket, he spared a glance at Bouncer to see if his face had given him away, but the trainee jogged to the garage bay without a second look. Sienna repeated the information, as dispatchers always did, and he filled in the missing bits.

Bouncer suited up in his turnout jacket and helmet, then hopped on the back of the truck and clipped in. Captain Mac emerged from the kitchen and walked briskly to the passenger side of the engine. Jan hustled from the bunkroom and took her place in the back jump seat. As the engineer, Troy climbed into the driver's seat. He hit the remote to open the big garage bay door, did a quick instrument check, flipped on the emergency lights, pulled out to the end of the driveway and turned on the siren. He blared the air horn once and spun the large steering wheel to guide the thirty-five-foot fire truck onto the street, keeping an eye out for Bouncer when the back wheels hit the gutter.

Troy had been the one to dub Brett Singh with his nickname. Brett's first day on the job, he'd kept his knees too stiff when the truck went through a big dip, and he'd bounced right off the running board. Spotting his feet flying in the side mirror had nearly given Troy a stroke. A good grip on the hand bar and the belt around

Brett's waist saved him from falling or getting hurt, but the nickname had stuck.

Jan had entered the address into a touch-screen tablet containing downloaded city maps. She told Troy to turn right at the next street, but he already had his indicator on. At just over ten thousand people, Alamosa was one of the largest towns in far Southern Colorado and boasted an odd mix of college students, generational ranchers, legalized marijuana dispensaries, chain stores and small businesses. It was also small enough that Troy knew nearly every street by heart—even here, in the little warren of cross streets between downtown and Adams State College.

A car pulled out from the curb and stopped halfway into the street, like a rabbit spotting a coyote and not knowing whether to run or stay still. He navigated around it, scanning for traffic lights, turn signals, brake lights and pedestrians. His hands ached, and he realized he held the steering wheel in clenched fists. Emergency response was second nature to him after all these years; it was the words "possible cardiac arrest" that had wound him tight as a spool of fence wire.

He forced his hands to relax, but his thoughts tugged him back seven months to the January day when he'd found his father on the floor of the hay barn. There'd been no pulse or respirations. The family's 3600-acre ranch lay fifteen minutes from Burgess and even farther from the hospital in Alamosa. Troy had performed CPR by himself for nearly twenty minutes on a body growing progressively stiffer and colder. And when the local volunteer ambulance had shown up, he'd gotten in the back of the rig with the volunteers and continued to trade off on respirations and compressions for another twenty minutes until his father was pronounced dead by the emergency room physician in Alamosa.

It had taken two months after the funeral for the daily questions in his head to slow to more occasional what-ifs: What if he'd gone looking ten minutes earlier when his father was late coming in for dinner? What if his father had asked their ranch foreman, Dustin, to move the hay bales instead of sending him off to help the wranglers feed the herd?

What if—for once—Troy had offered to help his dad out with the evening farm chores?

Turning left, he saw a police car halfway down the block and parked in the street in front of it. He would have preferred to see the ambulance, but they hadn't arrived yet. Bouncer grabbed the med kit, Jan brought the Automatic External Defibrillator, and the four of them headed inside.

The police officer in the living room pointed

down the hall. "Patient is Roberto Pérez. Wife is Maria."

Mac, as usual, stayed in the living room with the police officer. Nearing retirement now, his captain had said frequently that if he'd wanted to practice medicine, he would've become a doctor.

"The bathroom," Mac said under his breath as Troy passed him. "It's always the bathroom."

A woman, probably in her seventies, stood at the end of the hall. She wore a dark navy dress printed with tiny pink flowers. It fell to her knees over dark stockings and heavy black shoes. Salt-and-pepper black hair was pulled back in a bun, and her hands were tightly clasped over her thick waist. Her face was a picture of worry and sorrow that clutched at Troy's heart.

He felt an elbow in his ribs as Jan pushed ahead of him and squeezed in with Bouncer next to the unconscious patient on the floor. Even though Jan had been the one to put their struggling three-year relationship out of its misery a couple of months ago, she'd been at his side for his father's funeral in January, just like she'd been there for the aftershocks over the following months. She was the only person who knew how these cardiac calls affected him. He hadn't even talked about it with Cole.

She dropped to her knees and checked for pulse and respirations. Troy vividly recalled the sensation of his father's chest under his hands as he did compressions, the feel and sound of the rib that broke before the ambulance showed up.

"He's breathing and he has a pulse," Jan said. Troy let out a sigh of relief. "The pulse feels irregular. We better hook him up."

Bouncer opened the AED and handed her the pads. He pushed the on button, and the digitized voice of the defibrillator machine walked them through the rest of the process. The AED confirmed a viable heartbeat. No CPR or defibrillation needed.

Troy said a few supportive words to Mrs. Pérez and explained what the other two firefighters were doing, then asked about her husband's medical history and what had taken place prior to their arrival. She answered in heavily accented English with a few words of Spanish sprinkled in. He asked if she preferred Spanish. She relaxed when he switched, then gave him more detailed information.

High school language classes and two semesters in college had given Troy a foundation in conversational Spanish, but constant practice at work had made him fluent. An essential skill in a town forty-five minutes from the New Mexico border with a population that was nearly 50 percent Hispanic.

A siren grew closer, then shut off. A moment

later, the paramedics from the hospital's private ambulance company entered. Troy filled them in on the history he'd obtained and the vitals Jan had taken. The medics took over, removing the AED pads and hooking the patient to an electrocardiogram monitor. Jan and Bouncer assisted the medics, then helped with the awkward process of extracting the patient from the bathroom, loading him onto a backboard to lift him out of the small room to the gurney and navigating the gurney through the narrow rooms of the old house.

"Always the bathroom," the captain said again to Troy while the others wheeled the patient out and lifted the gurney down the front steps. "Smallest room in the whole house."

As long as it wasn't a CPR case, Troy thought. He wondered how many months or years it was going to take him to overcome the memories haunting him. He used to pride himself on his CPR skills and his professional detachment. These days, he felt anything but detached.

CHAPTER THREE

Sunday, July 26th

SIENNA GLANCED AT the clock in the bottom corner of her work computer. Ten minutes more and her twelve-hour shift would be over. She'd be off for the next three days. There was a burger with her name on it at one of her favorite restaurants, and—though Troy had been evasive and challenging the past few days—they would finally be getting together to work on the wedding. Also, dinner with a blond-haired, blue-eyed firefighter sure beat fast food while driving or leftovers by herself at home—especially now that she'd made a few inquiries and learned that Troy and his firefighter girlfriend had broken up two months ago. Meaning they'd split up a couple of weeks before that day he'd been flirting with her when she'd helped Kelli move her stuff. Also meaning maybe he was a little less problematic than she'd thought.

Her relief dispatcher arrived right on time but

there were a surprising number of calls in progress for a Sunday evening. By the time she got Marty up to speed, she had nine minutes to get to the restaurant. The last thing she needed was to show up late after implying that Troy had been unreliable.

She hustled to her car, made the short drive to the restaurant and scooted inside the front door a minute and a half before their 7:15 p.m. meeting time. Waiting to be seated, she scanned the few customers there but didn't spot Troy. She'd hurried to be here on time after work. He'd had the entire day off and hadn't shown yet. This didn't bode well.

The hostess seated her in a booth facing the front of the restaurant. Sienna held off ordering a drink and watched the clock above the register tick past 7:20. At 7:25, she broke her staredown when it brought back shades of checking the school's hallway clock, waiting for her late-again mother to pick her up. She pulled her wedding to-do list from her purse and studied the sheet. She'd prioritized it by importance, color-coded it and subheaded it with deadlines for each item. Her father would have glowed with pride. Her mother would have laughed.

There was *so much* to do and so little time. Thanks to Kelli and Cole's whirlwind romance, Cole's proposal had come only two months after they'd started dating. No one had batted an eye at the speed of the commitment. They were perfect for each other, and like Kelli had said, they knew from the beginning that they'd be together forever, so why wait. But moving their Christmas wedding to mid-August had been a surprise. They were telling people a summer wedding would be better for weather and travel, and would allow them to have an outdoor ceremony. But after her talk with Kelli the other night, Sienna learned the real reason—one that few others knew. Maybe not even Troy.

She glanced reflexively at the clock again, then looked at the number of things assigned to Troy and sighed. Sienna's whole life, on duty and off, revolved around being organized, while Troy struck her as the classic caveman type: *Need food, must hunt. Sleep now.* A leave-the-seat-up kind of guy. And the worst: a "Don't worry, it'll be fine" guy. Sienna had enough on her plate with her mother's flightiness; she had no patience left over for disorganized, laissez-faire men. She was mentally shuffling how many of Troy's tasks she could shoulder on top of her own when he walked in. She muttered a few colorful adjectives, but all the while her interest in him betrayed her.

He wore an olive-green, lightweight pullover shirt that outlined the lean muscles of his shoulders, torso and arms. The sleeves were pushed up nearly to his elbows and the three buttons at the neck were undone. The shirt was untucked over standard-issue blue jeans, and he rounded out the image of classic masculinity with a well-worn pair of brown cowboy boots.

At nearly five-eleven herself, thanks to her father's Spanish ancestry and some tall relatives on her mother's side, Sienna could appraise most men's height to the centimeter. The day they'd moved Kelli's clinic stuff she'd judged him a solid six-three in sneakers. Those boots would push him to nearly six-five. A flush of warmth bloomed in the pit of her stomach as she imagined being wrapped in his embrace. What it would feel like to press the side of her face into Troy's shoulder instead of the side of a shorter date's head. To tip her mouth *up* for a kiss. To wear heels without worrying about emasculating some guy.

Troy spotted her and broke into an easy grin that accented his handsome features. The heat in her belly spread through her like ink in a glass of water. Her spirits rose as he threaded his way to the booth. Maybe it wasn't his fault he was late. Maybe there'd been an emergency at the ranch or an accident on the highway.

"Sorry if I kept you waiting," he said, sliding

onto the bench across from her. "I got a phone call as I was heading out the door."

And just like that the melty feeling inside her cooled.

"It's too bad no one's invented some kind of portable phone." She refrained from rolling her eyes. He was only a few minutes late and, besides, she really did need his help. "It's okay. I appreciate you driving into town to get together with me tonight."

The waiter appeared and took their drink orders. They both ordered the same beer.

The waiter left and Troy pointed to the piece of paper tucked under the edge of her purse. Only the top half showed, covered in her small, neat writing and checkerboarded with color. He raised his eyebrows. "Is that the list?" She thought she detected mild panic in his voice.

She'd planned to ease into it, but best just to come clean now. "Look, I know I committed us both to a lot, but Kelli is my best friend. I've promised to help plan her wedding since seventh grade. It's important to me that this day is perfect for her, and if you knew what she'd been through with her other boyfriends, you'd understand why." She fingered the edge of the list, hoping she was getting through to him. "Even without my promise to her, she and Cole really need our help. They're both strapped for time, and they're paying for everything themselves. Between veterinary school and the start-up costs for her clinic, Kelli is buried in debt, and I'm sure Cole's money is tied up in the ranch. They can't afford to hire out the work, and they certainly can't afford a wedding planner. The more you and I can do for them, the better."

Sienna had thought Kelli hit the jackpot when she started dating Cole. The ranch he'd taken over when old Ben Tyler died was the largest cattle operation in Southern Colorado, and she'd grown up believing the Tylers were rich. Kelli had popped that bubble. Apparently, the larger the ranch, the more likely the owners were "land poor." Family money went to the property, buildings, livestock and equipment. Fertilizer, water bills, salaries and the cattle purchases and losses soaked up most of the summer and fall income. Spring and winter were all about money going out instead of coming in. Daydreams of Kelli throwing fancy shindigs at the ranch where Sienna could meet wealthy ranchers' sons had dwindled to accepting the fact that an occasional kegger with the locals was going to be as good as it got.

"I understand what you're trying to do," Troy said. "I want them to have a great wedding too, but they've said they want to keep it small and simple. Maybe it's best if we don't go overboard, yeah?" He tapped the edge of her list and smiled again. She liked the way it crinkled the corners of his eyes.

But no, he didn't get it.

"Even just getting married at the county courthouse takes planning. You have to reserve the date for someone to officiate, get a license before and a certificate after, pick out the clothes, arrange for witnesses… And this wedding isn't that small. They have nearly fifty people coming, not counting the wedding party. There's seating, decorations, food, the band, bridesmaids' and groomsmens' clothes, a rehearsal dinner, the bachelor party and a dozen other things to see to. There's no way they'll be able to pull it off without a lot of help from us."

She watched his smile fade as he realized his charm and good looks weren't going to get him out of anything.

"Look at it this way, helping to plan their wedding is part of my gift to them. And it can be yours too, if you want. But their jobs aren't nine-to-five like ours." He raised his eyebrows.

"Okay. I work twelve-hour shifts and you work twenty-four and we have weird days off. We have stressful jobs and crazy schedules. But, if you do the math, over a month's time, we average around forty hours a week. A bit more for you, but you're asleep at night when you're not out on a call. Cole probably puts in that many hours by Wednesday, and he works seven days a week, every week. Kelli works long days *plus* nights on call, and also six or seven days a week a lot of the time. And with your parents gone and Kelli's parents not able to afford much, this is something big we can do to help them. In fact, there's so much to do, I don't know how all four of us can get it done in time."

Troy's face tightened, and she hoped she hadn't lost ground with him.

Cole and Kelli had taken care of more than just the invitations and, fortunately, she and Kelli had picked out the dress in early June—a gift from Kelli's parents. A beautiful western-style wedding dress she'd wanted instead of the ivory cocktail dress she'd planned to get from a department store. And if this wedding didn't take place soon, there was a chance that Kelli's dad may never see her in it. A small chance, but still… He'd retired early from state patrol a couple of years ago due to a heart attack, but his heart muscle had been damaged and was getting progressively weaker. Now, his doctor was insisting on open-heart surgery to place a heart pump in the ventricle, but his heart failure made the procedure high risk. Apparently, eclipsing concern for himself, her father's chief worry was that he might not get to walk his daughter down the aisle. And so, Kelli and Cole had moved the wedding to three days before his surgery date.

The waiter brought their drinks and asked if they were ready to order. Sienna had been ready since picking this restaurant yesterday. She didn't even look at the menu.

"Black and blue burger with onion rings instead of fries."

Troy glanced up from his menu, interested. She pointed it out to him. "Blackened Cajun spice, crumbled blue cheese, bacon and Southwest sauce."

"Put me down for one of those too," he said.

The waiter gathered their menus and headed for the kitchen.

With their meal ordered, her mind boomeranged back to the list of wedding logistics she'd rattled off to him. Until she had a sudden, awful thought.

"Hey, speaking of the band, Kelli told me the lead singer is a friend of yours. Are they confirmed for the new date? 'Cause that would be a major hurdle if we need to book a different band on three weeks' notice."

"Uh, yeah. About that. That was actually the phone call I got on my way here." He fiddled with his beer glass. "Chris said they broke up a couple of days ago. Some fight over money or something." The vessels in Sienna's neck burned as her blood pressure probably doubled. "Don't worry," he said. "I already took care of it. I know a local rodeo clown—Joe Fitzpatrick, you know him? He's super funny. I called and he's available. It'll be great."

She pursed her lips and narrowed her eyes at him, catching on despite his flawless deadpan.

"Yes, they know," he said with a small chuckle, saving her from her impending stroke. "I put Kelli in touch with Chris ages ago. I heard her on the phone confirming the date change with him the other day."

"Jerk," Sienna said, hiding her smile in her beer glass.

"All right. Let me see this list of Herculean tasks." Troy reached to pull it from beneath her purse. The fine hairs on her arm raised in gooseflesh when his bare forearm brushed her lightly as he grabbed it. He scanned the list and winced.

His attitude and his track record so far had her spooked. What could she possibly entrust to him that wouldn't ruin some part of the wedding if he failed?

"How come my stuff is in pink?"

"It was the closest I could get to fire-engine red and still see the writing," she lied. In truth, it had been a harmless retaliation when she'd spent two days trying to get him to call her back.

Her own color was orange, of course. Sienna, after all.

He leaned against the back of the booth, still reading, then looked at her. His sky-blue eyes held a puppy-dog helplessness before the look shifted to something a tiny bit wicked.

"You know I'm going to be inept at half the things you've given me."

"Troy, there's no way I can get all this done without—"

"Hear me out," he said, holding up a hand to stop her objection. "What if we do these together? I know it won't be as fast as splitting up the tasks, but think how much it'll slow things down if you don't like what I pick out or how I do something, and then it needs to be redone. And if I have to get samples or estimates and run them past you, it'll still be slow. Besides, it'll be more fun together."

Having fun and getting out of responsibility were starting to look like his hallmarks, but he did have a point. She had just been thinking that she could see herself needing to double-check everything he did. She chewed her lip, then took a swig of her beer. It wouldn't be as efficient as splitting the list, but some things *would* be easier with the two of them together. Besides, a little extra time spent in the company of a tall, gorgeous and verified-single man was not altogether a bad thing.

Their food showed up, giving her a moment to consider the proposition. "You have five more days off, right?" she said once the waiter left.

"Right."

"I only have Monday, Tuesday and Wednesday this week, but we can probably knock out some of the most pressing things if you're willing to put in the time."

"Okay. I can put off my own errands until Thursday, when you go back to work. I'm all yours until then."

She eyed him, wondering if he'd intentionally loaded that statement.

"Deal," she said, reaching across the table.

"Deal," he said, giving her a firm handshake.

"So how long have you known Kelli?" he asked, picking up his burger, clearly marking the end of wedding planning for now.

She'd wanted to move on to sorting out what tasks they would get done each day. In the spirit of working together, though, she decided to make a show of getting to know him better.

"My mom moved us here from Albuquerque at the start of junior high, after she and my dad divorced. It was the same year Cole switched schools, so Kelli had just lost her best friend and I'd arrived in town not knowing anybody. She and I have been best buds ever since, even while she was away at college up in Fort Collins."

"I was three years ahead at Burgess Elementary, so I never really knew either of you. I vaguely remember Kelli through her connection to Cole, but I didn't really get to know her until Cole started using her as the ranch vet this past April."

"And you have an older brother too, right?" Troy nodded his answer since he'd just taken another big bite of his burger. "I've never met Lane," she said. "Will he be coming to the wedding?"

He shook his head and downed a swig of beer. "Wow. That really is good."

She smiled. The atmosphere of a restaurant meant nothing to her, but good food was everything. For the times she couldn't do the cooking herself, she'd long ago ferreted out the best food in a hundred-mile radius.

"No," he said, taking a break from wolfing down his supper to answer her question. "Lane was in Dubai for the past year and just moved to Singapore last month. Cole called him to let him know the new wedding date, but he said he won't be able to get away on such short notice."

"Kelli said she wasn't exactly sure what it is he does."

"Nobody's exactly sure what he does. He

got a civil engineering degree and then a master's in international finance. He works all over the world. Something to do with large-scale city planning and finance that none of us mere mortals understand, but I think he makes more money than the rest of us put together." He started in on his onion rings. "And how about you? How'd you get into emergency dispatch?"

They'd nearly finished their beers and, while Sienna was no stranger to a drink or two in social situations, when she caught herself watching Troy a little too closely as he lifted another onion ring to his mouth, she knew she'd better slow down.

"Kelli's dad," she answered. "You know he's retired Colorado State Patrol, right?" Troy nodded. "I spent a lot of time at Kelli's house as a kid. We'd sneak into her parents' bedroom and listen to his police scanner and pretend we were the cops or superheroes or whatever. By the time I went to college, emergency services was pretty much a foregone conclusion. My dad's a university professor. He insisted I finish my degree, so I got it in communications, then went straight into dispatching." She didn't ask him about college. Through Kelli, she already knew that he'd dropped out from the local college after only a year or so.

She also knew through Kelli that Troy's father

had managed their huge ranch into his late sixties and held positions on the water board and city council. His mother had been a successful artist until her death five years ago from cancer. Cole had a bachelor's degree in ranch management and a master's degree in agricultural economics, and Kelli said he was shaping up to be a better rancher than all the previous Tylers. And now she'd learned that Lane was some big whoop-de-do in international business. It was surprising that the whole family could be so successful, and Troy was…well Troy.

Not that being a firefighter wasn't a dangerous and difficult and admirable job, but it seemed with the advantages that Troy had growing up, he would have wanted more than Alamosa had to offer. Sienna had stayed in Burgess to look out for her mom, but Troy seemed unconcerned about wanting more. That "good enough," and "it'll be fine" attitude again. It was too close to her mother's airy-fairy approach to everything, drifting through life and having no follow through for goals. Sienna knew all too well how that attitude spilled over into every aspect of life for the people close to them—being late, forgetting important tasks, not bothering with specifics so the fallout landed on someone else. Her father had railed against it for years before leaving.

Good enough. She'd better start mentally stamping it on Troy's forehead every time she looked at that blue-eyed boatload of charm. After all, this was the same man who'd blown her off for days, shown up late for dinner, and who would without question frustrate her beyond reason when they spent more than a few hours together. She most definitely didn't need another runaway train in her life that she'd constantly need to keep on the tracks.

The check came and Troy picked it up, waving her off as she reached for her wallet. She appreciated the gesture and snapped her purse shut. The waiter collected the bill and credit card. While Troy finished off the last of his beer, she brought the conversation back to the wedding.

"So, I have no idea what the wedding site looks like or what we'll need for decorations. I think that'll be the best thing to start on tomorrow morning."

"Okay." He set his glass down and paused, then gave her an amused smile. "Why don't you come out to the ranch around ten tomorrow, and I'll take you out there?"

She wasn't sure what that mischievous look was about. Maybe for trying out the ten o'clock start time to see her reaction?

"How about eight o'clock? Decorations aren't the only thing on our agenda."

His lips pursed. "Ten works better. I have some things to do in the morning."

Like sleep in? These next few days were going to be like herding a feral cat across a busy street.

"Nine," she suggested, compromising.

"Nine," he said with a wince.

The waiter returned for the credit card signature, and Sienna stood. "Thank you for dinner."

She grabbed her windbreaker from the hook on the booth. Troy stood as well and took the coat from her, holding it while she slipped her arms in. Just as she'd thought, with him in those boots, the top of her head came just below his chin.

"I'll see you tomorrow," he said.

Yes, he would. And he'd better be up and ready to work.

CHAPTER FOUR

Monday, July 27th

TROY WOKE WITH the light, as usual, but when he trundled downstairs at 6:30 a.m., barefoot and wearing a T-shirt and pajama bottoms, Cole and Kelli were already finishing breakfast. With their busy schedules, the pair carved out any time to be together they could, including breakfast at the ranch if she had a livestock patient to check on in the morning. Their long-term plan was for Kelli's small-animal clinic to remain in the converted outbuilding behind her home, but she'd rent her house out once she and Cole were married. They'd already shifted her large-animal practice to one of the secondary barns here. Besides making more sense for her clients than the two-stall shed and corral at her house, she'd also officially transitioned to being the veterinarian for the ranch.

The three of them navigated the necessary traffic patterns for Cole and Kelli's cleanup and

Troy's all-important mission to achieve his first cup of coffee of the day. They circled each other in wide orbits between the dishwasher, cabinets, refrigerator and coffee maker, while Cole's border collie and Kelli's giant shepherd mix were asteroids on collision courses with everyone. Cole had already appropriated the coffee maker, so Troy began with his setup: measuring out his special beans and grinding them.

After the years of quiet here—just Troy and his dad in the house—things had changed rapidly once his father died. Cole moved home from grad school that same month with his dog, Baxter, and five months later, Kelli and Cole were engaged. With the accelerated timeline for the wedding, things would be changing again in just a few weeks with Kelli and her dog moving into the house. And Troy would bet that children would follow soon.

Troy was fond of Kelli, and he'd always been one to roll with a situation, but it did get him thinking. Thirty years old, and this was the only home he'd ever known. Soon, the time would come to turn the house over to Cole and his new family. Not that Cole or Kelli would expect him to move out; it was simply the right thing to do.

His little brother's broad shoulders seemed uncharacteristically tight today. Cole stared into space, distracted, while he rinsed his and Kelli's plates and placed them in the dishwasher, per their housekeeper's rules.

"Busy day?" Troy asked.

"Mmm," Cole grunted, returning from wherever his mind had drifted. "All three hayfields came ready at the same time."

"I heard they're increasing the chance of rain next week," Kelli said, bringing Cole the frying pan they'd used.

The coffee maker hissed a slow stream of liquid into the pot. Cole's thermos sat beside it, ready. The aroma drifting through the kitchen on the steam lit up the pleasure and frustration centers equally in Troy's brain.

"I heard that too," his brother said. "I'm not sure what's worse. The risk of losing that hay to mold if I don't have it baled before it rains, or the rain passing us by again, and the drought and heat stunting the new growth for the next cutting." He threw a water bottle and two Ziploc bagged sandwiches into a daypack, then glanced up at Troy. "I could always use a hand if you're off today."

Troy debated the lesser of the two evils: working out in the pasture his whole day off or wedding planning with Sienna. It was close, but at least Sienna was more fun to look at than Cole.

"Sorry, Kelli's maid of honor has me busy for the next few days with your wedding stuff."

His brother's dark eyes lit with mischief.

"Think that's funny?" Troy asked.

"You wedding shopping with Sienna? Yes."

"Okay, you have a point, but it's not all bad. She's wound kinda tight, but still, a day with a beautiful woman..."

"Hey now," Kelli said from the front door where she was searching all her pockets, "that's my best friend you're talking about." She checked the mail basket next and started back through her jeans. "Has anyone seen my truck keys?"

Troy eyed the coffeepot again. Half full. He leaned back against the counter and waited.

"You gotta admit," Cole said to Kelli, "she's tall and she's fiery. Just Troy's type."

"Tall, yes. Fiery personality...okay, I'll give you that one," Kelli conceded. "Troy's type, though? Not in a million years."

"Like either of you'd know my type," Troy said, feeling slightly defensive now.

"Sure I do," Cole shot back. "You set me up with them when I moved back from Texas, remember? The string of wannabe models you picked out for me online? That Italian one, *fiery*."

"Babe," Kelli warned him, though Troy knew Cole had only reluctantly gone out with any of them, and then only on one dinner date each.

"Sorry, sweetie," Cole said. "You know there's

never been anyone for me but you." He bent and kissed her. Then kissed her again longer.

"That's better," she said.

"Don't worry," Troy assured her. "Your friend is safe with me. You ought to see the color-coded list she has for us." He frowned when Cole huffed a laugh. "It's no joke. It's terrifying."

He said it to be funny, but honestly, it *was* kinda terrifying. He hated people expecting things from him, and Sienna was going to be expecting *a lot*. What had he been thinking when he agreed to this? The hay crop was more important anyway, right? Even a couple hours of his time would help his brother out, then he'd have the rest of the day to work out and do some of the errands he needed to get done.

On the second search of her windbreaker hanging on her chair, Kelli exclaimed, "Found them!" She held her keys up and jangled them, grinning.

"You know, I met with Sienna last night and it sounds like she's got everything planned already," Troy said, warming to the idea. "It's still early. Maybe I should call and let her know you need help today."

"So Sienna can blame me?" Cole said. "No, thanks. Besides, I'd probably only get an hour or two out of you anyway."

Troy tried to keep his expression neutral, hiding the fact that Cole had just read his mind.

The coffee maker finally spit the last of the brew into the pot, steamed for a moment, gave a last dribble and fell quiet. Cole poured the entire pot into his thermos. Slinging his daypack over one shoulder, he pulled his trademark black Stetson hat from the coat stand and pushed it securely on his head. A high of ninety-six degrees predicted today, and Cole still wore all the cowboy trappings: checkered western shirt with jeans, boots and hat. A pair of leather gloves stuck out of his back pocket. Then again, Cole would look like a cowboy buck naked.

"If that Thoroughbred looks good this morning," Kelli said to Cole, "I'll probably send her home today. Unless I get another overnight patient, I might not see you for a day or two. That colic really did a number on my clinic schedule."

With a quick goodbye to Troy, they swirled out the door, still talking. The dogs followed: Baxter to put in a day's work on the ranch. Tillie—who'd been renamed from Millie to commemorate her upcoming new life here at Tillacos Creek Ranch—to accompany Kelli to her clinic or ranch visits or whatever else she had lined up. And that was that. Troy was stuck tagging along with Sienna today.

So, they both thought she was fiery, huh? She

certainly had a spark to her. He'd noticed it when they were moving Kelli's stuff last month, and again last night after a couple of beers when she'd finally quit talking about wedding plans.

Thinking of sparks, he'd meant to check this morning on that wildfire in Washington State. Last he'd heard, it was over sixty thousand acres. High winds were expected today, and he needed to stay abreast with how the crews were handling this one. The wildfire situation grew worse every year in the western US, and he'd been one of only eight firefighters in the Alamosa Fire Department to cross-certify for their new Wildland Fire Team.

He decided to grab his laptop from his bedroom before starting his coffee, so he could check on the fires while it brewed. Punching the power button on his computer before unplugging it, he found he'd left it on and it opened to the site he wanted. Sitting for a minute, he read the update, then pulled up a couple of national news stories on the fire, and then a newscast from Washington for more specifics. He followed the links to videos of the latest planning sessions that the department released to keep the community up to date and off the emergency services phone lines. Listening to the daily recorded taskforce meetings was the next best thing to being there in person. From there, he browsed the national incident website and checked on the couple of growing fires in Colorado, plus the ones in northern New Mexico. Engrossed in the stories and videos, he even forgot about starting his coffee.

The doorbell rang and he glanced at the clock on the computer.

"Oh, no."

Somehow, it was 8:58 a.m. already and, of course, Sienna was right on time.

It would be fine. It would only take him a few minutes to shower and grab the coffee and breakfast he'd missed. Anyway, they had all day. More than all day. Three days.

Coming down the stairs, he saw her through the window. She'd worn practical clothing, which was good as he hadn't warned her what he had in mind. Dark-blue skinny stretch jeans and her top, patterned in shades of turquoise, looked beautiful against her light brown skin and dark hair.

The doorbell rang a second time. She cupped her hand and peered in the window, her mouth tight when she spotted him on the stairs, still wearing his flannel pajama bottoms. The look hit him like a cold shower.

Yep. It was going to be a long three days.

CHAPTER FIVE

SIENNA RANG THE doorbell for the second time.

Honest to Pete, if he was still in bed she might have to kill him in his sleep, even if it meant doing everything for this wedding on her own. She peered through the window and saw him coming down the stairs barefoot and in a plain gray T-shirt and…and pajama pants! *Unbelievable.* He really had overslept. Even if he didn't care about the wedding or helping his brother, he could have at least shown a little respect for the fact she'd told him last night how important this was to her. And why the flippin' frogs did he have to look so cute all tousled and unshaven?

The door opened.

"Ready to get this show on the road?" she said, stepping back as if he'd follow her to her car right that minute. "If we can see the wedding site and get a list of decorations together in the next hour, we can be in Alamosa before lunch. I have a few places lined out where we can price professional decorators and florists before we hit the rental place and hobby shops."

"Good morning to you too," he said with a wry grin.

He wasn't supposed to smile when she'd just passively aggressively cut him with the precision of a surgeon, pointing out that he was blatantly *not* ready to go. Maybe his snark detector was malfunctioning. He held the door open wide, inviting her in. Apparently, this show wasn't getting on the road anytime soon. She followed him inside.

Sienna had only been out to the ranch a couple of times. The elegant, log cabin–style home with its open layout impressed her yet again. Beyond the large living room and kitchen, a hallway ran to a mudroom and bathroom, then to a TV den, a spare room that Kelli said used to be their mother's studio, and Cole's office at the end.

The two-story, open-beam ceiling drew her gaze to the upstairs balcony. She remembered from the tour Kelli gave her after moving her large-animal practice out here that those polished wooden stairs led to three large bedrooms. Cole had the gorgeous primary suite on the right; Troy, the bedroom at the opposite end of the hall. Cole's old room, now the main guest room, lay in the middle. The place was neat as a pin, but Sienna wasn't giving Troy credit for that. Kelli had also told her about their cook and housekeeper, Sally Netzler, who'd been with the family for years, ever since Troy's mom had first been diagnosed with cancer. A no-nonsense, former mountaineering guide who had kept the household going through the ups and downs of the past few years.

Troy continued to the kitchen. He reached up into a cabinet for a large coffee mug, revealing a few small, milk-pale scars etched into the farmer's tan on his arms.

"Can I get you a cup of coffee?"

She startled slightly at his words, relieved he hadn't caught her staring at him. "Thanks. I had some *a couple of hours ago*."

He didn't even flinch at her verbal bullet. Sarcasm was obviously getting her nowhere.

So far, he'd dodged her phone calls until she'd pressed him, refused to discuss any planning last night at dinner and now had overslept so that he wasn't remotely ready at the time they'd agreed to meet this morning. All this on top of him being minimal help with the move last month. It didn't take Sherlock Holmes to detect a pattern of behavior here. Fine. He needed someone to be the adult in this endeavor? That was something at which she had plenty of experience.

She set her purse on the granite island, with the row of gleaming brass pans hanging above, and pulled herself to her full five-eleven, plus whatever her low-heeled fashion boots added. Gripping the edge of the counter, she said reasonably, "Troy, I thought you understood how much there is to get done. We need to get going."

Grabbing a blender cup full of dark coffee grounds, he went to dump them in the coffee maker, but found the basket full.

"Don't worry," he said. "Kelli told me the other day she's going to take a week off before the wedding. She has the dress already and they got their rings last month. The invitations are done, they've got the Baptist preacher from Burgess lined up and she and Cole were working on a list of caterers last night." He emptied the old grounds into a compost bucket on the counter. "Oh, and they both said they don't want a gift registry, and they applied for the license and name change last week. You know already that the band is sorted. They've even picked out their wedding song. It's practically all done. I'll bet we can knock the rest out today, no problem."

His casual dismissal nearly made her brain explode, so why did she keep shooting glances at him being all amiable and unshaven and rinsing his little coffee basket under the faucet. The happy, fun-guy demeanor made it seem like she was the one being unreasonable. Just like her party-girl mother made her feel so often—except she'd learned from her father how untrue that was. Giving an inch led to a mile of chaos. She unsnapped her purse, pulled out her list and slid it to him. He'd probably mentioned fewer than a quarter of the things on there. It was only thanks to three years in dispatch and a lifetime with her mom that she kept her voice level but firm.

"No, Troy, it's not practically all done. But you don't know that, because I couldn't even get you to read this last night." She thought he'd take the list from her now. He didn't. Instead, he glanced at it and sighed. He must have heard her nerves fraying and snapping because he arrested the sigh mid-exhale and managed a tenuous "you win" smile.

"Okay. Let me toss a couple of breakfast burritos in the microwave and grab a quick shower while they're heating up. I'll be down in ten minutes tops."

Nope. Nope. Nope. She knew this routine.

"Ten minutes will turn into half an hour, and I need your help. This is my day off too. I tried last night to plan an eight o'clock start. You pushed it back to nine. I was here on time, and it's not my fault you're running late because you slept in." He opened his mouth to say something, but she picked up the list, folded it, put it away and snapped her purse shut more aggressively than strictly necessary. "Let's just get going and get as much done in these three days as we can. Whatever's left, I'll finish it on my own. Okay?"

It meant more for her and Kelli and Cole to do, and shouldering that on top of their work schedules. But once the wedding was over, she could stay away from the ranch, go back to meeting Kelli in town, and let this teenager in a man's body saunter through the rest of his life dodging obligations.

Troy held out his hands in surrender.

"Yes, ma'am. Got it." He flipped his palms up, swinging his arms out to his sides, as if presenting himself. "Okay if I dress first?"

She couldn't help but take him up on his invitation to inspect him. Not trusting her voice, she fluttered her fingers in a casual shooing motion toward the stairs, then took a steadying breath when he vanished to his bedroom.

Distracting herself with her list helped to shift her focus from "cute Troy" back to "late Troy." She could practically hear a clock ticking the seconds away in her head and realized she was no longer reading her list, but had fixated on the staircase, just like her father used to do when waiting for her mother. Shaking herself free of that as well, she went to one of the large picture windows and took in the stunning view. She'd last been here in early June, always a beautiful month in Colorado. But now, in the third week of July, the ranch looked like something out of a painting. Acres of green, irrigated fields, the trees lush and shady, and behind the house, fourteen thousand-foot Blanca Peak towering to the east.

Thankfully, Troy reappeared quickly and, judging by the stubble still present, had been true to his word to do no more than get dressed. He now wore a navy-blue Alamosa Fire Department T-shirt over a well-worn pair of blue jeans. He rummaged in a cupboard, grabbed a couple of energy bars, and offered one to her. She shook her head. He stuck it in a back pocket and unwrapped the other, scarfing it down as he pulled on his boots. Raking his fingers through his thick blond hair, he then pulled on his boots, grabbed a brown cowboy hat from the coat rack and pushed it on his head.

She'd never seen him in one before, and Sienna was starting to understand why Kelli had fallen for a cowboy. Troy cast a final wistful glance toward the coffee machine, and she couldn't help feeling a pang of sympathy for him. What if he could have been ready in ten minutes? Her brain caught up to her emotions a second later. Not a chance. She knew his type too well.

"Let's get started," he said, opening the front door for her. There was no hint of irritation in his voice. Also like her mother, he apparently took it well when he didn't get his way. As frustrating as the flip side of the "it'll be fine" coin could be, the ability to let go, shift course and sail forward uncomplaining was an enviable quality. One she still fought to master.

They descended the porch steps to the driveway together. Sienna stopped next to his truck, but Troy kept going, past his truck and her car, then across the drive to a small gravel road that led to the barn and the pastures and corrals beyond.

"I thought we were going to the wedding site first. Kelli said it was an old cabin at the north end of the property."

"It is." He winked one sky-blue eye at her.

"The barn? Why are you going to the barn?" she said, hurrying to catch up. "Are we going on a four-wheeler? But wait, if we have to take a four-wheeler out there, how will the guests get there?"

They reached the barn, and she followed him inside. He passed the only four-wheeler parked there and led her down an aisle of horse stalls.

"Wait, what? Are you kidding me?"

He grinned at her over his shoulder. "You do ride, don't you?"

"My mom put me on a pony once at a carnival. It walked in a circle around a pole with other ponies. I think I cried."

He laughed aloud. It made those nice crinkles at the corners of his eyes again, the ones she wished she didn't like so much. She looked at the time on her phone.

"There has to be another way to get there than this. Some of the guests will be in dresses. Some are elderly. Are you telling me there's no way to drive out there?" How could they even get the wedding site set up if no road led to it?

"Did you see the wagon outside?"

"Yeah," she said slowly, remembering a large hay wagon by the barn door.

"We have two, and a neighboring ranch has another two we can borrow. The wranglers can all drive horse teams. With less than fifty people coming, we should be able to get all the guests out there in one trip."

She could picture the quaintness of it. "That is pretty cool," she said. "Wait. When did this plan get dreamed up? Kelli didn't mention it."

"Just last night. She and Cole were talking about how they could make sure everyone found the cabin. I suggested the wagons, and they liked the idea now that the wedding's moved up from winter to summer." He stopped in front of a stall.

"Oh, no," she said, realizing the implications. "Four wagons. It's another thing we'll have to find decorations for." She opened her purse and pulled out her list and a pen.

He slid open the wooden, chestnut-stained stall door with its black iron bars on the upper half. Even the barn was elegant here. What she didn't know about horse stalls was a lot, but it seemed large and roomy with thick shavings on the floor, hay in a wall-mounted feeder and a shiny metal basin mounted in the opposite corner for what looked like automatic water.

He haltered the dappled steel-gray horse and led it out. The thing was huge.

"I did tell you I rode a pony, right? Once."

"You did. This is Willie. We put our friends' kids on him. If you're scared, I can clip a rope to him and lead him behind my horse."

Of course she was scared of that massive beast. And not a chance she'd let him see that. "I'll manage."

She hoped she would, anyway. Images of her at five years old returned. Holding on to the saddle horn with both hands and crying while the pony walked in a sedate circle, one of a few hooked to a spoke on a thing that looked like a giant spinning clothesline.

He pulled a saddle and bridle from a nearby rack and had the horse ready in minutes flat. From another stall, he brought out a beautiful creamy-golden horse with a long white mane and tail. When both horses were ready to go, he led them outside into the sunshine.

"Okay, show me what to do," she said, resigned. With the gray horse between them, she surreptitiously wiped sweat from her upper lip.

Instructing her to come around to him on the left side of the horse, he held her stirrup for her. "Grab onto the horn and put your left foot in here."

He rested his other hand on the small of her back, as if to help balance her, but her legs were strong. She lifted herself smoothly into the saddle.

"This must be Kelli's saddle," he said. "Kick your foot out so I can adjust the length."

She bent her knee and scooched her foot back. He flipped the stirrup up in front of her and worked on the buckle beneath as she watched from above. His shoulder pressed into her knee and his arm bumped her shin while he unbuckled the strap and let it out two notches. She felt like Cinderella with the handsome prince kneeling before her like a servant to slide her foot into her shoe. It seemed almost too soon that he pulled the stirrup down and held it for her foot again.

"Try that."

She slipped her boot back in. Her knee was only slightly bent now, comfortable, like a bicycle pedal at full extension. He moved to her right leg and repeated the process. She kind of liked looking down from this height to his cowboy hat and bent head, the side of his stubbled jaw, his arms flexing as he worked at the strap.

"Okay, you're all set," he said, pulling the right stirrup into place and seating her foot in it. "This is your accelerator if he falls too far back." He grasped her foot and touched her heel softly to Willie's flank.

"This is your steering wheel." He took her hands in a two-fisted grip where she held the reins and lifted them. She experienced a jolt at the touch of his large, rough hands unexpectedly cupping both of hers. He swung their hands gently to her right until the left rein lay against the horse's neck. "Right turn." Then he moved them the other direction. "Left turn. This is your brake—" he pulled back slightly "—and reverse if you need it." He tugged a little harder, and Willie obediently backed up a step.

"We ride western-style here. Hold your reins in one hand." He removed her right hand, then wrapped the fingers of her left hand around both reins about a foot above the knot. "That's a comfortable amount of slack for both of you. Not tight enough to hurt his mouth, but snug enough that you can pull back if you need to stop." He let go, and she found she missed the warmth of his hands on hers.

A moment later, she forgot all about the pleasant sensations of the past few minutes when he moved away to mount his own horse. Like an airplane pilot suddenly handing over control of a plane to a passenger who'd never learned to fly, she gripped the reins in one hand and clung to the saddle horn with her other. Her palms were slick on both. The horse felt massive under her: hundreds of pounds of muscle shifting, a freight train with no emergency brake. Willie suddenly inhaled so deeply she thought her hips might pop out of joint. Then he sighed noisily and shook from nose to tail, nearly rattling her teeth loose. She swore a sailor's curse and would've bet the soft noise she heard from Troy had been a chuckle.

"Okay then. We're off," he said with an easy smile, lifting his reins and steering his horse into a walk.

She tapped Willie gently with her heels and lurched in the saddle as he stepped forward.

CHAPTER SIX

"HOW YOU DOING?" Troy asked her as they rode past the hay barn to the first pasture gate.

"Great," she said a bit louder and brighter than necessary, though he could see her hands were white-knuckled on the reins and he'd noticed her wiping sweat off her face before she mounted.

He turned away from her and grinned. He'd planned to take the horses today, even before she arrived, but the fact she was out of her element made it all a little more fun.

"Ease up on the reins a bit. Like this," he said, demonstrating.

She loosened her grip and gave Willie a little slack.

"Sweet, isn't he?" he said as he dismounted to open the first gate.

"He sure is." Sienna smiled and clenched her reins harder, letting go of the saddle horn long enough to pat Willie awkwardly on the neck. "So how far is this cabin?"

"Not far."

With the gate closed behind them, he set off again. Over his shoulder he said, "You'll have to touch your heels to his flanks now and then to speed him up if you want to ride side by side. It's in a horse's nature to walk single file."

She followed his instructions, which caused Willie to trot a couple of steps and her to sway alarmingly in the saddle before he settled into a faster walk. Troy ate his second energy bar, glad he'd brought it along, but when a light headache kicked in, he mourned his missed pot of coffee yet again. It was good to see Sienna relaxing in small increments, though. She looked around with interest at the green pastures of the ranch, the brown prairie surrounding it and the massive bulk of Blanca Peak on their right.

"How do you like dispatching?" he asked, to break the silence.

"It can be intense, but I enjoy it. It's a bit like playing high-stakes chess all day. Moving the pieces, keeping track of everything and all the potential contingencies, guessing what'll happen next and trying to keep everything covered. It's exhausting, though. Especially the phones. Going through that trauma and stress with people when you're their lifeline—literally, sometimes."

They rode stirrup to stirrup and he glanced at

her, thinking about the job from her perspective for the first time.

"I hadn't really thought about it like that. I mean, I know what you guys do, of course, but at my end, I just hear you sending us out to an address. It's easy to forget all the other stuff going on that we don't hear."

"Some things are harder than others. Frightened children calling in domestic abuse while it's happening in their home, concerned adults calling about child welfare, people calling minutes after being the victim of a crime or in the middle of a medical crisis or a fire. But other things are draining in a different way, like our 'frequent fliers.' We have one person with an anxiety disorder who calls most every day, and another who has delusions. But you can't ever dismiss what they call in about because it might be the one time it's for real."

He'd done a "sit-along" in dispatch years ago as a probational firefighter. It was supposed to make him appreciate the difficulty involved with emergency dispatch, but he'd come away from a quiet couple of hours with an impression of four people and a supervisor doing armchair emergency work while the frontline workers they dispatched did the heavy lifting. Obviously, he'd been wrong.

"I never thought about the emotional challenges of being a dispatcher."

"It's rough sometimes. Everything that your fire department gets sent to and every call the police go on, we've already been on the phone with the victims or bystanders, trying to provide safety advice or first aid while working blind. Everything's recorded, and our tapes often end up in court and sometimes on the news. You can't mess up the smallest detail because the well-being of the victims is in your hands until help arrives, but the dispatch center might be juggling multiple calls at a time. People think it's all car accidents and heart attacks..."

The memory of calling in his father's heart attack sprang vividly into Troy's mind, like he'd turned on a TV to find the event playing out full screen. He glanced down, hoping she hadn't noticed him wince, but she continued on.

"...but it's not. We hear it all. Every illness, false alarm, fire or crime in the city that warrants a 911 call."

Caught up in describing her work, she'd relaxed into the saddle and rode like a real cowgirl.

"Why do you stay?"

"Because I'm good at it." He could tell she wasn't boasting, just stating a fact. "I can keep calm, remember details, hold multiple incidents in my head at once. Answer phones for twelve hours straight while responding to the radio and keeping track of my units and resources on the computer. Honestly, the challenge of the job is what I like about it. What's hard is brushing off the judgment and second-guessing from our own units. A couple of weeks ago, I had to send an officer all the way to the east end of town ten minutes before he went off duty. It was for a robbery report with a victim, and I could tell by how flustered the victim was that it was going to be difficult and take a lot of time."

"Ouch."

"Yeah. But he didn't know that in the background I heard another police dispatcher taking a call for an in-progress break-in. We had two vehicles closer than he was, so I had to send the first officer to the robbery report. He used to come into dispatch to chat when he was at the station. I've been waiting two weeks to explain the situation to him but haven't seen him since that day."

Troy remembered something similar that had happened to his crew once when Sienna had been dispatching. He'd questioned her judgment—out loud—and realized now, almost certainly unfairly.

They both fell silent until she shot him a sidelong glance. "Look at you, though," she said. "A cowboy and a firefighter. Bet you're in all the charity calendars."

He barked a surprised laugh, warming as a rare blush flushed his neck and cheeks. "You know our department doesn't do a calendar."

"Maybe you ought to think about it. Just sayin'."

She bounced her eyebrows then chuckled. He couldn't tell if it had been flirtatious or a joke. He hoped for the former. Last night he'd wondered if he'd seen a bit of interest in her eyes after a couple of beers.

"So, can you rope and rodeo and all that stuff too?" she asked.

"I grew up roping and branding, helping with spring vaccinations and castrations, and all the rest. But rodeo? No way. I was never much interested in competitive sports. I'm glad now, with all the things I've seen since then as a first responder. Bodies are tough in some ways but ridiculously fragile in others. Cole's done a bit of rodeo, though. Nothing serious, but he's a fair bronc rider."

"And Lane?"

"No rodeo, but he can ride and herd like the rest of us. His big thing was always skiing, especially after he left for college. He doesn't compete anymore, but he still does black diamond stuff all over the world."

"Sounds like a family of daredevils. I'm surprised you aren't a smoke jumper or working for a big-city fire department or something. What kept you in Alamosa?"

The question flustered him. It had been a long time since anyone had asked him about his modest goals. His family had finally learned to avoid the topic.

"Just the way things worked out."

With superb timing, his horse, Whiskey, shied at a garter snake slithering quickly out of the way. His horse trotted a couple of steps in excitement. Willie, despite his calm nature, reacted with typical prey-animal behavior and trotted as well, sending Sienna jouncing in the saddle and grabbing for the saddle horn. Troy turned away so she wouldn't see him choke down a laugh at her sudden expletive and ungainly floundering. Both horses settled quickly, and he caught her from the corner of his eye, smoothing her hair and trying to marshal her expression. Again, she wiped furtively at her upper lip. He had to admire the way she picked up the conversation once the horses were calm, acting as if nothing had happened.

"I guess not many firefighters get to do both structure and wildland fires. And by the way, thanks so much for that extra workload this year. Dispatch got a big, fat folder full of operating procedures for wildfires even though the odds of a wildfire within our boundaries are nearly nil." He glanced over to see her wry smile. "Really, though, congratulations. We were all pretty shocked when eight of you actually earned the full Wildland Fire Team Certification. I know it's not easy to get. Honestly, it surprised us that the city even went for it. Isn't it still pretty rare for metro districts to cross-certify their firefighters?"

"Used to be. But a lot of cities now are finding ways to get the funding to have their own wildland crews and equipment. With the droughts and global warming making fire seasons so bad, they pretty much have to. Then add that to the high winds that parts of Colorado can get."

The Spring Creek Fire still ranked as one of the largest fires in Colorado history—over one hundred thousand acres burned. It hadn't endangered Alamosa or Burgess, but it had come close enough to scare everyone in the county, which in turn had scared up the funding for brush trucks, equipment and training.

"Is it a pretty low percentage of people who pass?"

"Not super low. Anyone who can pass the fire academy can probably pass the academic half, but you have to be pretty fit to pass the physical and to handle the workload when you get sent to a wildfire as a trainee. If you pass, though, and certify as a wildland team member, then you get to go to wildfires outside your own district. That's the theory anyway."

It was mid-July of their first year of certification, and they'd done nothing more so far than mop up a couple of small hot spots.

"Are you the only one at your station who certified?"

"The only one on my shift. No one else went out for it. Mac's too old, Bouncer's still probationary and Jan said it was stupid to want to dig trenches up mountainsides in one-hundred-five-degree weather in front of an inferno." He steered his horse around an old piece of fence. "She could have a point."

"They wouldn't call you away for something in another state, would they?"

"No. Wildland Team members can go out of Alamosa County, and the regular metro guys can't, but the Hotshots and Forest Service wildland teams are still the only ones that travel all over the country. They're the big guns out there, kinda like navy SEALs versus regular sailors—there are only a few special teams but a whole lot of grunts, like me." He dismounted as they reached another gate and didn't add that he'd dreamed since childhood of joining one of those special teams.

After a few minutes' ride through the new pasture, an old single-room cabin came into view to their right.

"That's the original home my great-great-grandfather built when he and his wife homesteaded the ranch. This meadow in front is where Kelli and Cole want to be married."

"Oh, wow," she said, taking it all in. "This really *is* gorgeous. And that cabin is in amazing shape. I'm used to seeing the old falling-down ones around here, but this looks beautifully preserved."

"After the main house was built, the family kept it in its original condition, right down to the furnishings inside."

A moment later, she noticed the other thing that had come into view, as he'd known she would. The dirt road on the far side, leading directly to it.

"That road over there," she said. "Does it go all the way to the ranch house?"

"Uh, yeah."

"And we could have driven here."

"Well, yeah. But this was more fun, wasn't it?"

She shook her head and gave him an exasperated grunt, but he could see she wasn't genuinely mad. "So, anyone who can't ride in the wagons, like Kelli's folks, can drive in?"

"Right. Cole's going to bring them out in his truck. I wasn't kidding about it being hard to find the way out here, though. It's mostly a series of unmarked dirt tracks, and the condition of the road isn't great either. It really will be more practical to use the wagons. Besides, it'll add a little atmosphere for the guests."

They pulled their horses to a stop in front of the cabin. He dismounted and flipped his reins around the porch banister, then held Willie's head for her.

"Nope. This side," he said as she started to slide off to the right.

She stepped down and took a few tentative steps, wobbling like a sailor after a month at sea.

"You all right?"

"I'd just started getting used to the ground moving under me. Now my balance feels off, and my inner thighs and knee joints feel like they've stretched an extra couple of inches. Am I bowlegged yet?"

He tried not to take that as an invitation to look. "Mmm-hmm," he affirmed. "Somewhere between Popeye and Yosemite Sam. Don't worry. They'll probably go back to normal eventually."

"Very funny. Good thing it wasn't a longer ride." She hobbled up to the tiny front porch.

"It's okay to go inside if you want." He pushed the latch, and the door swung inward.

Her eyes danced across the interior with the same fascination as every guest he'd brought out to see it, like the door was a portal and they'd just stepped back in time to the Old West. She took in the potbellied stove, small table, the lamps and chairs, and the narrow metal-and-springs bedframe of the one-room home, then stared into some middle distance. He wondered if Kelli had told her that she and Cole shared their first kiss here. Then he wondered what would happen if he followed Sienna into the room, slipped his arms around that trim waist, pulled her into him and kissed her full lips.

She'd probably belt him.

"My great-great-grandfather and -grandmother lived here the rest of their lives. They're the ones who started ranching cattle and they're the reason why we have senior water rights in the valley. His oldest son built the main ranch house. And my father took the main house down to its bones seventy years later and renovated it to what it is today."

Cole might have been the only one of the three brothers to follow the family tradition of ranching, but Troy couldn't deny that his family's legacy made him proud. He might not work the land with Cole often, but he was a Tyler—a living part of the history of the ranch—and it pumped in his blood the same as the rest of his family.

But unlike them, it hadn't stuck. He and his older brother Lane had washed their hands of ranching for a living. For Lane, it had been disinterest; for Troy, the reasons had been quite different.

Unexpectedly, it was Cole, adopted into the family at seven years old, who'd embraced the lifestyle. When they were younger, Troy guessed it was out of gratitude for being taken out of the foster system, rescued from criminal neglect, and adopted into a loving family. He had to admit now, though, that Cole might have been a natural cowboy all along. He'd been running the ranch solo for more than half a year since their father's death. And running it well.

They walked back outside.

"Well," Sienna said, looking around and taking in the views: Blanca towering majestically behind the cabin and a hundred-mile stretch of her fellow Sangre de Cristo range winding away to the north. "I certainly see why they wanted this spot for the wedding."

Troy leaned against a post on the porch and watched her as she walked into the field, wandering to both sides of the cabin as she mapped the wedding in her head and pointed out the possible locations for the various elements. She moved with the grace of a mountain lion through the tall grass. He guessed she could be as fierce as one too.

"It really is beautiful," she said, turning back to him, genuinely impressed.

Framed against the grass around her and the mountain range behind, her dark hair drifting in the light breeze and a smile lighting up her face, he could say the same about her. Beautiful might not even be a strong enough word. Stunning. She hypnotized him so he couldn't look aside. She took his breath away.

Noticing his stare, she examined him in much the same way. Suddenly feeling uncharacteristically self-conscious, he straightened and came down the two wooden steps to join her.

She broke her gaze as if nothing special had passed between them. Pulling out her phone, she started taking photos. Troy followed her as she wove an erratic pattern back through the field, pointing as she talked.

"We'll need a wedding trellis here, maybe decorated with flowers and lights, chairs facing the cabin with an aisle down the middle." She gestured while she talked. "Oh, and the decorations for the wagons too." She looked up to the sky. "We'll have to find some kind of shade cloth to hang over the chairs because it's likely to be a hundred degrees out. Maybe we could rent those colorful fabric triangles, the kind people use for porch covers, and string them from the cabin down to the wagons, or something. I guess it's the one day we'll pray there isn't any rain. The cabin's so tiny I don't think everyone would fit if the weather was bad. I wish we could afford one of those giant wedding tents. That would take care of both shade and rain."

She studied the empty field again, then studied it some more. Her beautiful smile wilted.

"Oh, Troy. There's so much to do." She opened her purse and pulled out the dreaded, color-coded list. "No electricity here, right? And there's no stage for the band. It would be too hard to dance without a dance floor anyway. I wasn't sure until I saw this, but they're going to need a separate venue for the reception. That means a reservation, decorations for the reception room—lights, flowers, centerpieces." She read down her list, pointing out items. "Tables and chairs, and linens. A cake table and cake knife. Champagne flutes for toasting, plates and silverware, a gift table. Trash cans. A guest book." She sighed. "Guest favors and maybe a trivia game or something to keep the guests occupied until the meal and cake and all that."

She looked up, her entire body tense, her face strained and the mood of a moment ago ruined. Troy felt her stress hit him like a shock wave.

"Do you know if they settled on a caterer or photographer?" she asked.

"Kelli said this morning she was going to start

making calls after work today. She's also going to take care of the bridesmaids' dresses and Cole will take care of the groomsmen."

"And what about a rehearsal dinner? The last time I talked to Kelli she didn't think they needed one, but I don't see how we can skip it. And bachelor and bachelorette parties. That means planning two other whole events. And August is a popular month. I don't even know if we can still get reservations."

She glanced back at the list and shook her head.

"Troy, we have to leave for Alamosa. Now."

CHAPTER SEVEN

ALAMOSA WAS A NIGHTMARE.

They didn't arrive until nearly 1:00 p.m., and by then Troy was so hungry and caffeine deprived that finding a coffee shop for him with a breakfast and lunch menu moved to top priority. Next, she learned that hardly anything was open that day. The florist and party shop were closed on Monday, the photographer Kelli wanted worked Wednesday through Saturday, and the rental store with everything from farm equipment to dinnerware closed for lunch from 1:00 p.m. to 2:00 p.m. Sienna made a note in her calendar to call them back when they reopened.

By midafternoon they'd accomplished nothing more than finding a cake knife and wedding flutes at a kitchen store and a bag of birdseed for throwing at the end of the ceremony. She found netting for the birdseed bags at Walmart, but had roamed the hobby aisles for the past hour trying to come up with DIY decoration ideas while Troy wandered off repeatedly to look at electronics in the next department. He meandered back just as her phone rang. Kelli's avatar showed on the screen.

"Hey, girl," Sienna answered. "I saw the wedding site and the cabin this morning. I see why you chose the spot. It's perfect!"

"Thanks, Sienna." Kelli sounded distracted. Sad maybe.

She instantly laser-focused on her friend's mood. "What's up?"

"I just heard from my sister. My brother-in-law's been diagnosed with pancreatic cancer."

"Oh, no. I'm so sorry, Kelli."

Unable to hear the other side of the conversation, Troy shot her a questioning glance.

"Blair is beside herself. I mailed the invitations out on Saturday, but I told her we'd call the guests and postpone the wedding. She started crying and begged me not to. I'm booking a flight out to Connecticut this afternoon. Cole said he'd go with me, but he was trying to get the hay cut this morning and then his tractor broke down, so I told him to stay here. There's nothing he could do for them anyway, but I need to be there to support Blair and Mark and the kids. They're doing a PET scan of his whole body tomorrow, so they're hoping to know more by the end of the week." Kelli's voice came across the phone tight with suppressed emotion. Sienna shot Troy a worried grimace, and he furrowed his brow in concern.

"I've got Rikki rescheduling my appointments until next Monday," Kelli continued. "I'm sorry. I know you're already helping me with so much, but could I leave the bridesmaids' dresses to you? You know the colors, rose pink, and teal. Really, anything at this point will do. I guess it's just you and Rikki as bridesmaids now if Blair can't make it. If Cole still wants his friend Derek along with Dustin and Troy, then we'll just be uneven. Maybe Troy could pick out something for the guys. And at least I can work on my vows while I'm at Blair's. I feel bad leaving you with so much. I'm sure Cole will get the tractor fixed soon, then he can help you with things until I get back." She didn't sound sure at all.

"Of course. You go take care of your sister. Don't worry about anything here. I got this." Kelli gushed her thanks and they hung up.

Sienna dropped her phone to her side, her head spinning. Half a dozen emotions fought a championship battle inside her skull, but worry for Kelli and her family was the easy winner. She recapped the conversation for Troy.

"That's a tough break," he said. "I've never met Mark, but I used to know Blair pretty well. She was in the same grade as me at school, though I haven't seen her in years."

“Pancreatic, that’s one of the bad ones, isn’t it? The one Patrick Swayze died of?”

Troy nodded. “I don’t know a lot about oncology. It’s not really something we deal with, being first responders. If I’m remembering right, it has the potential to get diagnosed late and move fast. Not that it means that’ll happen to Mark,” he amended quickly. “Could be that they’ve caught his early.”

“I hope so. Still, poor Kelli. She moved the wedding up because of her dad’s health, and now she’s got this worry too. Between Kelli leaving and Cole with his tractor problems, it’s even more reason to do everything we can for them.” She fished her list out of her purse, and then an awful thought struck her. “Is Cole going to need your help with the tractor?” She glanced at the folded list in her hand like it might spontaneously burst into flames and burn to useless ash. “I’ve heard Kelli say how critical the timing is for getting the hay harvested.”

Troy looked briefly like he wanted to say yes. Panicked desperation must have blazed from her eyes and his expression softened.

“Nah. Cole and his ranch foreman probably already have the thing fixed. Cole’s a decent mechanic, and Dustin’s twice as good. In fact, if there’s anything Dustin can’t do, I haven’t seen it yet. On top of that, Cole has four full-time wranglers to do the other work while they get the tractor going. I'd probably just get in the way."

The fact that he chose to stay and help her nearly melted her with relief. She needed him more than ever now, but it wouldn't have been right not to ask. Helping Cole would have been an easy out if he'd decided to take it. Maybe Troy wasn't such a bad egg after all. Jotting bridesmaids and groomsmen on her list, Sienna glanced up to get her bearings.

"There's a formal wear store just down the road. We could swing by and see if they've got any dresses that would do. Maybe you'll find something for the groomsmen too. I wouldn't make any bets on Cole getting to it with everything else that's going on now."

"Your servant, madame." He gave her a smile and a little bow that were so adorable it couldn't help but lift her spirits. Three weeks to pull off the impossible, but at least she wasn't in this alone.

The formal wear store turned out to be about as big as the waiting room at Kelli's small-animal clinic and had little to choose from. There were dresses in lime green, dark purple, hot pink and navy blue, but no rose. Sienna was a size 6, and Kelli had told her Rikki was a twelve. None of the colors came in either size. In the end, she didn't find so much as a decorative hairpin.

She was headed for the men's side when she saw Troy striding for the checkout with an armload of clothes. He dropped a pile of four white shirts and four black vests at the register. Sienna picked up one of the vests, surprised it actually looked nice. Solid black material with silver embroidery on the front.

"We all have black jeans. And they can pick out their own bolo ties if they don't already have them. There you go. Groomsmen, done." He gave her a big smile.

She chewed her lip. "I like the vests, but their colors are rose and black. Did you happen to see anything rose colored? Shirts or vests?"

"Nope."

Maybe they could make up for it with accents, like boutonnieres. And if they found something better they could always return these. Meanwhile, at least it was a partial something to cross off.

"Okay. Well done, then."

They left the store, and she checked her phone for the time: 4:05 p.m.

"Oh, no." She stopped dead in the middle of the parking lot, glaring at the clock numbers like she could intimidate them into showing something different. She scrambled to find the rental store's number.

Punching the phone icon extra hard didn't, in

fact, make it dial faster. Voicemail picked up and told her what she already knew. They closed at 4:00 p.m. and wouldn't reopen until the following day at 10:00 a.m. She'd meant to call them two hours ago. It wasn't like her to forget something like this. She'd even put it in her calendar.

Sienna pressed a hand to her forehead like it might keep her brain from leaking out her ears. Heading for a sidewalk bench, she plopped onto it, holding on to her phone with both hands in her lap and staring at it forlornly. Troy sat next to her.

"You okay?"

"No. I'm really not. I forgot to call the rental place before they closed. Troy, there's no way we can get everything done in the two days we have left." She shook her head.

He shifted to face her. "You do know the wedding is nineteen days away, right?"

She met his naive, baby-blue gaze.

"What I know is I only had eight days off until the wedding, today being one of them. Once reservations are made and we've got the supplies we need for decorations and the bridesmaids' dresses are sorted, then we'd have two and a half weeks to put it all together. That's still tight, but at least we'd have the things we need to make it work. Right now, we don't even know if we can get the photographer. Or the florist, or the things for the reception. And the one big thing I could have accomplished today, I botched by forgetting to call the rental store."

Sienna had looked forward to planning Kelli's wedding for years, and it was all falling apart. Worse, now Kelli was depending on her more than ever. An image formed of guests standing in the field because there were no chairs. Sun beating down with no shade. Wilted grocery store flowers on the porch of the cabin and mismatched bridesmaids' dresses—and on a long banner behind a plane looping above the cabin, My Maid of Honor Failed Me.

"Hey. Don't worry." Troy slung one arm around her shoulders and pulled her against his side.

She wondered how depressed she must have looked for him to make such a gesture, but she fitted so perfectly against him that, honestly, right now all she cared about was the fact that he felt strong and solid and comforting.

He pulled her tighter, rubbing her upper arm in a consoling manner. "It'll be fine, you'll see."

It'll be fine.

She'd always hated that expression—the battle cry of the lazy and disorganized—and she didn't believe it for a minute in this case. But Troy hadn't made it sound like lip service; he sounded like he trusted to his core that this wedding was going to come off all right, and that was something she needed to believe right now. She just wished she had as much faith in it as he did.

"Thank you, Troy." She slumped her head onto his shoulder, registering distantly that it was something she wouldn't have been able to do with a shorter man. "I'm actually really glad you're doing this with me. I'm sorry if I get a bit spun."

Somewhere deep inside she knew he was right; all was not lost...but the "what-if" part of her brain wouldn't shut up. The Dad part. The self-criticism she'd learned to internalize from constantly trying to live up to her dad's expectations and hearing her mother relentlessly criticized the first eleven years of her life. Troy was so different. She'd just confessed to the biggest fail of the day by not securing the chairs and other things they'd need to rent—100 percent her fault—and he hadn't said a word about it. Not even an eye roll, just comfort and reassurance.

He tipped his head to rest atop hers and massaged her shoulder. He smelled of clean laundry and the natural muskiness that came with sitting in the July sunshine. His fingers expertly caressed her tight muscles, and she imagined he must give a great back rub. And just like that, her perception of him as a charismatic but unreliable don't-even-think-of-him-that-way guy landed on its butt and started a slippery-slope slide down into the quicksand pit of full-on attraction.

Sienna stood abruptly and moved away, putting distance between her and those blue eyes and magic hands. Not the right time. Not the right guy.

Retreating into her safety zone of organization and planning, she paced in front of him wondering how he stayed so relaxed all the time. He'd showed no reaction to her launching away like a fighter plane on takeoff, and sat with his arms spread across the top of the bench now, his gaze following her pacing. *Focus on the wedding, Sienna.*

Okay, she could still pull this off. Well, if she didn't have a heart attack or stroke first. Right now, it felt like the entire wedding party stood on her chest, making it hard to breathe, and reminding her she had more to do than seemed humanly possible.

"It was silly to come to Alamosa," she said. "We should have driven up to Pueblo today. In fact, I'm not sure Pueblo is big enough to find everything we need. We'd better go bigger. Colorado Springs, or maybe Denver."

"Pueblo is ten times the size of Alamosa. And Denver is a four-hour drive each way—we could be in Albuquerque quicker."

"Yes, but there'll be less selection in Pueblo. We don't have time to waste running from place to place and not finding what we need." She chewed her lip. "As far as the things we'll need to rent, those will have to be local. Otherwise, transporting chairs and dinnerware and whatever else right before the wedding would be a nightmare. For the rest, Colorado Springs, then. Six times bigger than Pueblo but only two and a half hours away."

"You sure?" he said cautiously. "Five hours of driving to go shopping?"

"I seem to recall you saying you were all mine until Thursday."

He spread his hands and gave her a wry smile. "I did at that." He looked at his wristwatch. "All right, since we've done all we can for today and I'm yours for another sixty hours, give or take, how about I take you out for an early dinner somewhere?"

"I'll tell you what. If you promise to help me cross the top half dozen things off this tomorrow—" she fluttered the list at him "—I'll make you dinner tonight."

"Deal. If you promise to put that thing away until morning. No planning tonight. Just relaxing."

She didn't think she could take any more worrying about the wedding today, anyway. Besides, cooking always relaxed her.

"Deal," she said.

CHAPTER EIGHT

TROY PULLED UP in front of the small home and parked in the dirt driveway next to Sienna's car.

"Nice place," he said, getting out. "You own it?"

"Technically, the bank owns it, but thanks for calling my itty-bitty, seventy-five-year-old house nice."

His compliment had been sincere. With the fire department's emergency calls he'd been in and out of plenty of these old homes, most of them run down. Hers sported a new tile roof, fresh white paint on the siding, and bright turquoise accents around the door and window frames. Following her inside, he discovered the real surprise, an entirely remodeled interior: modern furniture, a high-quality vinyl floor, fashionable door handles, modern baseboard heating and—through the arch into the kitchen—a glimpse of contemporary cabinets and counters.

"Wow. Did you buy it like this?"

"Not even," she said, as she headed for a closed door in the middle of the hall. When she opened it, a ball of gray fluff bounced from the bathroom in a series of hopping, pouncing tackles aimed at Sienna's shoelaces. "You're looking at four years of room-by-room blood, sweat and elbow grease." She lifted the baby wildcat to her chin. "This is Tiger, by the way."

Troy gave the little guy scritches on the head, which earned him a finger full of claws in thanks. He extracted his hand gently before the teeth sank in too.

"*Your* blood, sweat and elbow grease?"

"All me. Well, not the roofing, but I did all the rest."

She set the kitten on the couch and retrieved a few toys from the bathroom. Leading Troy into the kitchen, his eyebrows lifted in surprise when his gaze landed on the coffee maker. "Oh, baby, you could make me a happy man." He ran his hands over it like he might the steering wheel of a new Ferrari. Coffee maker didn't begin to describe the elegant stainless espresso machine with temperature control, steamer and shot timer. Bottles of flavors and toppings stood in a neat row at the side.

"At least you appreciate it. Kelli can't tell the difference between a freshly ground espresso and warm water over instant coffee crystals."

"Tell me about it. Her *or* Cole. Those two are perfectly happy with their no name–brand grounds in their twelve-dollar coffee maker. And you could carbon date the coffee stains in Cole's thermos. I've been lobbying for them to go in on something like this, but they couldn't care less."

She opened a cupboard and then her fridge, studying the contents. "Spaghetti, enchiladas or corn chowder for dinner?"

"Cook's choice. It all sounds great to me. What can I do to help?"

"You like to cook?"

"Like is a strong word. Willing is closer. I've been told I'm better at doing the dishes."

"Dishes for you then. I love cooking. Always have. Before I went into dispatch, I thought about becoming a chef. In high school, I used to fantasize about getting into the cooking school in France. Cordon Bleu." She washed her hands. "You can sous chef. Spicy okay for the enchiladas?"

"Spicy's great."

She set the oven to preheat and poured some leftover beans stored in a thick sauce into a pot on the stove, then handed him a package of artisan tortillas. "Would you warm those up?" She pointed to a cabinet near his knees.

He rummaged through the neatly stacked pan cabinet and chose a well-seasoned cast-iron skillet while she chopped and sautéed onions, garlic and jalapenos, mixed them with spices and began a quick homemade enchilada sauce. Removing a cooked chicken breast from the fridge, she asked him to shred it while the tortillas warmed.

They danced around each other in the small space, bumping elbows and shoulders in the nicest way: relaxed and companionable. It relieved him to see that her DEFCON 1, imminent-nuclear-meltdown state in Alamosa seemed to have dropped to a nice, mellow DEFCON 5 here at home.

"Cordon Bleu, huh? That's a far cry from 911 dispatch."

"Not as far as you'd think." She ladled sauce into the bottom of a Pyrex dish. "Being a chef probably ranks up there with dispatch and air-traffic control on the stress scale. Organization too. Juggling a lot of balls at once and massive pressure not to mess up even the smallest thing."

At her direction, he set the kitchen table while she grated a bowl of cheese and then rolled the marinated beans, cheese and shredded chicken into the warm corn tortillas and placed them in the baking dish. She added the rest of the sauce to the top of the enchiladas, covered the baking dish with foil and popped it in the oven, setting a timer for twenty minutes.

Next, she had him spoon sour cream and

homemade salsa into small bowls painted dark blue with yellow sunflowers while she chopped some garnishes and whipped up a bowl of fresh guacamole.

"So you can handle a stressful job, do construction and cook. What else?"

"Hey, a gal's gotta have some mystery to her. What about you? What job did you imagine yourself doing when you were in high school?"

He gave her a big grin that belied the overwound spring that tightened his gut whenever conversation steered too near to his unrealized goals. He deflected out of habit. "A guy's gotta have some mystery to him, you know," he quipped.

Pulling two beers out of the refrigerator, she settled in one of the chairs at the kitchen table. He took the other seat.

Tiger, tired of the toys, pogoed from the living room to jump on his leg—digging claws into his jeans the way a climber wielded crampons and ice axes—and scaled his shin to his lap. Baby fur stuck out in all directions like a cartoon character getting electrocuted. He stroked it flat, but it puffed up again every time the kitten moved.

"I can take him if he's bothering you."

"No, he's fine. The ranch always has friendly barn cats. I grew up playing with them." They'd had dogs too, but cats came with fewer responsibilities.

With five minutes left on the timer, she removed the foil and sprinkled some of the extra cheese on top.

Much to his surprise, he was discovering that he really liked Sienna. When they'd moved Kelli's equipment to the ranch there'd been attraction, but even then, like these past couple of days, he'd been leery of her take-charge attitude. Coming here to her home, though, seeing this new side of her, a switch in his brain had flipped. She felt whole and real. The laughter and the intelligence, the spark in her eyes, the kitten, her dreams of Cordon Bleu and a growing list of mighty impressive skills, they were all as much a part of her as her list-making and her ability to track and dispatch multiple emergencies at a time. She was as multifaceted as a diamond and sparkled just as brightly.

However much his impressions of her might be favorably changing, though, he guessed her opinions of him might not be quite as flattering. He probably hadn't made the best impression on her the first time they'd met, and he might not have moved the needle much today. He picked at his beer label with one thumbnail, studying her while she stirred the guacamole to keep it from turning brown. What he needed was a way to find out if his suspicions were correct and a chance to explain himself if it turned out they were.

"You know," he said, risking whatever goodwill he might have accumulated over the latter half of the day, "we could always try finding the things you need in Pueblo first. If it didn't work out, then we could go on to Colorado Springs."

"Hey," she said, turning to him, guacamole spoon in hand. "No weaseling out now. If we waste time in Pueblo and don't find everything, and I think our odds are low, there wouldn't be enough of the day left to shop in the Springs."

"Truth or Dare," he said.

"What?" She gestured her confusion with the spoon she held in the air.

"Play three rounds of Truth or Dare with me and I won't bring it up again. We'll go straight to Colorado Springs."

She sat back in her chair with a deep look of suspicion, though a small smile tugged at her lips. Her measuring gaze held a wicked spark of interest.

"We were already going straight to Colorado Springs, mister. You just want to play Truth or Dare, don't you?"

She was no easy mark, that was for certain. He was pretty sure she'd go for it, though. Cole and Kelli had been right about her. She was clever, but also fiery. He was betting on her bold personality, and he had a feeling he'd only seen the tip of the iceberg.

"Tiger wants us to." He held the kitten up and looked him in the face. Blue eyes starburst with yellow stared back. He turned him to Sienna. Tiger's little hind feet paddled in the air.

She chuckled. "And just what do you have in mind as a dare?"

"That's up to the question asker."

"Well, then I'm reserving the right to veto."

"Kind of changes the game," he said with mock disappointment. He set Tiger back in his lap and twirled his beer bottle on the table. "Okay, how about this, you got anything hotter than jalapenos here?" She nodded. "How hot?"

"I bought some habaneros the other day at the farmers market to make jam."

"Perfect. We slice, say, half-inch strips lengthwise. Whoever refuses to tell a truth *and* refuses the dare picked for them gets the default dare—eating one slice with three seeds on it. I know I don't want to. And I definitely wouldn't want to do it more than once. But you have to confess now if you're better than the average hot pepper eater." She shook her head no. "All right, then. What do you think?"

She pursed her lips, probably still trying to divine his reasons for suggesting this, then smiled. "Done."

He reached out his hand and they shook. Skin soft as silk and manicured nails belied the firmness of her handshake.

A timer on the oven dinged.

"After dinner, though," she said.

"After dinner."

She pulled the enchiladas from the oven, scooped them dripping with sauce and cheese onto thick ceramic plates, garnished them with chopped lettuce and tomato and set a plate before him. The aroma filled the air. He plunked Tiger unceremoniously on the floor to fend for himself and topped his enchiladas with guacamole, sour cream and salsa. The second Sienna picked up her fork, he dived in.

Best enchiladas he'd had in his life. Hands down. He might have moaned just a little. "This is amazing."

"Thanks," she said, sounding genuinely pleased. "I'm glad you like them."

"I do. Just don't think this dinner is going to get you out of Truth or Dare."

"I'd never," she said with mock affront. "We made a deal."

CHAPTER NINE

"WHO GOES FIRST?" Sienna said as she scooped leftovers into containers and stacked the dirty dishes by the sink. As promised, Troy was washing up and doing a good job, even considering her high standards. Plus, she liked the look of all six feet three inches of him standing at her sink, forearms plunged into the soapy water.

"You can if you want."

"Hmm. I haven't decided on a question or a dare yet. You go first."

"Okay, slice up one of those habaneros and give me a minute."

He rinsed the dish in his hands and set it in the drying rack while she pulled a bag of reddish-orange peppers from the refrigerator. His smile faded and his brows pulled together in concentration while he dried his hands. If she had to guess, she'd say he seemed reluctant to start, even though this had been his idea. Yes, there was some point to this, she felt sure, and she was curious to find out what.

"Are you ready?" he asked, nodding his chin to the pepper she was slicing.

"Ready as I'm going to get, I think." She finished slicing and put the leftover peppers back in the refrigerator.

"Okay. Truth or Dare. What was your honest opinion of me the first time we met, that day we were moving Kelli's stuff? If you don't answer truthfully, you have to dance by yourself to a song I pick."

He put the saucepan in the soapy water to soak and turned to her, waiting. The slight tension in his shoulders as he rested his palms on the counter behind him made her wonder how much her answer meant to him.

"I consider that dare well within reason," he added, "but you know your default if you veto it. And I get to be the seed inspector."

Her heart rate picked up slightly. Was this the reason for the game? Well, she certainly wasn't going to dance for him, and while she liked spicy food, raw habaneros with seeds were not an attractive option. They were having such a nice evening that she didn't want to spoil it with a truth like this—but game or no, she was never anything less than honest. Besides, maybe it was time to clear the air about that day.

"So that's how we're going to play this?" she said, starting with a bit of jesting bravado to cover her worry that things might go downhill from here. "Okay, buddy. Game on. Truth." She washed the pepper oil from her hands with soap and hot water, and said, "You might want to sit down for this."

She gestured to the couch in the other room, dried her hands and carried the plate of sliced peppers to the coffee table. They sat facing each other at opposite ends, but as the "couch" was technically a love seat, their knees nearly touched.

No point in easing into this, she decided. "The first thing you did was flirt with me when I pulled up. Right after that you answered a phone call and went into another room to talk privately to what was obviously a girlfriend. Then you took off an hour later to pick up the lunch we'd ordered and didn't come back until midafternoon, leaving us hungry and doing the majority of the work. When you finally did come back, we got cold pizza. Gotta say, it wasn't the greatest first impression." She quirked a smile at him to take the sting out of her honesty. Strangely, instead of seeming upset, his shoulders relaxed.

"I've wondered for weeks if you heard me talking to Jan that day, or if you were miffed about the pizza, or if you just didn't like me much because of something else, maybe something you'd heard at work. I only knew that things seemed friendly when you showed up and not so much after that."

"In your defense, I learned just the other day that you and your girlfriend broke up before we met." Tiger sauntered over to them. Sienna leaned down to pick him up, but he bypassed her and jumped onto Troy's lap again.

"Jan and I had broken up about two weeks before. I mean we'd broken up a dozen times, but that time I knew she meant it. The relationship had been dying a slow death for a long time, dragging both of us down with it. I was glad she did it. She called me that day because there were some things I'd loaned her that she wanted to return. I volunteered to get lunch so I could swing by and get them. Turned out, what she really wanted was to have a last heart-to-heart chat to be sure we were still friends and weren't going to have a problem working together. I didn't want to cut her short, but it turned out she had a lot to say. I told Cole later, but I'd just met you. It wasn't something I really wanted to explain when I got back."

Sienna's perspective shifted so suddenly the room seemed to tilt. She replayed the day in her mind. The snippet of conversation she'd heard hadn't sounded flirty, it had been subdued. His mood when he returned with lunch had been one of forced cheerfulness. She'd thought at the time both had been subterfuge, hiding the girlfriend, then trying to avoid getting called out for dodging work. In hindsight, this explanation made more sense.

"Good to know," she said airily, as if she didn't feel the ACME-sized anvil of judgment she'd been carrying lifting from her. Maybe the real Troy Tyler was the person she'd enjoyed tonight over dinner instead of the one she'd thought she knew. "Well, it's a good thing then that you can make it up to all of us at once by helping out with the wedding."

Hoping she didn't look flustered over her newfound hopes for him, she plunged straight into her question. "My turn. If I went through your bedroom, what would I be surprised to find? Same dare. You dance for me to a song I choose or…" She fluttered her fingers at the plate of sliced pepper where a few dreaded habanero seeds shone pale yellow against the reddish flesh.

He laughed out loud.

"Easy. Truth. Nothing nefarious in my room. And, sorry to disappoint, nothing embarrassing." A small twitch at the side of his mouth—a hint of a grimace—like maybe he'd thought of something after all.

"Mmm-hmm." She pulled out her phone, tapped in a search for songs from *Dirty Danc-*

ing and hit play. The first strains of "Time of My Life" filled the room.

He lifted his hands palm out to her in a gesture of surrender. "Okay. Okay. It's nothing, really. Just an old poster from when I was a kid. Maybe not the best look for a thirty-year-old man that it's still up on the inside of my closet door."

"Megan Fox?" she guessed. "Miley Cyrus?" She couldn't remember who boys had posters of twenty years ago.

"Red Adair."

No one she'd heard of. Maybe some redheaded bombshell?

"Is she a singer?"

He chuckled, and she melted a little at his grin and the timbre of his laugh. "An oil-well firefighter. *He* died two or three decades ago at nearly ninety years old. The guy was fearless. He pioneered a method of capping oil- and gas-well fires burning out of control. John Wayne played him in a movie after he extinguished a four-hundred-and-fifty-foot column of fire in the Sahara that had burned for over a year."

"Oh, wow. How long have you had the poster?"

"I'll give you that as a bonus question. I think I was eight or nine when I got it."

"So you've always wanted to be a firefighter?"

"Yep. Ever since grade school."

"With someone like that as your hero, I'm surprised you didn't end up working in downtown Chicago or being a smokejumper or something."

His expression shuttered again, just for a second, then brightened with the false cheer she was learning to recognize as masking.

He made a loud buzzer sound. "Baaaaaa. You have asked entirely too many questions for your turn. For my turn, I invoke the right to reuse my dare again, and your song will be..." He pulled out his phone and punched at it a few times. The noise of shrill techno-pop with a record-scratching beat started, followed by squawking chicken noises over the music. On his screen, a chicken strutted and bobbed.

"The Chicken Dance song? Oh, no you don't," she said, horrified, though she couldn't hold back a laugh.

"Fine, then answer my question truthfully or your peppers await you. What's the best kiss you've ever had?"

A little flutter flitted up the underside of her sternum. This game was Slip 'N Sliding fast into genuine flirting. Though she had to confess that when he'd first proposed Truth or Dare, this was the direction she'd wondered—okay, hoped—it might take.

She didn't even have to pause to think about it. "About six years ago, I went to New Mexico to visit my dad for summer break during college. A cousin introduced me to her boyfriend's friend Jorge. We'd double-dated a bit with them, and then one day he took me to Carlsbad Caverns. I'd been there before, but he'd signed us up for a special tour to a really deep part of the cave. At one point in the tour, the ranger turned out all the lights. I've never experienced absolute darkness like that before or since. So I'm looking around, trying to see anything at all, and all of a sudden I felt him right in front of me. Then he kissed me."

They'd kissed a couple of times before that, but not like this. It was sweet, but something about the total blackness turned up the dial. "And then the lights went on again quicker than he expected, and we were busted." She still remembered the chuckles from the rest of the group.

"Wow. I may have to steal that one."

"Yeah, well, when I told my cousin about it, I found out it was his standard move with all the girls. Your turn. What did you think of me that first day we met?"

"Hey, that's reusing a question. What about a little originality, huh?"

"You made the rules, bub. There was nothing in there about not reusing a question."

"You're right," he said, then fidgeted with a cat toy left between the couch cushions by

Tiger, a small mouse that vibrated when touched. "Okay, truth. So, I may have come off a bit flirty at first." She shot him a look. "Yes, more than a bit," he amended, "and right when you first drove up, like you said. It wasn't a playbook move, though. I came out to help you unload your car and I was…well…you kinda knocked my socks off when I first saw you." Then he endeared himself to her forever by blushing. "I'm sorry. I hope that doesn't come off as rude or objectifying." She quirked her eyebrows, waiting for the rest. He grimaced and plowed ahead. "And then you got out of the car…well, I adore tall women. Enough said."

Tiger leaped from his lap and pounced after some bug, real or imaginary, then meandered toward the litter box in the bathroom. Good thing. The distraction pulled Sienna from a long fall into Troy's sky-blue eyes, golden scruff of beard, adorable smile and deepening blush.

She'd been attracted to Troy from the get-go—and apparently he'd felt the same—but all the more reason to keep reminding herself that the two of them were polar opposites in personality, just like her mom and dad. And she'd seen firsthand how well that had worked out. She'd more than seen it, she'd lived it: her father's criticism and constant stress over her mother's flightiness; her mother pretending not to notice, trying to remain cheerful and true to herself; the growing gulf between them until they were living such separate lives they were like two renters in the same house; and in the end, the divorce.

She and Troy would be working closely for three days and that needed to be all there was to this. Developing romantic feelings for him—even the stray fanciful thoughts this evening that kept flitting through her brain, how maybe they could do better than her parents—wouldn't change the facts.

"I think it's time to get rid of these pepper slices," she said, standing to put distance between them and grabbing the plate.

"Agreed. We're both too brave with the truth card to be pepper people. Though I am a little sorry about not getting my chicken dance." She felt certain now, though, that the dare had nothing to do with this. His whole purpose in suggesting the game had been served when he cleared the air about his breakup with Jan and why he'd bailed on them that day.

"Me too," she said, feeling slightly awkward for ending his game so abruptly. "About my 'Patrick Swayze big finale dance'… I would have loved to see you re-create that one down the aisle of the theater just before the big lift."

He snorted a laugh. "Would you have gone for it? The lift?"

It was her turn to snicker, glad the tension between them had broken. "Guess we'll never know now."

She put the peppers in the compost, washed the plate and thoroughly cleaned her hands again. Returning to the archway she had to look twice before finding him squatting on the floor, examining the bottom of her bookcase.

"You have a ton of games here," he said, touching the various boxes and cases. "Yahtzee, Scrabble, Monopoly, Pente, dominoes, backgammon, Settlers of Catan, chess, a cribbage board, four decks of cards..."

"My whole family enjoys games."

Game nights comprised some of her happiest memories growing up. Her father might have been an inflexible man who could be judgmental of others, but he was also a good teacher and a gracious loser. As a brainiac who excelled at strategy, he enjoyed a wide variety of games, but had always been generous with praise for anyone who beat him. At heart, he really wanted to help everyone be their best self, though he could never see more than one path to any goal. And her mother...well, her mother loved anything fun. As a result, all three children had grown up playing cards and board games often.

"Do you like online gaming?" he asked, still sifting through her stack.

"I do, but I don't dare play. They're so addictive, I'd never get anything else done. If you're a gamer, though, these probably look pretty boring."

"Not at all. We have most of these at the station. I have a hard time getting anyone else interested, though."

"Pick one out if you want."

"Mmm. I'd like to but I feel kind of sloth-like after that big dinner." He shifted onto his knees, browsing her shelf of DVDs. "How about a movie instead?" She crossed the room to stand behind him, looking at the selection over his shoulder.

"Those are pretty old. I keep meaning to box them up. You know I do have actual streaming channels. Modern movies and everything."

"Oh, old movies!" He turned to her with a grin. "I have an idea. Do you mind?" He gestured to the TV.

She shrugged and handed him the remote.

They took their places on the love seat again and he punched in the search term, "Hellfighters." His face lit up. "Bingo. There it is. Streaming is awesome."

The movie poster thumbnail showed an illustrated John Wayne posed dramatically in front of a giant column of smoke and fire. He hit the select button.

CHAPTER TEN

"I DON'T KNOW if something this old is going to interest you," Troy said, having second thoughts about his movie pick. "I've already seen it so don't feel you have to watch it for my sake."

"My mom and I watch old movies together all the time. Most aren't even from her era. They were the ones she'd grown up watching with her mom. Gotta confess, I still kind of have a thing for Cary Grant."

He chuckled, trying to remember the last time someone had made him smile as much as she did.

"I normally never offer food that isn't homemade, but I do happen to have a box of microwave popcorn," she suggested.

"Buttered?"

"Extra movie-theater butter."

"I'll never be so full that I turn down extra-butter popcorn with a movie."

By the time the opening credits had run, Sienna returned with a large glass bowl filled with steaming popcorn. Leaving a table lamp on, she turned off the overhead light and scooted a little closer on the sofa so they could both easily reach the bowl between them. The popcorn was good; the company was better.

Movies this old didn't demand close attention. Not exactly intricate plotting or profound dialogue in most of them. He filled her in here and there on the differences between the fictional character of Chance Buckman, and the real-life firefighter, Red Adair. When they finished the popcorn, she pulled a throw blanket from the back of the sofa for them to share. It was a warm evening and he didn't need the light cover, but it kept them snuggled close together, so he wasn't about to object. Seemed perfect timing for the ol' stretch and drop an arm around her shoulders move, but he was enjoying their improved rapport so much that he didn't want to risk ruining it.

He'd hinted at his interest in a kiss earlier with Truth or Dare, and then he'd been honest about finding her attractive. She'd ended up pulling back, the same as she had when he'd put an arm around her on the bench in town this afternoon. It was for the best anyway. After three years with Jan, he had no desire to leap back into a relationship that wouldn't go anywhere. Better to go slow and get to know each other.

"You smell good," she said out of the blue. "Like rawhide."

Dried sweat on his day-old shirt from the hot day layered over horses and sandalwood soap more likely. He wasn't going to ruin her flattering perception with such a mundane truth, though. She smelled far better than horses and sweat. Gardenia and rose on a rainy summer day.

"Why aren't you a cowboy?" she added.

"What?"

"I saw you this morning, decked out in your boots and hat, and riding your horse like you were born to it…which I guess you literally were. So why firefighting? You said this morning it's all you've wanted to do since you were a kid. Why's that when you grew up on a ranch?"

"I suppose when I was little I wanted to be a cowboy. It was all I really knew. Wooden rocking horse in my room as soon as I could walk. Horse-head stick toy later. Cowboy boots in preschool. But around fourth or fifth grade we had a career week. The usuals came to the classroom—police officer, doctor, dancer, scientist, forest ranger. We had some hands-on stuff with a dog trainer and a chef and florist. Video lectures from an astronaut, an actor, a UN delegate, I think. But when the teacher played the video from the New York City firefighter… I don't know how to explain it… I just knew that was it. All those interesting people and that one hit me like lightning."

On TV, Chance Buckman swaggered onto the scene of yet another raging fire. The movie pyrotechnics spurred a weird trifecta in his brain: the bravado of John Wayne, Troy's own childhood goals and his current everyday work reality. He had certainly landed short of his grand dreams of big cities and hellfighters.

He continued. "The captain in the video had moved into teaching at the New York Fire Academy. He stressed the importance of giving back to the community, protecting people, being brave even when you thought you couldn't be. He described the promotions from firefighter to engineer to captain to chief, and specialties like arson investigation, and how it was a career and not just a job. He had a slideshow too. I still remember some of them, like an engineer checking water pressure gauges on the engine with a three-alarm fire blazing in the background. A firefighter sitting on a curb, hair matted with sweat and covered in soot. A rescue on one of the bridges. It all looked so exciting. By the time that video ended, I was hooked. From that day on, I never doubted it."

"How'd your parents feel about your choice?"

He loved the feel of her under the blanket with him, nestled against him, the sound of her voice, the shadows on her face in the flickering light of the TV. In the comfort of her company, he floated back through the memories of those years.

"They were supportive, even though it wasn't really what my dad wanted for me. Later, they offered to send me to college—anywhere, any major. I think after Lane decided at eighteen to major in international business, they hoped I'd either go big like him or stay home and go into ranching with my dad. By the time I graduated high school, it was clear that I wasn't going to change my mind. It was okay, though. By then everyone could see that Cole was a cowboy through and through, and Dad had already taken him under his wing, mentoring him to take over. It's good that things worked out like they did. I can't imagine Cole doing anything else, and his goal of ranching freed Lane and me up to pursue what we really wanted."

"Which interests you more, wildland firefighting or urban?"

"I'm not sure yet. We haven't been out on more than a couple wildland hotspots so far. I was watching some videos this morning of that big wildfire blowing up in Washington. More and more places are putting the tactical commanders' meetings online. The videos are great for studying how they handle things in real time."

"You were watching the videos this morning? Before I came over?"

"Mmm-hmm."

"So when you came downstairs all frumpy in your pajamas, you'd been watching videos?"

"Frumpy?"

She ignored his tone of indignation and fell silent, chewing her lip, considering. And then he remembered that she'd accused him of sleeping in. He couldn't blame her for the mistake, and she'd been so riled up at him for not being ready that he hadn't bothered to correct her. Hard to believe that the color-coding, list-making, time-obsessive woman who had shown up on his doorstep was the same woman he practically cuddled with now. The woman who was smart, funny, an amazing cook and could remodel her home.

She seemed to shrug off her reassessment of the morning before another thought struck her. "Huh," she grunted.

"What?"

Her focus returned and she turned her head to look up at him. "I don't know. I guess I'm still surprised that you find New York Metro and wildland fires and oil fires so exciting—" she flicked a finger at the movie "—and here you are in Alamosa. I mean, you have family here and I get that. I've dreamed of moving to Southern California for years, but I stay here mainly to watch out for my mom." She tipped her head to meet his eyes. "With your parents gone and Cole getting married now, do you think you'll stay on here?"

The warmth receded, leaving his fingertips cold. He could feel the acid increasing in his stomach. He'd been so content and comfortable with her that he'd walked right into this without noticing.

His family had never come right out and said *do more with yourself*, but the implication had lurked in every question about his grades, his efforts, his ambitions. *Why Alamosa College instead of a big university? Why drop out before getting your degree?* Their mild disappointment had bruised him, but it had been less stressful than their expectations.

His parents had excelled at everything. His brothers had excelled. His grandparents and great-grandparents had. The fear that he wouldn't had dogged him all his life and made it easier for him to simply not try in the first place.

Lane, as the oldest, had received the brunt of their parents' attention until it shifted to Cole, adopted at seven years old, with his emotional wounds and more extreme and imperative needs. Troy, the middle child, had floated under the radar, happy to be invisible. Inevitably, he grew up enough that people started noticing his mediocrity. Lectures from his teachers and coaches—the encouragement to *just try*—only put more pressure on him, making him retreat further, which made those around him focus on him more. Anything he expressed an interest in might as well have summoned a magnifying glass to float above him wherever he went, stirring everyone to anticipate "maybe he'll shine at *this*, or show ambition at *that*." It made trying even more unbearable.

Class clown. Deflection. Mediocre goals and mediocre achievement. Those had been his comfort zones as long as he could remember. His Wildland Fire Team certification had been the most ambitious pursuit he'd tackled, but he'd done that one just for himself. Something he'd wanted since childhood. He told no one in the family he was training for it until he passed the course. By then, his father was gone. He never got to share that accomplishment with him. Still, even that was for Alamosa, like Sienna said. He'd never gone to New York or LA or Chicago, as he'd imagined as a child.

"What?" he said mockingly. "Alamosa isn't exciting? Seriously, have you seen our crime rating? New York's got nothing on us. If they want high risk, they should come work here."

"Yeah, I know, I just—"

Now was the time for the stretch and drop. He spread his arms like wings across the back of the sofa and let one hand slide to her shoulder. "Were you working the day that drug ring out of Arkansas got busted?"

As he'd done this afternoon, he massaged the muscles under his fingers: levator tendon, neck muscles, deltoids, all of them peppered with tight trigger points. Little land mines that he gently defused with steady pressure and kneading fingers.

"I was working nights then," she mumbled, relaxing into it. "I came in to hear about all the excitement I'd missed. Hey, while you're at it, could you move down lower between my shoulder blades?" She turned her back to him, and he began massaging with both hands. She reached out to turn off the table lamp shining in her eyes then puddled like a jellyfish, sitting slumped and boneless under his ministrations.

He increased the pressure carefully—not enough to send her trigger points into spasm but enough to feel some of the knots unkinking.

"You're very good at this," she said, her chin almost on her chest.

Yes, he was. He knew his strengths. And he knew how to stick to them.

"This part of the movie," he said after a couple of minutes of quiet massage, "where they go to Venezuela, that's bunk, like most of this plot, but Adair did work all over the world. The Sahara, Australia, the Middle East. Right into his seventies, I think."

Troy stopped the massage and she turned back to the movie, her body loose and her line of questioning dropped or forgotten, as he'd hoped.

He sat back with her and pulled the blanket up again, the coziness and gentle heat adding to her relaxation, and then to his own. A few minutes later, the warmth of their combined body heat under the blanket brought a soft drowsiness creeping over him like fog. His eyelids grew heavy.

"I DRIFTED OFF, didn't I?" he said, stretching.

The movie had ended so long ago that the TV was in sleep mode. They'd tilted toward each other in sleep, arms touching, her head against his shoulder. She looked so sweetly drowsy—tousled and gorgeous in the faint light of the half-moon outside and the various electronics and chargers in the room—that he didn't want to move.

"I guess we both did," she mumbled.

"What time is it?"

"Mmph," she said, stretching for her phone on the side table. "Oh, wow. One thirty."

"Ugh. I'd better get going."

"If we're going to be on the road by seven thirty, why don't you just stay here?"

He looked askance at her love seat. "I don't think I'll fit."

"I do have a guest room, you know."

And he had his work duffel in his truck, where he kept basics like a change of underwear, and a shaving bag. He debated the twenty-minute drive home versus imposing here. If he left, Baxter would bark and disturb Cole, and Sienna would have to swing by on the way out of town to pick him up in the morning.

She turned on the table lamp and through the kitchen arch he could see the edge of that marvelous coffee maker.

"Do I get an expresso in the morning?"

"A *double* expresso."

CHAPTER ELEVEN

Tuesday, July 28th

"AAAAAAAAAEEEEEE" CAME JAMES BROWN'S loud screech in a continually rising register, not unlike the upward wail of a police siren. "Ugh," Sienna said aloud, lifting Tiger from her head and reaching her other hand from under the covers to slap blindly at her nightstand.

Drums and bass guitar joined in on the final "ow!" of the song's opening vocal. Grunts and whistles interlaced with the heavy funk beat before James Brown admonished Sienna to GET UP OFFA THAT THING! The alarm looped back to begin again with the opening screech of the song before she managed to find the kill button.

Dozing on the sofa in the evening hadn't been as restful as genuine sleep, and by the time she'd gotten Troy settled in the spare room around two in the morning, brushed her teeth and made it into bed, she'd found she was no longer sleepy.

Especially since a tall, gorgeous, single firefighter, who just happened to also be a surprisingly fun and genuinely nice person, slept just the other side of her bedroom wall. Not that she'd changed her mind about him. A relationship with him would be doomed to fail, but it didn't stop her from lying awake for an extra half hour thinking about the what-ifs.

The light through the curtains crept tentatively into the room, thin and gray. It would be so easy to roll over and go back to sleep, but Sienna's superpower had always been her ability to stay on task. She turned on the bedside light and got up. Slipping into a bathrobe, she knocked on the door of the guest bedroom.

"Come on in," Troy said with an early-morning rasp to his voice.

She opened the door a crack to find Troy sitting up in bed. She poked her head inside. "You're awake."

"Hard not to be with that noise. Did you step on little Tiger's tail?"

"I need something that can get my attention after a long night shift and bad day's sleep."

"That would do it. If your alarm woke me up in here, I can't imagine what it was like in there. You would've had to scrape me off the ceiling." He scooted back down until his head reached the pillow. His eyes closed.

She opened the door wider. “Hey, none of that. Up and at ’em, sleepyhead. We’ve got miles to cover and lots to do.”

“Mmph,” he replied.

“If this is how you are when there’s an emergency call in the middle of the night, it would explain why your shift’s response time is so slow.”

Their response time was no different than any other shift or station, and they both knew it. He lifted his head and shoulders to brace on his elbows.

“Why? Is there an emergency I’m unaware of? A grease fire in the kitchen from making me breakfast? Has Tiger learned to drive a car overnight and been in a collision?”

“The emergency is that my best friend’s wedding is eighteen days from now.”

“Well, I seem to remember somebody promising me a double espresso.”

“It’ll be ready by the time you’re out of the shower.”

“Do that, and I’ll be yours to command.”

“All day?”

He slapped his right hand over his heart. “All day.”

She liked the sound of that.

After fueling him up in Alamosa yesterday, she had the basics of how he took his coffee. Ten minutes later, she returned with a large mug of double cappuccino with just a hint of caramel and amaretto flavoring and one for herself. She knocked on the bathroom door and he emerged fully dressed. He took a sip and his eyes closed in sheer ecstasy.

"I'll be out of the shower in ten," she said. "If we're on the road by seven thirty, we'll hit our first stop in the Springs just as they open."

SIENNA BACKED OUT of the driveway at 7:29 a.m., both of them showered, caffeinated and fed. A work-from-home neighbor who checked on Tiger during her long shifts had been notified that she'd be gone for the day.

"You listen to music on your commute?" he asked.

"Spotify through my phone, usually. Feel free to start it up if you want. The jack is there." She pointed to the black cable snaking out from the console between them.

He lifted her phone from its cradle on the dash, plugged it to the speakers and held it for her to tap in her lock-screen code. Another couple of taps from him, and the acoustic guitar chords of Jamestown Revival's "Cast Iron Soul" began.

"Did you choose that?" she asked, surprised.

"No. I just started your 'favorites' playlist." Troy cocked his head, trying to place the song or the singers. "So you like folk? Alternative bluegrass? Americana? What is this?"

"A little bit of all of that." She bobbed her head along with the two-man harmonies.

He scrolled down her playlist. "I don't recognize half these names. Am I that old?"

"I don't know. Maybe. You told me you're thirty, but how do I really know?"

"I was three years ahead of you in school."

"Yeah, but you could have repeated a grade like eight times."

"It was only five."

She snorted a laugh as he went back to scrolling through her playlist.

"It's mostly Americana and mellow alternative," she said, "but the rest is pretty eclectic. Country. Rock. Some alternative rock like Kaleo and Pearl Jam. Blues. Some older stuff—Pink Floyd, Elvis." She turned to him. "What do you listen to?"

"I feel so boring now. Contemporary country, I guess. Mostly. I mean, I was kind of funneled into it. It played at home, in Dad's truck, in the stores in town. I like these guys a lot, though."

"That's not surprising. Country music has its roots in folk, and Americana has its roots in country."

For the next dozen songs, he jumped around in her playlist, sampling artists he didn't know.

When they ran out of downloaded songs and lost internet on the pass, she turned it off and they made fun of billboards for a bit, then chatted about past road trips and weird roadside attractions.

They were nearly an hour and a half north of Burgess, on I-25 now and about halfway between Walsenburg and Pueblo, when her phone rang. She answered it on speakerphone.

"Hey, Mama."

"Oh, Sienna. I'm so glad I reached you. Listen, honey, I need you to do something for me."

"I'm not in town. I'm on my way to Colorado Springs for the day, but I should be back around dinnertime or so."

"Oh, that's fine. I'm sure they'll let me stay until you get here."

"Who'll let you stay where?"

"The hospital."

"What hospital? Why are you in a hospital?"

"Because of the accident," her mother patiently explained, as if Sienna was five years old.

Sienna squeezed her eyes shut as long as she dared while driving. She'd played Twenty Questions with her mom more times than she could count. "Mama, what accident? Tell me what happened."

"I told you I was coming down to see my new grandbaby. Well, your brother and Louise too, but especially my new grandbaby." Sienna's nephew was fourteen months old. Hardly new. "I figured it was a good time to go, what with the oil change and tune-up the car got last week. Besides, Dan had to go to some financial conference thing all week somewhere. Arizona? Utah? Oh, I don't remember now. So I just popped down."

"No, you didn't tell me. So you drove down to Albuquerque and you got in a car accident? Are you okay?"

"No, no. Not a car accident. I slipped off the windowsill trying to get inside through their living room window. I broke my right ankle and the doctor won't let me drive back. The orthopedist here says I have to have surgery on it, but we've got to wait a day or two for the swelling to go down some."

Sienna shook her head, unsure where to start. "Mama, why are you calling me instead of Carlos?"

"Well, because they aren't here, silly. That's why I was trying to get in the window."

Sienna bugged her eyes at Troy in exasperation. "I'm not following any of this, okay? Start at the beginning."

"Well, my car caught on fire the other day and got all fixed up, and so I decided it was a good time to come to Albuquerque and see Carlos and Louise and my grandbaby. Especially my grandbaby."

Sienna sighed, but she *had* asked her to start at the beginning. There seemed to be more at work here than her mother's routine spaciness; framed against heavy pain medication, things made a bit more sense. Not her mom, of course… just the number of non sequiturs. Though traffic was sparse, she pulled over on the shoulder to focus better on the conversation.

"Right. I got that part. Then what?"

"Then I got here, and they weren't here, and I called them, and they'd gone…somewhere." Sienna could almost see her mother wave away the annoying details.

"Mama, is this the week they'd planned to go to Kansas for her folks' fiftieth anniversary?"

"Oh, yes. That was it."

"And you didn't call first to let them know you wanted to visit."

"I thought I'd surprise them."

"And you were climbing in the window because…"

"Because they weren't home, dear. I didn't want to drive all the way back that same day, and hotels are outrageously expensive. The screen on the living room window looked loose, and I knew they wouldn't mind."

Sienna shot Troy another look. He shook his

head, but he was smiling. No, *worse*. He was trying not to laugh. Sienna's brows drew together. His shoulders quit shaking, but the smile didn't fade.

"Mama, I'm probably, I don't know, five hours or more from you." She glanced to Troy who shrugged, then nodded in agreement. He pulled out his phone and opened his maps app. "Have you called Tommy?" She didn't hold out much hope for her other brother. He worked as an engineering technician for the railroad and was usually out of state at least five days a week.

"He's in Sacramento until Saturday."

"Dad?" she said weakly.

"Oh, honey, don't be silly. He's with that Nancy woman now. I'm not going to call there."

That "Nancy woman" had been Sienna's stepmother for twelve years.

"Okay. I'll give Uncle Marco a call. If you've been there long enough to be seen and get diagnosed, the ER will probably discharge you before I can get there. If he can drive down from Santa Fe to get you, then I can pick you up at his house."

She got the name of the hospital and they signed off. Sienna leaned back into the headrest and propped one elbow on the car's windowsill with her hand across her eyes as it occurred to her that she not only had her mother's injury and the logistics of helping her out to deal with, but also the blow this would deliver to the wedding shopping.

Dropping her arm to her lap, she half turned to Troy and shook her head. "Rose Herrera strikes again." She started the car and pulled onto the interstate, heading for an exit where she could turn around. "Once I drop you off at your ranch, do you think maybe you could go to the rental place in Alamosa today? You could call me from there and I'd talk you through what we need."

"Dropping me off would add nearly an hour to your trip. Better to shoot straight down the interstate all the way to Santa Fe."

"What? You can't come to New Mexico." He looked taken aback, and she regretted her phrasing. "I mean, you don't *want* to come, right? An hour isn't all that big a deal considering how much driving I'm going to be doing in the next couple of days."

"Probably more than a couple of days. But either way, you're going to need to figure out a way to bring your mom's car back up here for her. Unless you can drive them both like a stunt rider riding two horses, you'll need another driver, and it sounds like your brothers are out of the picture."

She hadn't thought that far ahead, but he was right. "But… New Mexico. Are you sure?"

"Sure I'm sure. I'm off work until Saturday. We'll get the wedding stuff done when we get back, okay? Don't worry. It'll be fine."

It'll be fine.

CHAPTER TWELVE

AS FAR AS Troy was concerned, going to Santa Fe in place of a full day of wedding shopping in Colorado Springs felt like a kid getting a surprise snow day off school. While he appreciated the reprieve, though, he couldn't help but notice Sienna's drooped posture and the sad line of her mouth. He'd offered to drive when they turned around so she could make her phone call and relax a bit, but his gaze kept wandering from the road to her staring out the passenger window. For her, this had to be a perfect storm of concern for her mom, delays to her plans and a sad farewell wave to her remaining two days off.

"Worried about your mom?" he asked, when she'd been silent a while.

"Not exactly. I mean, yes, but the accident already happened. It's fortunate she didn't injure anything but her ankle, and she's being treated at a hospital. It doesn't do much good to worry about it now."

The calm with which she approached the

whole situation impressed him. But maybe it wasn't all that surprising considering she handled emergencies every day at work.

It seemed hard to believe how much his image of her had evolved in the past twenty-four hours from a two-dimensional, detail-oriented dispatcher to this smart and complex woman. He kept sneaking looks at the sunrise colors of orange and yellow on her light, spaghetti-strap top, her sandals that exposed toenails painted candy red, her jean shorts, ragged at the hem and her one long leg bent, foot on the dash, while she pulled up her uncle's phone number. She was like a firecracker on a winter night. Something bright and fun and unexpected. A burst of color and sparkle that warmed you just looking at it.

"Frustrated then?" The moue that puckered her mouth was answer enough.

She shrugged. "Trying not to be. Not frustrated with my mom, anyway. Believe me, you're just seeing a slice of everyday life with Rose Herrera. But losing time with the wedding coming up so soon..." She shook her head. "I promised them, Troy. Kelli has so much on her shoulders, and I told her to leave it all to me." She shrugged again, as if struggling to embrace her only option, reluctant acceptance. "Nothing I can do about it for now, though. 'When a plan gets foiled, change the plan,' as my father would say. I'll deal with my mom first, then figure a way forward, right?"

"Right."

She'd found the number she'd been looking up and hit dial. Her uncle picked up and she explained the situation to him. From Troy's side of the conversation, it sounded like he was happy to pick her mom up from the hospital. Sienna thanked him, hung up and fell silent again, staring out the side window.

Despite her saying that worry would do no good, she obviously wasn't taking her own advice. It made him want to pull over and give her a hug of reassurance. Her head against the headrest made him wish she could nap the drive away to distract her from her troubles. When she flipped her long hair back, he wanted to massage her scalp and feel her unwind under his hands, as she'd done with the back rub last night. He realized that her worry was causing him to worry, and he used her silence to examine his reaction to her.

She was the first woman he'd spent significant time alone with since Jan, but it wasn't the newness that made her company so stimulating. Though he appreciated Sienna's height and her looks, it was more than just physical attraction. Something intangible had begun to hum in his veins. Like walking under one of those immense highline transformers, electricity vibrated through him when he was near her. The current had begun when they first met, but it sparked to life while making dinner last night, strengthened during Truth or Dare and intensified again when they shared a blanket, a movie and a nap. It had warmed him to be the first person she'd talked to this morning, and if he hadn't been with her today, he would have missed that singing in his blood. At last, he put a name to the sensation. Chemistry.

Fifteen years of dating and he'd finally found that elusive, more-than-attraction, more-than-common-ground connection. He'd finally found chemistry. And because of it, her concern and worry was able to insinuate itself into his own emotions.

He spoke without preamble into the silence.

"I swam with sharks without a cage on a family vacation in Mexico. My mother has paintings in two world-famous galleries. My great-great grandfather knew Kit Carson."

Her melancholy study of the roadside broke off and she stared at him.

"I... What?"

"Haven't you ever played Two Truths and a Lie?"

She laughed. He liked the sound of it, rich and throaty.

"Not in a long time," she said. "About as long as Truth or Dare, I guess." Pulled from her funk for the time being, she said, "Okay, give those to me again." He did, and she squinted in concentration. "Kelli mentioned your mom was an artist, and I saw the cabin your ancestor homesteaded. I'm going with swimming with sharks is the lie."

"Nope," he said with the smugness of a winner. "It happened during the only family vacation we took out of the country. It was for a wedding in Mexico for some friends of our parents. I went down to the beach by myself and heard about a tour for swimming with sharks. I traded in my ticket for the scenic tour my dad had booked for the family the next day and got a ride on the shark boat. When they stopped, I jumped in the water."

"You what?"

"I was thirteen. I didn't know they went down in cages."

She gasped and slapped a hand over her open mouth.

He shrugged, though, older and wiser now, he had to agree with her assessment of his stupidity at the time. "What can I say? My enthusiasm was bigger than my brain. I guess I figured the boat crew kept it safe somehow or they wouldn't do the tours. Turns out, the way they kept it safe was with cages, which they were just about to instruct everyone on."

"So were there sharks?"

"Yeah. One. I about levitated out of the water when I saw it. The crewman who hauled me in told me it was a reef shark. Nonaggressive. About five minutes later, we saw a bull shark. Very aggressive."

"Did you go back down in a cage?"

"No, they wouldn't let me. By then they'd realized I didn't have parents with me, plus they said I'd already taken up too much of everyone's time. I think at that point they were afraid I'd open the cage door or something."

"So Kit Carson was the lie?"

"It was. Though my great-great-grandfather did come up here on the Santa Fe Trail and was two weeks behind a group being led by Kit Carson. He never did meet him, but apparently he talked about it for the rest of his life saying if he'd arrived in Santa Fe two weeks earlier he would've signed on to ride with him." He turned to her with a smile. "Okay. Your turn."

She caught her lower lip in her teeth and thought for a moment.

"I'm fluent in three languages. I've been skydiving six times. I can strip down and rebuild a car engine." She raised her eyebrows at him in challenge.

It was his turn to narrow his eyes, holding her gaze. "I call bunk on that last one."

"Wrong," she said with a smirk.

"Really?" He'd been pretty confident about it too, but he loved that she kept surprising him.

"I have two brothers. The oldest one was into mechanics. My other brother and I learned from him."

"Skydiving then?"

"I've only been once."

"So, barely a lie."

She shrugged. "A handful of friends went to Las Vegas one spring break in college. We'd had a bit to drink that first night—okay, more than a bit—and one of the gals saw a poster for the skydiving outfit. She drunk-dialed, signed us up and paid ahead with her credit card, so we had to go through with it. It was horrifying. Especially hung over."

He laughed. "I can only imagine. So, languages are English—being a Herrera and living here and working dispatch, I'm going to guess Spanish, right?" She nodded. "What else?"

"American Sign Language. I have a cousin who's deaf, so I learned it to talk to her. And I grew up with Castilian Spanish. My dad's family was from Spain."

"Is it similar to the Spanish spoken in Mexico?"

"Similar enough for conversation, but I learned Latin American Spanish too." She shifted in her seat to face him. "Okay. We're tied now and I love winning. You got another one?"

He watched the lines on the road flash by as he searched for three things that might stump her.

"All right. I'm deathly allergic to peanuts. Even one could kill me. I hate watching sports on TV. All of them. I've lived the 'firefighter saves a cat in a tree' cliché."

"Peanuts," she said without hesitation.

It surprised him she got it so easily. "How'd you know?"

"Someone that allergic would've mentioned it before I cooked for you last night. Even a surface or utensil with peanut residue on it could put you in hospital."

"You're right. Busted. I did go on an anaphylaxis call once, though. An airline pilot who'd retired in Alamosa. Passed out cold on his living room floor. Swollen lips and throat. Turning blue. Two doses of epi later he came to. First thing he said was there must've been a peanut hiding in an appetizer at a party they'd just come home from."

"And the cat rescue?"

"Well, I think that one speaks for itself," he

said with a haughty air, hoping belatedly to bury the topic.

"Oh, no you don't. You started this game. Asking a follow-up question is totes legit."

He winced convincingly, but knew already he'd tell the story in hopes it would cheer her up. He gave a theatrically deep sigh.

"All right. The cat story. Here goes." He clicked on the cruise control and scooched lower in his seat.

"I know it's a stereotype, right? But in seven years with the department, I swear it's the only cat-in-a-tree call I've ever been on. It happened last fall, but if this doesn't sound familiar to you, you must have been off work or dispatching police that day." He cast his mind back to the event. "So, first call of the day—I haven't even finished my morning check sheet on the fire engine—and we get sent to an unknown emergency. Elderly woman in distress. We drive there hot, lights and sirens. Police respond because 'unknown,' right?"

She nodded. The potential danger of sending a crew into an unknown situation meant dispatchers always sent a police unit as well.

"An ambulance crew responds too. We arrive, and dear, elderly Mrs. Metz is beside herself yelling 'he's stuck' and 'quick, help him' and 'he's going to fall' over and over."

"Oh no. Mrs. Metz on Elm Drive?"

"You know her?"

"She's one of our frequent fliers."

"Okay, so you get the picture. She points up in the tree, and there, thirty feet off the ground, hidden by leaves, is this fuzzy, orange face." He paused for dramatic effect, and Sienna gave a twirling motion with her finger to continue.

"So, by all rights, Bouncer, being brand-new, should've been the one to get the cat, but he begs off saying he's allergic. Like peanut-anaphylaxis allergic. Then Jan pipes up that she's allergic too, even though I'd known her for two years by that point and I'm more than certain she's not. And it's not like the captain was going to do it. So guess who went after the cat?"

She smiled.

"I know it was thirty feet up because the ladder we carry on that truck is twenty-five feet. We unload the ladder and brace it, and up I go. The cat is just out of reach, so I'm balanced on the top rung, hanging on to branches. Elderly Mrs. Metz is still pointing and dancing and about to have a stroke saying her cat is going to fall. I'm fighting to push limbs and leaves out of the way, and all of a sudden I get a better view of this cat. It's *big*, and my brain is going 'maybe it's a Maine Coon.' So I move the last branch out of my way and realize this thing's head is as big as a golden retriever's. The black markings on its fur register about the same time I see a paw the size of my hand." Sienna is laughing out loud now. "Amber eyes lock onto mine, and then this thing growls. Not a cat growl. A bobcat growl."

"No," she said.

"Yes. Deep in the chest, low in pitch, rough. Sounds almost like a bear. And the dead giveaway? The teeth. Canines as big as my fingers." He waggled the fingers of one hand.

"Somebody's dog must've treed it at dawn or something. Anyway, I'm hurrying so much I nearly fall twice trying to get back down through the branches to get my hands on the rungs."

Sienna was bent forward with laughter now, elbows on knees, one hand over her mouth. Tears filled her gorgeous dark eyes.

"Once I get hold of the ladder, I'm down faster than greased lightning. As soon as my feet hit the ground, I shoot dear Mrs. Metz a death-ray glare, which she doesn't notice because there's this small ginger cat winding around her legs. And she's all, 'Oh, there you are, Charlie,' and picks up her cat and goes in her house without so much as a thank you."

Sienna wiped her tears away, her little finger dabbing at the corners. It drew his attention to her long, black lashes, thick and curled, framing her dark eyes. Realizing he'd paused, he jumped back into the story hoping she hadn't noticed him staring.

"So, you'd think that's the end, wouldn't you? But you've never worked in a fire station. They're born pranksters. Want to know what they put me through?"

She nodded, nearly choking from trying to stifle fits of mirth that kept bubbling up and making her eyes tear.

"I'm now the proud owner of the total Hello Kitty line of merchandise. Mug, lunch pail, thermos, backpack, sweatshirt…you name it, I have it. It went on for about a week. My clothes stashed and my towel swapped out while I'm in the shower so that the Hello Kitty beach towel is all I have to walk around in looking for my uniform. A T-shirt swapped out for my department T-shirt while I slept, so I ended up going to a middle-of-the-night call wearing the Hello Kitty one. Yeah. Good times."

A fresh fit of laughter gripped her so hard she couldn't control her breathing or the small squeaky sounds she made. If her picturing his myriad humiliations meant him getting to see her like this—joyful, unguarded, unscripted—it was worth it a hundred times over.

The game ended there, and the rest of the drive was spent in companionable conversation and laughter. They stopped for an early lunch in

Las Vegas, New Mexico, at the historic hotel on the plaza, where they shared the biggest plate of loaded nachos Troy had ever seen. Once back in the car, she called her uncle again.

"Hi, Uncle Marco. How's Mom doing?" She listened to his reply. "That's good. Thanks again for going down to Albuquerque and checking her out of the hospital. Don't wake her, but we're just leaving Las Vegas so we'll be in Santa Fe in about forty-five minutes. See you soon."

CHAPTER THIRTEEN

SIENNA AND TROY arrived shortly after lunchtime. Her Uncle Marco met them on the front porch of his beautiful Spanish-style home and gave her a big hug. He shook hands with Troy, clapping him on one shoulder when she introduced him. Fun, gregarious and less than twenty years older than Sienna, her uncle had always felt more like an older cousin than her father's younger brother.

"Is Mom still asleep?" she asked as they headed inside.

"Sure is. Whatever they gave her at the hospital really knocked her out. She's been asleep since I got her here about lunchtime."

His home was large and elegant, with gleaming tile floors and heavy, carved wooden furniture. Somehow the house managed to feel both contemporary and yet essentially unchanged from her childhood memories.

She'd let Troy know on the drive down that her uncle had been a widower for ten years, but the photos of her Uncle Marco and Aunt Maria on the built-in shelving still tugged at her heartstrings. They'd been so in love. She wished her own parents had kept that same closeness with each other. Growing up, she'd spent more than a few holidays here, witnessing the contrast between her parents' relationship and her aunt and uncle's. She'd often wondered if the differences between the two half brothers boiled down to the fact they had different fathers from vastly different marriages, or if they might have been opposite personalities even if they'd been full brothers.

"Oh, sweetie, you made it." The enthusiastic, though somewhat slurred, words came from the arch to the hallway leading to the bedrooms. Sienna's mom emerged, tilting unsteadily on a knee scooter. Troy reached her in two quick steps, gripping her elbow to keep her from tipping over. Her shoulder-length, flame-colored hair—normally a masterpiece of bangs and perfectly hair-sprayed layered cut—lay flattened now to one side of her head. The sparkly gold eye shadow, no doubt skillfully applied this morning, had smudged across one temple. And if she'd been a cartoon, her eyes would have been spinning.

"How much pain medicine did they give her?" Sienna asked her uncle.

He shrugged.

"Let's get you to the couch," Troy said.

"Oh my," her mom said, giving Troy's upper arm a firm squeeze when he swung her expertly from her knee scooter and lowered her to the dark leather cushions. Her fingers spanned less than halfway around his flexed muscles. "Honey, is he yours? If so, hang on to this one." She giggled.

"Oh, my stars," Sienna muttered. Drugged Rose Herrera might even top tipsy Rose Herrera. She needed to get Troy out of here before her mother embarrassed her any further. "Is her car still at my brother's house?" she asked her uncle.

"As far as I know. She went to the hospital by ambulance from there. The nurse gave me her car keys when I signed her out." He plucked them from a nearby bookshelf and handed them to Sienna along with a hospital bag containing her pain meds and discharge instructions, including a follow-up appointment with the orthopedist the following day.

"If my mom's suitcase is in the car and my brother's out of town," she said to Troy, "the sooner we bring her car back here, the better."

And with any luck, maybe her mom would have come down off her high by the time they got back with it. Getting some food into her mom wouldn't hurt either, and she said as much to her uncle.

IN THE TIME it took them to drive to Albuquerque, retrieve her mom's car, stop at a grocery store and drive back to her uncle's, her mom had thankfully returned to a more normal level of ditzy energy and inappropriate conversation.

Sienna had taken stock of her uncle's bare refrigerator on the way out. Now she unpacked the frozen shrimp, mussels, whitefish, poblano peppers, onion, celery, milk, corn, potatoes and fish stock for dinner, along with an accompanying loaf of crusty French bread and stick of butter, plus a dozen additional staples she'd noticed he needed. While she got a large stockpot and started the spicy seafood chowder, Troy put away the remaining groceries and then slipped naturally into his role of sous chef, expertly chopping, dicing and mincing.

"If you grew up with a housekeeper cooking for your family, how'd you learn to do that?" Sienna asked, pointing her wooden spoon at the growing pile of cut vegetables on the chopping board.

"Work. Some shifts have a designated cook who gets out of all the cleaning chores, but no one on our shift likes cooking that much, so we rotate the duty. Every fourth shift, I have to decide the menu and cook lunch and dinner for all four of us. Trust me, if you cook for your crew, it had better turn out edible. I may not be fancy, but in seven years I've at least learned the basics."

Sienna tilted her head in a sideways nod to say that made sense, then passed him another pepper to chop.

Her uncle watched the news in the living room, and her mother had retreated to her room with a borrowed book after Sienna chased her out of the kitchen. The spicy seafood chowder—one of her best quick recipes, a favorite of Kelli's and a dish especially good for multiple people—was ready half an hour later. Troy rounded everyone up and Sienna ladled the chowder, setting the steaming bowls on the table with the platter of bread and butter and a pitcher of water.

"White wine or beer with dinner?" her uncle offered. They both picked beer.

"Wine, please, Marco," her mom said.

A chorus of noes volleyed back at her, with Sienna's the loudest and firmest. Her mom on pain pills was bad enough without throwing alcohol into the mix. Her mother shrugged with her penciled eyebrows in a nothing-ventured-nothing-gained gesture and allowed Marco to pour her a glass of water.

Dinner conversation began with the usual "what do you do, where are you from, and how did you meet" questions and responses, though Sienna smiled to herself when talk dwindled to an appreciative silence as everyone tried the chowder.

"Masterful, dear," her mother said. "As usual."

Near the end of the meal, with a little directed prompting, Sienna had Uncle Marco telling stories about his work in experimental geochemistry at Los Alamos, researching hydrogen clean energy. Initially, he'd told Troy straight-faced that he'd have to kill him if he divulged anything about his work, but soon he was like a lecturing professor, expounding on the science and challenges, yet in a way they could all follow along.

With dinner finished, her uncle, always the good host, carried their dishes from the table into the open kitchen and set them on the counter.

"Anyone for a game of Go Fish?" her mom asked hopefully.

"Aren't you tired?" Sienna asked.

"I had such a long rest this afternoon, I feel like I won't sleep again until next week."

Her mom really did amaze her sometimes, in all the best ways. Her trip had been ruined and her ankle broken. The ankle was swollen and had to be painful—even with the medications and elevating it on her scooter—and she faced surgery in the next couple of days. Despite all that, her mom hadn't complained or expressed worry once. Not about the accident, not about her pain…not about anything. She appeared unfazed by the injury and the complications it would be sure to cause for the next few weeks. But then, her mother always had been the poster child for making the best of a situation. Sienna had vacillated her whole life between finding it naïve, like her father did, and admiring the heck out of her for her ability to sail forward through anything, seemingly without a worry in the world.

And then there was Troy, switching gears and heading down here with her like it was nothing. On top of that, there hadn't been a single joke or snarky comment from him about her mother's foolishness for forgetting that her son would be out of town. Not a word uttered about her not calling ahead, or her falling out a window while trying to break in. Her father would have had plenty to say. The contrast made Sienna appreciate Troy's easygoing acceptance more than she could have put into words. Moreover, it seemed to be infectious, relaxing her more than she might have been on her own here, worrying about the challenges of the next few days and weeks.

"I'll get the cards," her uncle said.

"Oh, I'll come with you," Sienna's mom chimed in. "I just thought of a perfect something in my suitcase that I brought to have some fun with Carlos and Louise."

Troy sprang to his feet, but her mother was faster, sliding out of her chair and pulling the knee scooter to her before he reached her. At least she looked more stable than earlier in the day, Sienna observed, as her mother kicked past her like a kid on a two-wheeled toy scooter.

When they were alone, Troy plucked at his T-shirt and sniffed. "Whew. I wish I had my duffel bag I left at your house. Between the heat today and my clothes being on their second day, that shower this morning isn't helping much anymore. Good thing I'll be driving back alone tomorrow when this shirt's on day three."

"Oh, right," she said. "Easy enough to fix. Wait here a minute."

She followed her mother and uncle into the hallway and had a quick conversation with her uncle. She returned a moment later with a bright floral bathrobe from her mother's suitcase and a dark blue, checkered flannel one from her uncle. "Here you go," she said, handing Troy the flannel robe.

"I'm sorry," her uncle said, returning with the cards. "With no luggage to put away, I didn't think to show you to your rooms yet. They're just down this hall." Troy and Sienna followed him.

"The middle door is the guest bathroom. I've set some toiletries out for you both. The bedrooms are to either side of the bathroom. Go ahead and change into the robes, and you can get your clothes in the washing machine."

Her mother kick-wheeled herself down the hall from her room at the far end of the hallway. A large flat package dangled from one hand wrapped around the scooter bars. "You know what, Marco? I think a year from now these two kids won't be needing separate rooms, and I'll have myself a fireman son-in-law." She gave a little smile and wink to Sienna, who felt her face heat. She grabbed Troy's arm and pushed him toward the left-hand room, then vanished as quickly as possible into the other one.

Sienna threw on the borrowed bathrobe and gathered her small pile of laundry, then met Troy in the laundry room. They took one look at each other and burst out laughing. Troy's robe barely came to his knees while her mom's—even shorter on her than his was—practically glowed neon with bright pink and orange flowers.

"Please tell me this isn't what I'm going to look like forty years from now," Sienna said, examining the damage in the laundry room mirror.

Troy placed his hands on her shoulders from behind, gazing at her in the reflection. "You'd be gorgeous in sackcloth." Her belly warmed, not just from the flattery, but from the sincerity in his voice. "Besides, forty years from now, I might be wearing powder-blue polyester jumpsuits and sneakers with Velcro straps. Think of the fashion statement we could make together."

She snickered. "Well, we've got a good start on it," she said, half turning and waving a game-show hostess sweep of her hand at his attire.

He chuckled, then held her gaze, staring down into her face. A brief charged instant passed between them. A moment where time stretched longer than the couple of seconds that ticked by in real time. A moment that held a kiss somewhere within its protracted silence.

Her father had been impulsive one time in his life, attracted to a woman his complete opposite. They'd probably started out thinking it a fun and casual fling, forgetting that emotions had a life of their own. Give them a little leeway and they spiraled out of control, pulling hearts and bodies and logic bouncing helplessly in their wake on any trajectory they chose. But she and Troy weren't her mother and father. Doubt and attraction waged a lively war within her.

"Hurry up, you two." Her mother's voice came from nearby, making Sienna jump. "I'm looking forward to a game of cards, and you both need to get your clothes in the wash so they'll be dry for tomorrow."

The moment spoiled, they started the washing machine and headed back to the dining room to appease her mother with a couple of hands of Go Fish.

CHAPTER FOURTEEN

TROY RETURNED TO the dining room behind Sienna to find Marco had cleared the rest of the table except for their drink coasters, moved the centerpiece of silk flowers to one side and set out two decks of cards along with fresh beers. The dishwasher hummed industriously in the kitchen.

Marco and Rose sat on the far side of the table. Troy took the seat across from Rose and next to Sienna. Marco pulled the jokers and handed the two decks to Rose. She expertly shuffled them together and dealt them each five cards, then spread the rest face down in the middle of the table. As Troy moved to scoop up his hand, Rose reached across and stopped him.

"Uh-uh," she chided, singsong. "Not yet. One more thing before we start."

Troy watched with curiosity as Rose picked up the flat, school-notebook-sized package lying next to her. The opaque gold of the cellophane bag hid the contents, and with no telltale markings on the back, he couldn't guess what the packet might contain. Sienna seemed not to know what lay within either, but it didn't stop her from eyeing it with dread.

Her mother peeled back the flap and pulled out a stack of oddly shaped paperboard, still upside down and plain white on the back. They did, however, have what looked suspiciously like ear loops near the sides.

"No, no, no," Sienna said, horrified.

"Don't be a party pooper, Sienna." Her mother flipped the stack over, and Elvis Presley stared back at them.

She fanned what Troy now saw were masks of six different popular figures. They were well made: cut precisely to cover the wearer from the cheeks and ears to above the hairline, with only a cutout for the nose. The features were realistic, as if based on photos, but painted in full-color artwork that made them even more bright and fun.

"Everyone pick one," Rose said.

Sienna turned to Troy with a mortified expression. "You *absolutely* do not have to do this," she said, fixing him with her gaze.

"Are you kidding? These are great." He grabbed the Clint Eastwood mask, à la Italian spaghetti western era, complete with two-dimensional battered brown cowboy hat above the brow.

"Pish. What fun is that?" Rose said, snatching it from his hand and passing him the Carmen Miranda mask.

Sienna did a facepalm, spreading her fingers to roll her eyes at him.

"Good call, Rose," Troy said. "Way better." He put it on immediately and secured the ear loops. "In fact, I think everyone should choose the mask for the person to their left," he said. Sienna, of course, was to his left.

He seized the Eastwood mask back from Rose and handed it to Sienna. "Here you go, No Name."

She held it limp in one hand and stared at him, then fought to smother a smile. He could imagine what she saw. His exposed mouth and two-day bearded chin beneath the mask with the flamboyant singer's blush-glazed cheeks, bright eyes, thick eyelashes and thin, peaked eyebrows. The eyeholes of the mask were tiny, just large enough for the pupils, so to others, the eyes would appear realistic but unmoving. At a jaunty angle, atop the singer's trademark yellow headscarf was, of all things, a painted hat in the shape of a basket filled with tropical fruits. The mask, in combination with the borrowed, blue-checked flannel bathrobe, must have presented quite the spectacle. Sienna couldn't hold it in anymore and burst out laughing.

He wagged his finger at Clint Eastwood in her hand. She rolled her eyes again but donned the mask with its squinty eyes, ruddy cheeks and battered cowboy hat above her beautiful, full-lipped mouth, smooth neck and *Golden Girls*–worthy floral robe. Now it was Troy's turn to laugh.

"All right, Uncle Marco," she said ominously. "Your turn." Sienna handed him Marilyn Monroe.

All four of them cracked up when he had it in place. Then Marco reached for the Elvis mask but changed his mind and handed Rose Charlie Chaplin, leaving Elvis and Audrey Hepburn unused. Troy picked up his cards but couldn't stop chuckling at the absurd sight the four of them made.

Rose had dealt, so Troy was up first. He shifted his cards into order: a two, five, two sevens and a jack. He turned to Sienna and demanded she hand over any sevens she might have. Squinty eyes staring him down, the Man with No Name told him to go fish. Troy laughed so hard he bent over the cards in his hand, which started everyone else laughing again.

Once Sienna saw him enjoying Rose's party trick, her shoulders relaxed and she settled back in her chair, embracing the hilarity as thoroughly as everyone else. As the game progressed, he couldn't help but glance over to enjoy her immersion in the carefree silliness and wonder if she was less different from Rose than she thought. Several times she reached under her mask to wipe away tears of laughter, like she had the night before. And he had to admit that the adorable squeaky, choking sounds when she tried to suppress an aftershock of giggles might have him falling a little bit in love.

Eventually, normal conversation reemerged, though the masks continued to punctuate the banter with absurdity. At one point, Troy mentioned the collection of seashells and starfish around the room.

"Uncle Marco is a dive instructor," Clint Eastwood informed him.

"Did you live on the coast before your job at Los Alamos?" he asked Marco.

"No, I grew up in Albuquerque and moved to Los Alamos right out of graduate school," Marilyn Monroe explained. "After I got my PhD and a couple of promotions, I moved here to Santa Fe, since it's only forty-five minutes from the lab."

"He taught at the Blue Hole two weekends a month," Rose said.

"You flew to the ocean every other week?" Troy asked, stunned.

"The Blue Hole is about two hours southeast of here," Sienna said.

Troy screwed up his face in confusion, though his Carmen mask would still be presenting her bubbly, basket-hatted, ready-to-burst-into-song face. His silence must have conveyed his puzzlement well enough, though.

"It's an enormous sinkhole used for diving certification," Sienna explained. "Only about eighty feet across, but also eighty feet deep. There's an underwater cave system going down another eighty feet or so below that, though that's closed off now for public safety. Uncle Marco and Aunt Maria both taught there a couple weekends a month for years. All three of their kids dive too."

"My work sent our whole Geochem team there one Christmas, years ago, as a bonus vacation for a breakthrough we'd made. After that, I was hooked."

"That would've been a great one for Two Truths and a Lie today if I'd realized you didn't know about it," Sienna said.

"Ooh, I haven't thought of that game in years!" Rose exclaimed. Her voice brimmed with excitement, but the wide-eyed, powder-white face below the dusty bowler hat stared with silent-picture intensity.

"*No way*, Mom," Sienna said with a finality like anyone who disagreed might find themselves staring down the barrel of a gun. "You got your Go Fish and your masks. You are *not* listing off your most outlandish truths in front of a guest."

"Oh, fine," said Rose, "but now I'm curious. What was the most surprising thing that came out of your game with Sienna?"

The way she made him feel every time she looked at him, he wanted to say.

"Well, there was that cat story..." Sienna offered.

"No, there wasn't," Troy said firmly.

She snickered. "All right, the shark one then?"

Her mother clapped her hands and exclaimed, "Yes, the shark story. I want to hear the shark story!"

The card game continued, and Troy told his shark-diving story for the second time in two days, this time expanding it into a proper tale with all the details. That led to an inspired conversation about *Jaws*, including quoted dialogue of favorite bits, then segued into a discussion of favorite movies. With a casual matter-of-fact delivery, Marco mentioned the time Rose had drinks with an A-list celebrity whose name made Troy's jaw drop.

"Ooh, I had the biggest crush on him for years," Sienna said with an enthusiasm that sparked an unexpected twinge of jealousy in Troy, but the fleeting emotion was overshadowed by his curiosity.

"No. Hold on. Go back. What was that about having drinks together?"

"We had a couple of drinks at that little steakhouse in Old Town," Rose said, her Charlie Chaplin face studying her hand with wide-eyed intensity. "He was very funny. I hadn't expected that. His movies were all so serious up to that point." The face turned to him. "Do you have any threes?"

"I...uh..." It took him a moment to refocus on the game. He had two and handed them over. Rose added them to her own two and placed the set of four with the many other piles she'd accumulated. She was killing it at Go Fish.

"They were filming some scenes in town," Sienna said, continuing the story for him. "She was looking at the menu board in the restaurant's courtyard and literally bumped into him."

"I'm surprised that led to drinks together, though," he said. "I would have guessed celebrities would be more standoffish than that in public."

Troy asked Sienna for her jacks, which she handed over.

"Not if you talk to them like normal people," Rose said. "I didn't make any big deal about who he was, and something I said made him laugh… I don't remember what now. He asked if I had any recommendations on the menu. I'd never been inside, but I'd heard about the place. We ended up going in to check it out together and had drinks while he ordered something to go." She shrugged.

Sienna asked Troy right back for his twos, which she seemed to know he had. "He's not the only one she's met," she said. "She's kind of a celebrity magnet."

"Got any sevens?" Marco asked Sienna. He'd switched to the Audrey Hepburn mask in the hopes it might change his luck. Sienna shook her head and continued. "A lot of movies have been filmed in New Mexico. A whole lot. Some TV shows too. Somehow my mom just keeps running into folks from them. What is it? Four or five big names you've chatted up now? More?"

"Oh, I don't know." She waved the question away with her free hand. "It's not like I keep count."

Troy shook his head in amazement.

Using two card decks instead of one made the Go Fish rounds longer and more challenging to keep track of what other people might be holding. He and Sienna took a quick break to move their clothes to the dryer, and when the game ended around 9:30 p.m., they all demasked. Rose had won with ten piles of four of a kind to everyone else's four or five piles.

As Marco gathered up the cards and took the beer bottles to a recycling container in the garage, Rose's phone rang. She hopped on her scooter and paddled away at alarming speed, saying it was Dan and she had to tell him about her day.

Sienna told Troy to take the first turn in the guest bathroom. By the time he finished, she had their clothes out of the dryer, folded and was carrying his pile to his room to set them on his bed.

"Your mom is a blast," he said, standing in the doorway.

"She makes me crazy a lot of the time, but she's always been fun. There were a lot of happy times when I was little, but also plenty of unexpected incidents like this ankle thing." She tipped her head toward her mother's room where they could hear her on the phone with her beau. "They constantly frustrated my dad. You haven't met him, but my dad is actually really nice too. A little intense sometimes, but he's kind. It's just that he likes everything a certain way. He's got his reasons, and they make sense, but it just wasn't something my mom could live up to. It's too bad they weren't both a little less extreme. Dad fell in love with the beautiful party girl and my mom fell in love with the smart, stable university professor. They were so close to being like Uncle Marco and Aunt Maria. Just not close enough."

The memories melted her reflective expression into something melancholy that made Troy want to take her in his arms. Before he could think of anything helpful to say or do, she shrugged and said good-night.

CHAPTER FIFTEEN

Wednesday, July 29th

The next morning, Sienna drove her mom back down to Albuquerque for her follow-up appointment with the orthopedic specialist who'd seen her in the ER. Troy, continuing to impress, had gotten up early and offered to go along.

The surgeon told them the fracture still required internal fixation, but the good news was the swelling had decreased enough to do surgery the following day and he had an urgent slot open. They all agreed it would be better to get the surgery done at the large hospital in Albuquerque rather than transporting her mother five hours home with an unstable fracture and a surgery appointment that might be days out.

Next up, Sienna needed to get time off work, so Troy guided her mom through her pre-op screening while Sienna made her phone calls.

"Is she still getting her labs done?" Sienna

said a few minutes later, having tracked him down in the waiting room of the lab.

"Mmm-hmm. I'm not sure why it's taking so long. It's just bloodwork and a urine sample. Maybe she's having performance anxiety. So how'd things go for you?"

She plunked down in the hard plastic chair bolted next to his. "The bad news is that with our newest hire still in training, they won't let me take vacation days off until the intern is ready to work solo. The good news is that Marty's willing to switch with me and give me Thursday and Friday off, but that means I'll need to work this weekend for him on top of my weekday shifts next week. It gives Marty nearly a week off, though, and he said his wife has been wanting to go out of town and see her folks."

Troy gave her a look that said he didn't even try to keep up. "What day do you go back to work?" He pulled his shift schedule out of his wallet.

"I'll be here tomorrow for my mom's surgery, then drive home Friday and go back to work on Saturday."

"And when's your next day off after you get back?"

"Not until that following Friday."

"I'm off through this Friday," he said. "I guess

if I leave today, our next day off together would be the end of next week, Saturday, the eighth."

She leaned into his arm to peer at the calendar with him. Her eyes flew wide and she slapped a hand to her mouth to cover a gasp.

"I know it's tough," he said, deadpan. "I have faith you can make it without me for that long."

"No. Look. My next day off won't be until Friday, August 7th." She pointed to the tiny square on the calendar.

"Right. You just told me that. Because your schedule switches to weekdays on the first of the month."

"August 7th, Troy! The wedding is the fifteenth. The only time I'm going to have off between now and the wedding is the seventh, eighth and nineth. That's it. Even those days will be divided between whatever my mom needs and all the other things I normally get done on my days off."

She rested her elbows on her knees and pressed both palms to her eyes as if she could blot out the sight of his calendar. "This is awful. Kelli's dealing with her father's upcoming heart surgery and her brother-in-law's cancer. Cole is dealing with the ranch and the hay. I promised them I'd take care of everything." She turned to him and saw his shock at the tears that burned her eyes. She wasn't a woman who cried easily, and he'd probably guessed that. He squeezed her hand in sympathy.

"Hey, hey, it's okay," he said. "I can handle it for you. Your mom's pre-op stuff is almost done. As soon as we're back at your uncle's house, I can take off and drive her car back to Burgess." He glanced at the clock above the reception desk. "I'll probably be home before dinner. It'll give me all day Thursday and Friday to get things done. Besides, you'll be waiting around tomorrow during your mom's surgery. Albuquerque's nearly as big as Colorado Springs. Maybe you could find those bridesmaids' dresses in the colors you want."

A glimmer of hope straightened her spine, followed almost immediately by doubt. She chewed her lip, thinking.

"I might find something," she conceded, "but there's so much left to do. I can't rent anything here or fill the car with decorations, even if I had the time to find them. Are you sure you're up for this? I'm not trying to bash your offer to take over for me and save my bacon, but…catering, reservations, so many details… You've as much as said it isn't your wheelhouse."

"Give me the chance to surprise you. Besides, I'm all you've got. Go ahead, say it. 'Help me, Obi-Wan. You're my only hope.'"

She didn't know whether to laugh or cry. "Oh,

my stars." She dropped her forehead back into her palm.

He pulled her hand away and held it in both of his. The warm, physical connection between them comforted her.

"Look, I know you think I don't get the importance of this, but I do. I understand that you've looked forward to planning this wedding for a long time. Kelli's your best friend, and you want her day to be perfect. Give me your ginormous list and I'll take over." He slid down on one knee and the older couple across from them elbowed each other and smiled, assuming it was a proposal. "I vow to take up my lightsaber and fight the Empire of Wedding Obstacles for you."

She could feel the blush burning her cheeks and tugged at his sleeve to pull him back into his chair, but she couldn't help the smile that twitched at the corners of her mouth. The sincerity of his words shone in his eyes, even though she'd bet this was the last thing on earth he wanted to do. Maybe it was just those darn tears of hers still threatening to unleash. He really did seem to be filling the role of knight in shining armor these last couple of days, though.

"I give you my word," he continued. "I'll take care of everything, but on one condition—you have to agree to leave it up to me and not worry.

I don't want you thinking about it on top of everything else you've got going on. Promise?"

She hesitated, then nodded.

"Good. Look, I'm so confident this will work out that I'll even make you a bet. I'm going to bet that I can make this wedding every bit as special as you imagined. And if I do, then you agree to do something completely spontaneous with me."

"Like what?" A small spark of intrigue lifted her spirits another notch.

He released her hand and placed one arm across her seat back, leaning in to stress his words. "The next time we have four days off together, we take a trip."

"Where?"

"That's the spontaneous part. You pack an all-purpose bag, and you don't find out where we're going until we get there. And when we get there, we plan nothing. We do everything spur of the moment, like your skydiving adventure in Las Vegas. Deal?"

"Troy, if you can pull off the wedding I'm picturing, I swear I'll go along with any crazy, impulsive idea you dream up."

"Great. You look for the dresses here and leave everything else to me. You've promised now. No checking up. The whole point of this is that you don't need to think about it, okay?" He gave her hand a squeeze for emphasis. "You'll see. It'll be fine."

CHAPTER SIXTEEN

TROY'S DRIVE HOME later that day seemed exceptionally quiet after the company and fun of the last couple of days. Moreover, the stillness of sitting alone for hours gave his doubts ample time to shout at him about his promise to Sienna. Even as the words left his mouth in that waiting room, he'd known that taking over the wedding was nothing he wanted to tackle. With her current commitments, though, there was no way she'd have had time to juggle everything, and he'd wanted so much to lift the burden from her shoulders and soothe the lines of worry between her brows. Now the dread of living up to expectations of this magnitude fell on him like a brick wall.

He'd had a vague outline of a plan that seemed like a good idea. One he now realized had the potential to disappoint her deeply if things went sideways, which they might for any number of reasons. Good thing he'd made her promise not to check up on him. The longer he kept her away from anything to do with the wedding, the better.

He dropped Rose's car at Sienna's house and drove his truck back to the ranch. Half an hour later, Cole took off for his monthly town water board meeting. Their housekeeper, Sally, had already left for the day, and with Cole gone until late, Kelli wouldn't come over to spend the evening here as she often did.

Troy rattled around in the house with only Baxter for company. Eating dinner alone for the first time in days opened an unexpected void in him. Perhaps spurred by the combination of the quiet and missing Sienna, the black hole of his father's absence pulled at him. A profound grief gripped him for the first time in weeks. It was like that. His grief never really left, only receded for a while, then snuck up on him again at unexpected moments. A mountain lion silently stalking him for days or weeks before pouncing, using the strength of his what-ifs and regrets and emptiness to knock him down, pinning him, helpless and overwhelmed.

To distract himself he brought his laptop downstairs and checked on the fire situation across the Western US. His attention soon drifted back to Sienna, though; one image after another winding through his thoughts and emotions like a weaver shuttling colors into a marvelous tapestry. Memories of chatting with her during their hours of driving, learning the stories about various points in her life, laughing with her over Go Fish, snuggling next to her to watch the John Wayne movie.

In just a matter of days, she had insinuated herself into his life. The physical attraction had been instantaneous, but it was so much more than that now. She was easier to be around than he ever could have guessed. Now he wanted to be around her all the time. The two days until she returned were going to feel like forever. He resolved to give her a call.

She answered on the second ring.

"Hey, you," she said.

He liked that she must have him in her phone contacts to have known it was him before he spoke.

"Hey back. Your mom feeling ready for her surgery tomorrow?"

"Yep. Approaching it like a brand-new adventure. If pain medicines made her loopy, I can hardly wait to see what she's like postanesthesia. That ought to be good for a few laughs."

Her soft chuckle sparkled through the phone connection, and he wondered again how much of her mother's effervescent personality simmered just below the surface of her professional demeanor.

"Is it still looking like you'll be coming back here on Friday?"

"We'll know for sure after the surgery tomorrow, but the doctor said the fixation should be pretty straightforward. We're expecting her to be out of hospital tomorrow night and hopefully able to travel on Friday. There's not a lot of wiggle room, anyway, as I have to be back at work on Saturday, but if it comes down to it, Uncle Marco or one of my brothers will bring her home on the weekend."

Troy registered her words but focused more on her voice. Smooth and confident, like hearing her over the station intercom. A voice he could listen to like ocean surf, a soothing soundtrack for his life. Overcome with a sudden desire to tell Sienna that he missed her, Troy choked back the words. Not the right time or place.

"Good," he said instead. "Well, drive safe. Call me when you get in to let me know you made it back, okay?"

Maybe they wouldn't have her mom or the wedding as an excuse to spend time together when she returned home, but he resolved that he wasn't going to leave things to fate like he so often did. This woman wasn't slipping through his fingers. As long as she wanted to see him too, he'd find a way to make it happen.

CHAPTER SEVENTEEN

Friday, July 31st

SIENNA CHECKED THAT her mom had packed everything and had her reading glasses in her purse. Next she swept the room, finding her mom's phone half under the bed where it had fallen off the nightstand. After loading the suitcase in the car, she double-checked her own room, including the closet and dresser she hadn't used, and then, just to be sure, Troy's room, even though he'd left two days ago.

Though three out of their group of four had remained in the house, her uncle's home had seemed empty without Troy. They'd spent three days almost constantly in each other's company and with him abruptly gone, she'd felt like a glacier with a piece calved off. Still whole and still her, yet different; missing something that had, for a while, made her more complete.

"BT"—before Troy—as she was coming to think of it, she'd convinced herself that she led a full and satisfying life. She'd had her work and her mother and occasional evenings out with Kelli or work friends. Now, it seemed glaringly obvious how much she'd missed having a man in her life. Okay, not *any* man, which is why she didn't think she'd missed it, but most definitely *that* man.

Troy had hinted at a kiss that night they played Truth or Dare. She'd had another opportunity with him when they stood close in the laundry room in their borrowed bathrobes. Or she could have kissed him goodbye before he drove back to Burgess, like his eyes told her he hoped she would. But she hadn't. And now she wished she had.

Sienna held her mom's elbow, helping her roll through the house on her knee scooter. The last thing either of them needed was another fall. Fortunately, the surgery had gone well, though, and her mom's pain seemed well-controlled.

Uncle Marco held the front door for them. There were hugs all around, and Sienna thanked him for the hospitality and the help with her mom.

"My pleasure," he said. "I've eaten better the past three days than I have in months. And, Rose, you're always a delight. Next time, though, skip the injury. You don't need an excuse to come visit."

Once Sienna had her mom settled in the back seat with her foot elevated, she stowed the knee scooter where they could access it for the inevitable bathroom stop—or stops. Her mom had a bladder the size of a peanut, and Sienna knew every gas station or store with a public restroom between Albuquerque and home.

As a bonus, while she'd been waiting during the surgery and post-op recovery, Sienna had dashed out with a handwritten list of local bridal stores. On her second stop, she'd found the perfect rose-colored bridesmaids' dresses. She nearly squeed out loud when she saw they carried the right sizes for herself and Rikki, plus an adorable matching dress for Rikki's niece, the flower girl. And in a light bulb moment, she'd realized that since the ceremony was expected to be short, they could have the eight-year-old stand with the bridesmaids, making the parties even again. The store also had beautiful, wide belts in black taffeta, each accented with a large black fabric flower, and in the men's department, burgundy silk boutonnieres.

She wished there'd been time to get more things, like decorations, but she wasn't here for that...she was here for her mother's surgery. Besides, Troy had the list now, and there would've been no sense in duplicating their efforts. He'd told her to trust him, and she'd vowed she would.

However difficult it might be.

THE DRIVE HOME proved uneventful, even the two bathroom stops. She got her mom settled at home, but still wished she could have taken vacation days off for her post-op care. Her mother assured her, though, that Dan was fine with taking over. They'd made plans for him to stay in her guest room all weekend, as well as check on her in the mornings and evenings during the workweek. He'd even promised to take time off from work to drive her to her follow-up appointments. Sienna didn't love it that a man she barely knew would be staying with her mother, but her aunt lived too far away to commute and there weren't any other options.

It was early evening by the time Sienna returned, at last, to her own house. She collected Tiger from her neighbor and gave him a big hug and scritches. His zoomies around the house let her know how happy he was to be home.

"Aw, peewee, you're getting big so fast." She swore she could see a change in him after being gone only a few days. Dangling a toy for him to bat, she said, "I think it's time to give you free run of the house. What do you think? Maybe get you a cat stand to hang out on when I'm at work? Oh, and I still need to take you in for your shots, don't I?"

Thinking of Tiger's vaccinations reminded her to check and see if Kelli had called her back.

They'd texted short updates but, with everything going on for them both, they hadn't had a chance to talk in person. Mark's PET scan results should have come in today, and Sienna was surprised not to find a message from Kelli. A bit worrying but, of course, they might just have been busy, or even out celebrating. Hitting dial, she got only voicemail, so she left a message for her friend to return her call when she could.

A shower revived her from the long drive and then, as promised, she called Troy to let him know she was home.

"Was traffic bad?" he asked, deadpan.

"The worst. Total gridlock around Wagon Mound."

They both chuckled. The interstate between Santa Fe and Highway 160 in Colorado was about as congested as driving across Death Valley.

"Work is going to have you pretty tied up this next week," he said. "I was thinking maybe I should take you out for dinner tonight so you can relax this evening. What do you think?"

Had he just sounded a tiny bit nervous? And what *did* she think? She'd called him because she missed hearing his voice, but she hadn't expected him to ask her out tonight on what sounded suspiciously like a date. The part of her brain her father influenced reminded her that being cautious about who she dated now might save a lot of heartache later. The part her mother influenced told her to go have fun. The mom side won out. Too much caution made for a mighty boring life.

"I think that sounds pretty marvelous."

TROY PICKED HER up an hour later. When he arrived in a burgundy western shirt, sleeves rolled and tails tucked into his jeans, with clean boots, hair freshly washed, and his beard trimmed to an attractive, light stubble, she got the impression a fair bit of effort had gone into getting ready. Not that she hadn't done the same, but she had to wonder if perhaps he'd missed her these last couple of days as much as she'd missed him.

They took his truck to Alamosa, to the burger place she liked. It seemed almost unbelievable that only five days had passed since they'd been here last. So much had changed. Not least of all—despite her arguments with herself on the topic—her feelings toward him.

She was dying to ask him about wedding preparations and what he'd done, but she'd made a promise. Hoping he might voluntarily update her, she'd avoided mentioning it on the drive into town, but he hadn't broached the subject. Once they'd ordered their meals, she tried dropping a hint he couldn't miss.

"You were right about Albuquerque. I found the perfect bridesmaids' dresses while my mom was in surgery." She spared him the detailed descriptions.

His face lit up. "That's great. I felt sure the thing with the dresses was all going to work out."

He said nothing more. Their drinks came.

"So," she said, trying again, "I guess the rest is up to you."

He nodded and took a sip of his beer. "Yep. The rest is up to me."

It was Friday night. If he hadn't called the rental store by now, their chances of getting any of the major items they needed would have probably run out. She understood the reasons why Troy had let them all down that day they'd moved Kelli's veterinary stuff, but that also meant she had yet to see him actually come through on something for someone else. The pressure building in her felt like a balloon left too long on the helium tank nozzle. If he didn't give her something soon, she might just pop.

"Soooo, how's that going?"

That won her nothing more than a knowing half smile.

"I gave you my word," he reminded her. "I also made you a bet that I really want to win.

You promised you were going to trust me on this."

They were having too nice an evening to ruin it by pushing harder. She'd be working 7:00 a.m. to 7:00 p.m. for the next six days, and there was no choice except to leave things in his hands. It was good practice, she told herself, delegating tasks to someone else. She had to repeat it to herself a second time to shove her curiosity and anxiety to a back burner. Their food came, and he paused to thank the server. She added that kindness to the growing list of things she liked about him.

"Did you hear about the fires in Idaho?" he asked.

"No. I've been so busy that I haven't heard any news for days."

"They had one near the state border blow up on them the other day, and they're afraid it might merge with that big one in northwestern Washington that I've been watching. The Hotshots are getting spread pretty thin."

"Any new fires in Colorado?"

"Thankfully, no. But that one north of Denver and the one out by Georgetown are still less than ten percent controlled."

"Fingers crossed we don't get one down here. It's getting scarier every year. Besides," she said, giving it one last college try, "we have a wedding to put on in a couple of weeks."

He gave her a smile and dived into his burger.

"How about I challenge you to one of those games you have in there?" Troy said, walking her to her door. He didn't seem any more ready to end their evening than she was, though somehow it was 9:30 p.m. already and Saturday was a workday for them both.

She wanted to say yes more than anything.

"I'd better not. I'm a bit tired from the drive and my alarm goes off at five thirty."

"I still have nightmares about that alarm." He shuddered, and she snickered.

They stopped on her front porch.

"All right, rain check then."

"Rain check."

They stood in front of her closed door, facing each other, an expectant silence filling the space between them like a column of ions gathering for a lightning strike. In a sweet and boyish gesture, Troy reached forward to take both of her hands in his, holding them loosely between them, gazing at her.

Yes, she and Troy were opposite personalities, and there'd been some red flags at first, but knowing him better now, she had to wonder again how different she and Troy might be together than her parents. She knew the answer to that question should matter. She should make informed decisions and avoid romantic entanglements unless she felt certain, but right now she just couldn't bring herself to care. Perhaps she was caught up in a temporary tidal wave of emotions and hormones, but at this moment, all she wanted was for him to kiss her.

Holding his gaze, she gave an unspoken yes to his unasked question. He leaned forward and touched his lips to hers.

Every cell in her body energized, sparking to life like bulbs on a Christmas tree at a tree-lighting ceremony. His hands slipped around her waist and hers went to his shoulders as their lips pressed together, expanding their relationship into new and exciting territory. The kiss ended and lightheadedness left her feeling tipsy and weak in the knees. Jorge's cave kiss couldn't hold a candle to this.

Troy pulled back, but held her tight another moment—fortunately for her, as she still fought to will strength back into her legs.

"Thank you," she said inanely, meaning thank you for the evening but sounding like she was thanking him for the kiss. Though maybe she was.

"*Thank you*," he said with a quirk of a smile before she could clarify.

She unlocked her door and stepped up to the threshold. “Good night.”

“Good night,” he said wistfully.

With difficulty, she closed the door. What was that old saying? *Always leave them wanting more.*

Unfortunately, that was supposed to apply to him, not to her.

CHAPTER EIGHTEEN

Saturday, August 1st

TROY'S SHIFT ON Saturday moved so slowly it felt like he'd worked his twenty-four hours before dinner. Doing the instrument checks on the fire engine in the morning had taken twice as long as usual, and the downtime between calls seemed to drag. It had taken him until midday to realize time ticked by so slowly because he was at work instead of somewhere with Sienna. He hadn't even gotten to hear her voice on the radio today. She must've been dispatching for the police department, which meant they might as well have been on different continents.

After lunch, he texted her a joke that one of the other firefighters had told, but she didn't respond. He didn't take it personally. She'd let him know the dispatchers rarely got proper breaks, ate at their desks if things were busy and that their department had a rule that personal phones stayed turned off except on break.

Watching TV in the bullpen room in the evening—some ridiculous reality show one of the others had picked—Troy felt his phone vibrate and nearly dropped it pulling it out of its holster too fast. It was 7:35 p.m., and he knew Sienna should be getting home about now. A smile tugged at his lips when he saw it was her texting back. It had been such a dad joke he'd sent earlier in the day: "What's the worst thing to hear your surgeon say during your operation? Literally anything."

She responded now with one of her own: What do you call a paper airplane that can't fly?

There was a pause, the little typing dots jumping, and then the answer:

Stationary.

He laughed so hard that Jan and Mac turned in their recliners to stare at him. He texted a laughing emoji and then:

How was your day?

She typed much faster than he did. Not surprising since she was on a keyboard all day long. Her reply was even grammatical and punctuated.

Brutal. I was so beat I hit the McDonald's drive-through for dinner. Going to bed very early tonight.

How about I bring takeout food tomorrow night when you get off work? You can relax and we'll pick out one of your board games to play.

That sounds wonderful. Tomorrow I'm on fire dispatch. You guys are such slackers, it'll be an easy day. I'll be nice and rested up for beating you at the game of your choice.

He snorted another laugh and wished her good-night. He put his phone away feeling more at ease than he had all day.

Sunday, August 2nd

THE WAIT FOR SIENNA to get off work Sunday evening felt interminable. The wildfire in Washington was still only 60 percent under control, so he'd spent part of the day watching videos of incident commanders giving their updates and studying maps of fire perimeters.

Around midday, he noticed a new incident listing for Colorado at the western edge of Huerfano County, just to the east of his own Alamosa County. He turned on his phone's police and fire scanner app and found the Huerfano County Fire

Protection District. The blaze had started with a lightning strike from a thunderstorm the night before. A hundred forty acres in the mountains had burned between the town of La Veta and La Veta Pass before the smoke had been spotted and the blaze investigated this morning. Local agencies were monitoring the fire and planning to request air support since the location was in steep and difficult country. As wildfires went, this one was still small, though decidedly too close for comfort.

He opted to spend the rest of his morning reviewing the coursework his station had done for their wildfire management certification, along with pertinent chapters in his handbook. Later, with postlunch drowsiness creeping up on him, he nodded off over the material. His crew had been out twice during the night: one traffic accident and one medical call. A nap was overdue, and he lay on top of the bed, still in his jeans and T-shirt.

He woke about an hour later to a fading impression of Sienna's laughter. Lying there between sleep and wakefulness, dream images and real memories swirled together behind his eyes: her standing sideways to him, unaware he watched her help her mom; the way her mouth pursed when suppressing a smile; the deftness of her manicured hands when dicing vegetables for a meal, chewing her lip in thought. And then a less comfortable image surfaced: the tension in her shoulders and voice when she tried oh-so nonchalantly to ask about the wedding plans.

Wide awake now, he explored the conflicting emotions around the fact that she'd been astoundingly good about respecting their deal to trust him, and yet, avoiding a discussion had become more challenging by the day for them both. As much as he loved the time they spent together, his nerves vibrated on yellow alert in the background the whole time, worried she'd break her promise and demand details. He'd never promised to follow her list, but he was sure that's what she was expecting, and if she found out too soon that he hadn't, she'd never understand.

Cole and Kelli would be fine; they weren't concerned as long as they got married on the fifteenth. The fancy wedding bash was all Sienna and her commitment to her childhood promise. The hardest part was not letting on to her that he wasn't staying up till midnight handcrafting centerpieces or working on seating charts and whatever else was on that list. It would all work out in the end, he felt sure, but he was banking hard on the fact that she'd come to see it the same way.

MEALS AT THE Dirty Dawg Bar and Grill in Burgess were surprisingly good for their tiny town, with dressings, sauces and desserts made from scratch. Plus, Sienna had mentioned she liked their grilled sandwiches. He ordered ahead and picked up two meals to go. Five minutes later, he knocked on her door and they opened the still-steaming bags with a warm Monte Cristo for her and Reuben for him, sides of fries, coleslaw, salad and two pieces of toffee cake for dessert.

"This is a ton of food!" she exclaimed, spreading it all out on the table. She lifted Tiger down after he jumped up to investigate, only to have him jump back up again.

"I figured you could use any leftovers tomorrow. I'll be at work, so I won't be able to rescue you again until Tuesday."

"Ah… Kelli has me booked for Tuesday." Her tone was apologetic and upbeat at the same time. "She's getting back from Connecticut tomorrow morning. She'll be spending every minute she can with Cole, but he has a town council meeting Tuesday night, so I grabbed her."

"Oh. Well, good. I'm sure you have a lot of catching up to do."

He hoped he covered his disappointment well. Somewhere along the line, he'd begun to assume they'd continue this pattern on his nights off. Foolish, but there it was.

They consumed their dinners in record time, then both retreated to the living room to digest. "All right," she said. "Your time of reckoning has arrived. Which game do you want to get beat at?"

He chuckled and glanced at the bottom shelf of the bookcase. "How about backgammon? I haven't played that in a million years."

"Backgammon it is."

She stood and retrieved the faux leather case about the size and shape of a small briefcase. Opening it fully so it lay flat on the coffee table in front of them, she sat cross-legged on the floor and he sat opposite her. She reached forward and took one beige and one brown disc from the two trays, then held the thick pieces hidden in her fists and let him choose. He picked brown, and she started laying her beige discs on the triangular "points" inset on her side. Tiger hopped on the coffee table and walked across the center of the board, sniffing.

"You're going to have to remind me how this goes," he said.

Jumping back down, tail high, Tiger crossed to his new, carpeted cat tower where he climbed to a platform and pounced on a stuffed toy he'd left there.

Sienna laid out all her pieces and had Troy mirror hers on his own side. After a brief run-down of the rules, they began. She went first, rolling a six and a five, giving her a good start moving her pieces clockwise around the board.

"It's good that you and Kelli are going to get some time together this week," he said, a bit more sincerely this time. "Cole's been worried about her. They've been talking on the phone every night, but he thinks she's holding back on unloading her feelings so that she won't worry him. And then he worries about her because of it." He shook his head. "Those two sometimes..."

"I know what you mean. It's hard to imagine two people more in love. I could totally see Kelli not letting on, though, if she's sad. Even with me, she hasn't said a whole lot about her brother-in-law except that the PET scan came out bad. I know her sister is having a hard time with Mark's diagnosis. Did you hear any details from Cole?"

He nodded. "It sounds like he may not have much time."

"That's what I gathered too. You were right about pancreatic cancer. It can move fast. And them with three kids and another on the way."

They shared a quiet moment. He thought not only of his soon-to-be extended family, but also how bittersweet it must be for Cole and Kelli to anticipate their wedding day knowing her sister and brother-in-law would be staying in Connecticut, dealing with all this.

"Did you hear the update on the fire between here and La Veta?" he said to change the subject.

"No. What's up?"

Her second dice roll had been low, and he'd rolled double fours, bringing them nearly even again. He filled her in on what little he knew.

"That's good that it's still fairly small," she said.

"As of this morning, anyway. Last I heard, we're supposed to get high winds tonight. Our normal wind pattern would blow the blaze away from us, but it sounds like they're expecting Chinook winds overnight and into tomorrow. Chinooks usually blow westerly."

The same as in parts of Montana or Wyoming—where the mountains sloped steeply down to open prairie—the windstorms in some parts of Colorado could easily gust to Level 1 hurricane speeds of 75 mph or more. The highest on record had been on Monarch Pass at 148 mph, the same as a Level 4 hurricane or an F3 tornado.

She'd thrown the dice, but instead of looking at her toss she studied him, her eyes tight with concern. "Do you think you'll get called out to the fire?"

"Too early to say. I haven't heard any updates

since this morning. Who knows, they might even have it out before the winds hit."

She moved her discs. "So how does it work if you do get called out?"

"Eight of us passed cross-certification as Wildland Fire Team members, but we're spread out across all three shifts and all three stations." She'd surged ahead in the game again—definitely winning now. He rolled his dice—a paltry two and a three—and moved his pieces, while he continued. "On duty or off, if we get called in, our team heads to Station One and loads up in the new brush vehicle. Off-duty firefighters would get called in to cover for us."

"How long would you go out for?"

He shrugged and handed her the dice. "Hard to say. We'd just be extra crew to the full-time wildland agencies so, at most, until the perimeter came under control. Probably less than a week."

It could be longer, but he wanted to give her the best-case scenario. In reality, a fire like this could get bad fast if it got out of hand. The Spring Creek Fire from a few years ago had also been in that steep terrain between Fort Garland and Cuchara. If Chinook winds blew this west, into the steep slopes of those mountains, it would be harder to fight and could burn for a month or more.

"So if this fire blew up, your chances of getting called out are pretty high." Her face remained passive, her voice conversational, but her delicate Adam's apple bobbed ever so slightly with a hard swallow. Her hand paused before moving her first backgammon piece off the board, decisively ahead now in the goal of moving all the pieces from the home side around the far side of the board and off.

Considering what she did for a living, it surprised him to see her so concerned about this. "Yeah, I guess so. Why? Does that bother you?" he asked.

"It just sounds dangerous," she said with a shrug, but didn't meet his eyes.

"I'm a firefighter. The whole job is dangerous. You know that better than anyone."

She threw her dice with less enthusiasm. They rolled to a one and a five, and she moved her two pieces before meeting his questioning gaze. "Wildfires are different, though. So huge. So uncontrolled… So unpredictable."

"Uh-huh. And that's why we train so hard for it. And why only a third of us who tried out passed the certification."

"I know. But I've also heard the stories. Storm King. Prescott."

Could it be that her concern wasn't just about the fire or the crews fighting it? Could it be that she cared specifically about the possibility of him being out there? It planted a small ball of warmth in the pit of his stomach to think so.

He knew the incidents she was talking about. Every wildland firefighter did. They'd been two of the deadliest fires for Hotshots and wildland teams in modern history. The Yarnell Hill fire in Arizona, where nineteen firefighters from Prescott were overrun by the blaze. South Canyon on the western side of Colorado, commonly called Storm King for the hiking trail, where fourteen died, forced to shelter in place when the fire made a hard uphill run. The scenarios, and the mistakes they'd led to, were still taught as cautionary tales.

"Storm King and Yarnell Hill were outliers," he continued. "There've been hundreds of wildland fires over the last few decades where nothing like that happened. Most wildfires are just hot, tedious and a lot of hard work."

"Hard, tedious work wouldn't make you want to do it so much. I'm betting it's the excitement and danger that are the big draw."

He shook his dice cup and threw.

"Most of it's grunt work, but sure, the big ones are challenging. Maybe dangerous sometimes, if you're close to the leading edge," he confessed. "I mean, I imagine they are. I haven't been on one yet except as a trainee, where they kept us well back from the main lines." He couldn't deny that he'd wanted to be closer to the action, though. "But I study the briefings and strategies because if we end up going to one, I want to be as educated about wildfire behavior and tactics as possible. That's how you stay safe." He moved his first disc off the board, and she threw the dice.

"Well, you better," she said, her tone commanding, her gaze determined.

He thought about her work in dispatch. Maybe hearing every emergency in the city on every shift she worked had its own cumulative effects, like some of the trauma he'd witnessed. Then again, maybe he'd been right about what he saw in her a moment ago. Maybe she was concerned because it was him…

She moved two more pieces off the board, then continued in her no-nonsense manner. "So, did the rental store have everything you needed?"

Dang. Now he wanted to go back to talking about fires. This was by far the most direct she'd been. Maybe it was her way of taking emotional control back after her worry about something over which she had no control at all.

"You promised you wouldn't ask."

"I promised I wouldn't ask what you'd done," she said, avoiding his eyes. "I'm just asking if the store had what we need so we could brainstorm if they didn't."

"I can't tell you," he said, just as firmly.

"What?" She looked up sharply from the game board. A blend of incredulity and alarm raised her voice a full register. "Why not?"

"Because it would spoil the surprise."

"What surprise? The surprise of what they did and didn't have at the rental store?" He'd wanted to make her smile, but her brow had furrowed instead. He was losing her. He needed a quick course correction before this went downhill and she boxed him into a corner.

"No, silly. The surprise of me pulling this off just as well as you would have done it. Remember? We have a big bet going, lady, and I plan to win it. No more questions. This is about you trusting me. Right?"

She chewed her lip.

He made a show of staring at the backgammon discs.

"Wait. What? How are you down to just three left?" He pulled a face and stared forlornly at his remaining six pieces. "Oh, man. You're going to wipe the floor with me, aren't you?"

It tugged the smile from her that he'd hoped it would. "Watch me," she said, shaking her dice cup. She threw double threes.

Inwardly he breathed a sigh of relief while

outwardly he shook his head in mock disappointment as she cleared the last of her discs.

"Another game?" he asked when they'd gathered all their pieces.

She glanced at the clock on the wall behind the couch, and he knew before she formed the words that she was going to say no.

"Better not."

They stacked their discs neatly in their respective trays. She closed the board back into its briefcase shape and snapped the latches, then walked with him to the door.

Instead of heading out the door, he turned to say a proper goodbye, bringing them abruptly face-to-face. She didn't back up.

"This was really nice, Troy."

"Yeah. It was." He slipped his arms around her waist and pulled her the last few inches toward him. "Any time I get to spend with you is really nice."

"You smooth talker."

"You bring it out in me."

He tipped his head down to hers as she tilted her face up. Their lips met and he tasted the hint of citrus in her lip gloss. The feel of her in his arms was like a sleepy weekend morning or a snowy evening at home by the fire. He found another name for it: *Love.* She felt like love. He held her like he never wanted to leave her again, finally admitting to himself that he'd fallen in love with her.

The kiss ended. Her liquid brown eyes searched his face, her lips near his. They both knew they needed to end the evening. He let her slip out of his arms.

"So," he said, glad his voice sounded steady, "workday for us both tomorrow, then you're spending Tuesday evening with Kelli, and then a twenty-four-hour shift for me on Wednesday. Got room for me on your social calendar on Thursday?"

"I'll see if I can fit you in," she said with a smile, and a glint in her eyes that said she most certainly would.

Thursday suddenly felt very far away.

CHAPTER NINETEEN

Tuesday, August 4th

AT THE END of four days into her unprecedented six-day run, all Sienna could think about was how much she'd like to go straight home and be in bed by eight. She'd promised to meet up with Kelli tonight, though, and she wanted to see her friend even more than she wanted the extra sleep. Plus, Kelli had been every bit as busy as Sienna, having her own work to catch up on after being in Connecticut for a week. The two of them had barely found time to text, much less call, and Sienna had missed her best friend, especially with all the non-work-related events going on in both their lives.

It was a warm summer evening and wouldn't get dark until nine, so they'd agreed to meet after work. They'd set the meeting at a small park near the grade school at the east end of Burgess, about halfway between their homes. It sported a little gazebo with a picnic table and no water features or ponds, so the mosquitoes weren't bad, and the breeze was keeping the smoke in the air to a minimum. With the playground empty due to the late hour, they had the park to themselves.

After a big hug, they sat across from each other at the picnic table. Kelli had brought leftovers from yesterday's dinner at the ranch and unpacked about a dozen Tupperware containers from a nylon shopping bag.

"Holy cow," Sienna said. "How much food does that woman cook?"

"*A lot.* Sally makes meals for Cole and Troy whether they're there or not, and one portion could feed Cole twice over." She popped the lids off each container and fished silverware and napkins from the bottom of the bag. "She knows I come over for dinner more often than not, and Cole shares with the wranglers when there's extra food or a whole cake or pie. I think he usually sends Billy home with something on Sunday nights too."

"Billy's the young kid he hired?"

Kelli nodded. "The sixteen-year-old. He stays with the wranglers Friday and Saturday nights in case his dad is on a bender."

"You sure found a good man when you found Cole."

"Didn't I, though?" Kelli looked up and smiled, then paused, spoon poised above the container of pot roast she was dividing up. "Wait. What's up?"

"What's up with what?"

"With that look on your face. That dreamy, googly-eyed look. I was only gone a week. Are you crushing on someone? Are you dating? Spill it, girl."

Sienna rolled her eyes. She hadn't hinted about Troy in her texts and wasn't sure she wanted to share her feelings this soon. It was so new that even *she* didn't know how she felt. "It's nothing."

"How could you possibly be seeing anyone new? You've been working ever since you got back from Santa Fe, and you were down there for days. What was it, a week ago today that you and Troy..." Kelli gasped so suddenly and so loudly that Sienna flinched. "No! Troy? Seriously, you and Troy? Holy mackerel, I didn't see that one coming."

There was no use denying it now. "Yeah, well, neither did I."

"Wow, Troy's sure been playing his cards close. He hasn't let on at all. And the last I heard from you, he was getting on your nerves because he wouldn't call you back about getting together for the wedding planning."

"I know. And then I spent time with him and discovered that he's actually really kind and funny and caring."

"And handsome," Kelli added. "I mean, not to me—don't tell Cole I said that—but in the looks department he's definitely your cup of tea. Better still, your cup of coffee."

"Soooo handsome," she agreed. "I think my brain melts a little bit every time I see him."

"Well? Are you flirting? Kissing? Are you—"

"No!" she said vehemently, stopping Kelli in her tracks. "I mean, not that, but yeah…the other two."

Kelli finished dividing the roast and vegetables, still warm enough to waft wonderful smells, the salad loaded with creamy dressing and a carrot cake that looked homemade and wonderful. She shuffled containers around like some kind of Tetris puzzle, processing Sienna's information in what appeared to be stunned silence.

"*Well*?" Sienna said at last, unable to take it anymore. "Go on. What are you thinking?"

"You know, maybe I do see it," Kelli said, pushing half the containers to Sienna's side of the table. "In fact, I'm not sure why I didn't before. You're both adrenaline junkies, you practically work the same job, and you like so many of the same things. You're definitely each other's types physically. And the best thing, you're both really good people who care about helping others."

"And…?" Sienna prompted. Kelli's words sounded affirming, but her expression held some reserve.

"It's just… I don't know… He seems a little laid-back for you. I always saw you with an international race car driver or some high-powered lawyer or something. Someone with focus, follow through. Drive, I guess." She stabbed a big forkful of pot roast swimming in gravy.

"I know. Me too," Sienna said, pushing her salad around. "That's the part that scares me. What if all the good stuff is making me overlook the most important thing—genuine compatibility?" She finally took a small bite. Wow, even the salad was exceptional.

"Do you really think the two of you don't have that?"

"I don't know. I didn't at first. Now, I'm not sure what to think. When I ask him about his career or goals, he clams up. I get the feeling it's something that runs deeper than not caring or not having drive, but I haven't been able to ferret it out yet. It's worrying, though. I mean, how could I not worry about it, growing up with my parents, but this feels different. I want to believe it's different, anyway. He's not spacey, like my mom. And he doesn't seem disorganized or forgetful." She waved her fork since she couldn't gesture with her hand. "It looks like laziness, but

I'm getting the feeling it isn't that either. I can't quite put my finger on it."

Sienna tried the pot roast next and made an involuntary groan of appreciation. She took pride in her cooking, but Sally was an artist.

"Maybe so," Kelli said. "I was being kind of charitable when I said laid-back. It's more like a master class in avoiding things he doesn't want to do. Still, you can't really call him inherently lazy."

"I know, right? Like his dedication to certifying for that Wildland Fire Team and studying wildfires, and even...well, I'm going to have to confess this to you sometime, even though you probably already guessed it..."

"Confess what?"

Not ready to meet Kelli's eyes, she took a deep breath before looking up. "With my mom's accident and now having to work extra days, I didn't get anything done for the wedding. Troy's taken over."

"Oh. Wow, you really *must* have that man wrapped around your finger to get him to commit to that!"

"He saw how upset I was, and he seemed so sincere. We both knew you and Cole had too many crises to deal with to plan the wedding yourselves, and I had a list for him to follow." She shrugged with another wave of her fork. "I didn't even ask. He offered, and he promised he'd see to everything. It's all laid out for him. All he needs to do is keep to the list and everything will be fine."

She did her best to sound confident, but she could feel her brows tighten and her gaze turn pleading, willing not only Kelli to believe her, but willing herself to believe it as well. Good friend that she was, instead of worrying about how the wedding might turn out Kelli tried to allay Sienna's guilt.

"I'm proud of you, girlfriend. Look at you, handing the reins to someone else. That can't have been easy."

It had been anything but easy. She'd been dying to call the rental place and the other businesses to check up on him and make certain he'd been getting things done, but for one thing she hadn't had time during business hours and, more importantly, she'd promised him, again, that she would trust him. And now, trusting him had tangled with other feelings for him. Tugging at that tangle could break things, like his faith in her if she checked up on him or, scarier still, it might break the fragile strand of hope that he really would come through for them all. Because, if he did pull this off, then maybe they truly were compatible. Baring all to Kelli, though, brought her worries rushing back threefold.

"I tried to get a progress report out of him a couple of times," she continued, "but he didn't budge. I promised him that I'd leave it up to him, but I don't want to let you down either. Has he said anything to you, by chance? Or have you seen the list lying around with things checked off? Heard him on the phone? Seen packages of wedding stuff?"

Kelli spread her hands palms up. "I don't know anything about anything. I just flew in yesterday morning, and Troy was at work when I went over in the evening. Don't worry about it, though. If he promised you he'd follow through, I'm sure he will." She took a bite of gravy-covered carrot, then tipped her head to the side as if reconsidering her words. "Probably."

Sienna dropped her forehead in her hand. "This is killing me. But there isn't anything I can do about it until Friday at the earliest. Oh," she said, looking up, excited. "I got the dresses though. Did you see the picture?"

"I did and I love them! They're perfect. And really, don't worry about the rest. There's been so much going on for all of us, I'm okay with Troy doing whatever he can."

"Oh gosh, I'm sorry. Here I am talking about me when you haven't even told me about your trip or how Mark and Blair are doing."

Kelli stabbed a forkful of meat, then just

twirled it in the container. “It’s not good. I wish I could have stayed longer. They’ve got so much to deal with. There’s not much that can be done, so they’re facing all these decisions and end-of-life planning, financial concerns, the kids. My mom took leave from work to help them. She got to Blair’s house a couple of hours after I left, then she’ll be coming back here for the wedding and Dad’s surgery. Mark’s mom is planning to get there before my mom leaves, then she’ll stay with them long-term to help with the kids.”

“So there’s nothing they can do?”

“They’re going to try what they can, but the odds aren’t good. The doctors told them both to be prepared.”

“I’m so sorry. Is there anything I can do to help?”

“Just what you always do. Be here for me.”

“Till my last breath.”

CHAPTER TWENTY

Wednesday, August 5th

TROY WASN'T THE only one on edge all day Wednesday; his entire crew radiated a restless energy, wondering if the shoe was going to drop and the Wildland Fire Team would be called out.

Jan had bumped into him as he turned from the coffeepot. He'd spilled enough from his full Hello Kitty mug that he needed to top it off again as well as clean up the mess. They both mumbled apologies instead of the verbal play-sparring that would normally have followed. Bouncer sat in the bullpen polishing his work boots for the second time that day. Captain Mac had been on his cell phone since their shift started, talking with the fire chief, Alamosa County authorities, Huerfano County authorities and the other captains with on-duty team members.

On top of that, windstorms always wound Troy like a spring: The incessant groan and whine. The air, like sandpaper, dragging over the streets and sidewalks and buildings without rest. And for anyone who ventured out in it, rubbing over skin, tugging at clothes and hair and hats; pushing at your back or chest like a bully, throwing sand and dirt in your eyes and sending loose paper and leaves and debris swirling into you.

No one liked the high-wind days, but maybe growing up on the ranch had made him hate it more than some people. All those open acres for grit to accumulate before peppering the windows and structures. The horses and cows and dogs restless, some on the edge of panic. The need for chores to be done regardless of the wind, and trying to feed hay without it all blowing away or refill water tanks while avoiding getting trampled. The whistling and buffeting against the second floor of the ranch house when his childhood chores were done and he was trying to sleep but couldn't for the howling.

The Chinook winds had begun around midnight and weren't expected to abate until this evening. Worse still, he'd woken last night to gusts rattling his bedroom windows and his first thought had been of the fire. The county had air-dropped chemical fire retardant the previous two days, trying to get ahead of the wildfire before the winds started, and yet the blaze had grown from 1,040 to 2,368 acres. From the ranch he'd seen the distant blue sky painted with streaks of red, but they couldn't fly overnight, and then the planes had been hamstrung today by winds gusting up to 82 mph. The last estimate he'd heard was that the fire now covered more than 7,200 acres. The beetle-kill trees and thick undergrowth in that steep, remote canyon, along with the Chinook winds, had combined into a perfect storm for an inferno.

The captain ended his call and walked into the kitchen just as Troy threw away the coffee-saturated paper towels he'd used to wipe the floor.

"What's the word?" Troy asked him.

"Just over ten thousand acres now. Odds are you won't get called out today. County officials are in online meetings with national admins for the Forest Service and Hotshots. They have more crews headed this way and are holding off on bringing in our Wildland Team for the time being. Stay ready, though. You could get a call anytime, day or night, to head to the staging area."

There wasn't much else to say, so Troy nodded and wandered into the bunkroom for the third time that day, unsure why he was there until he saw his large, packed duffel at the foot of his bunk. Some looping, restless worry kept prodding at his unconscious to be certain he had everything ready when, of course, he did.

He unzipped the bag anyway to reveal his helmet and hood, goggles and gloves, breathing apparatus, yellow wildland shirt and green pants and his heavy wildland work boots so different from the big, pull-on turnout boots for structure fires. Fifty-nine pounds of gear before adding the weight of a shovel, pickax, chain saw or other tools. The bag also held a couple of changes of T-shirts and underwear, some dehydrated food, a canteen and most important of all, his emergency fire shelter: five pounds of aluminum and silica in the size and shape of a sleeping bag that might save his life in the event a blaze overtook them and they had to shelter in place.

"Penny for your thoughts?"

Troy turned and found Jan standing behind him. Firefighters didn't talk about their fears, partly out of superstition and partly because refusing to acknowledge them made it easier to pretend they didn't exist. Pretty obvious what he was thinking, though, as he held the packaged fire shelter in his hands.

"Hard to believe that an eight-by-two-by-three-inch piece of tinfoil can trap breathable air and keep you safe in up to five hundred degrees of heat and flame roaring over you, huh?"

Harder to trust since it hadn't saved the crews in the Storm King and Yarnell fires where temperatures might have reached as much as 2000 degrees. Still, he'd meant it when he'd told Sienna that those were the outliers. Firefighters battled scores of wildland fires every summer that didn't result in those kinds of tragic outcomes. Every one of the eight firefighters in his department who'd certified had wanted this. He couldn't help but be a bit nervous—he imagined they all were—but he also couldn't deny the excitement and the hope that he'd get called out to test his new skills as part of a crew instead of as a trainee.

"At least you have that technology available to you if you need it," Jan said. "But the whole point is not to need it."

"Truer words..." He tossed the package back into his duffel and zipped it up. "Reconsidering going out for wildland next year?"

She shook her head. "You can have it. I always wanted to work the structure side. Air-conditioned station house. Go home in the morning after my shift."

"What's your new beau think about your profession? Working with thirty-one men, gone twenty-four hours at a time..."

She shrugged. "Taking it like a lawyer. He knew the facts going in." She retrieved her iPad from her locker and left the bunkroom.

Jan had talked openly for the past month about dating someone from the DA's office.

Not to make him jealous, which he wasn't, or to brag. Just Jan being Jan—upfront and matter-of-fact. An everybody-deal-with-the-situation-and-move-on gal. It was one of the big factors that helped them succeed at both dating and breaking up while also working together. Some folks in the department thought her emotionless sometimes, but he knew she was just pragmatic. It was surprising, really, as pragmatic as she was that she hadn't ended things with him much earlier. It had been obvious from the start that the two of them were never going to make it.

He shouldered a good chunk of the blame for not trying in case he failed, with Jan as with so many things. It was going to be different with Sienna, though. The way he felt when he was with her was nothing like with anyone else. Even when he wasn't with her, colors were brighter, jokes were funnier. The lightness of heart he'd been experiencing lately had made him realize how little he'd felt since his father died. Maybe longer.

He was self-aware enough to know he'd always been a man of middles: middle emotions, without much in the way of highs and lows; modest goals he couldn't fail; middling risks in his personal life to avoid breakups; restrained interaction with his family in case they pinned hopes on him that he didn't achieve. He regretted his restraint now with his parents. He would regret it someday with his brothers if he didn't change. And he would absolutely regret it if he lost Sienna over him not living up to his promise about the wedding.

His stomach twisted at that last thought, but he suppressed his concerns. They were getting to know each other better all the time, care about each other more. He'd made a hasty promise to help ease her stress, but he'd never been able to explain—to her or anyone else—how deeply pressure and expectations affected him. Her list was so meticulous. What if he did some of it wrong? All of it wrong? Cole and Kelli weren't worried about the details, so he felt confident that Sienna would relax over time too. She'd see. It would all be fine in the end; he felt sure of it. Well, *pretty sure*.

A piercing tone over the PA interrupted his thoughts. Sienna's clear voice filled every room of the station, sending them to a traffic accident on the highway.

BY THE END of the day, his crew had responded to three medical calls, one routine inspection and a burn pile left to smolder the day before, which had been brought back to life by the winds. It turned out to have toxic elements in it: magazines, plastic, particle board and tires. The owner had been cited and now faced a court date and fines that would make the cost of hauling it all to the dump seem like nothing.

Overnight, they responded to one traffic accident, but Troy had difficulty getting back to sleep when they returned. Every muscle in his body felt poised for the alert tone and callout that would send him to his brand-new brush truck, then east to the fire with his team.

He couldn't help wondering how he'd do. The wildland certification requirements had challenged him even more than the fire academy had. He'd never tried so hard at anything or wanted it so much. After growing up on stories of Red Adair and watching scores of hours of wildland firefighting strategy, when it came right down to it, he wouldn't know if he had what it took until he tried.

And when he wasn't lying awake thinking of the wildfire, he was thinking of Sienna. She'd dispatched until seven, so he'd heard her voice off and on all day. It pulled at him like a fishhook in his stomach to hear her and not be able to talk to her. He'd given her a quick call in the evening, but she'd been tired, and they hadn't chatted long. Long enough, though, for him to make a pitch to take her out somewhere special the next evening. She'd be starting her three days off Thursday evening, and he figured she'd be up for celebrating getting through her week. He'd been right. She had been up for it, even though he'd kept his plans for the date a surprise.

Thursday, August 6th

THE 7:00 A.M. TONE sounded through the station, signaling the official shift change. Most of the A-shift crew had arrived earlier than usual, two of them carrying their own Wildland Fire Team duffels. Tense nods were shared as C shift left and A shift settled in for the next twenty-four hours.

Troy poured a large cup of coffee in his stainless travel mug for the drive home. The winds had finally died down around 9:00 p.m. and the extra crews of smoke jumpers and Hotshots had arrived yesterday. If they could make significant progress on the containment lines today, the wildland team might not even be needed.

As usual, Cole was already out working when Troy got home. He and his foreman, Dustin, had fixed the tractor last week and baled the hay, but then the forklift had broken down while they were moving the enormous bales off the field. The forecast called for rain next week, and if it came before the hay was safely stored in the barns, they could lose the entire harvest to mold.

To Troy's surprise, though, the kitchen wasn't empty.

"Morning, Sally. You're here early. Training for a race?"

Sally turned from drying and putting away Cole's breakfast dishes. She wore her blade prosthetic today, the one that looked like an upside-down metal question mark, meaning she'd probably gone for a run before work.

She nodded. "Kurt and I signed up for the trail races in Fairplay later this month. He's doing the ultra and I'm doing the half-marathon."

They'd been world-class mountaineers and expedition guides until her husband had semiretired to film other people's expeditions and write books, and Sally had lost her lower leg to frostbite when she'd helped another climber descend in a storm. When his dad said he was hiring a housekeeper following their mother's cancer diagnosis, Troy had expected someone like Aunt Bea from *The Andy Griffith Show*. Sally had been as far from that as possible, but had turned out to be an amazing cook and a woman who'd become a close family friend.

Her eyes dropped to the large duffel in his hand. "Have you heard if you're getting called out?"

"No word yet," he said.

She nodded and returned to work. She'd not

been what he'd expected ten years ago; she'd been better. With ranching and firefighting among the hardest and most dangerous professions in the US, she'd fit right in. Another person who understood the risks and rewards inherent in challenging oneself.

After breakfast, he watched the fire updates. It turned out that between the high winds during the day and the overnight gusts, the fire had made an uphill run and more than tripled the acreage burning. Even with the extra crews showing up, they'd have their hands full.

Tired from his sleepless night, Troy waited for Sally to finish vacuuming the upstairs and then Cole to clomp around getting his lunch. Finally able to nap, he woke around 2:30 p.m. to his cell phone ringing. The screen showed it was his captain calling, setting off a flutter of butterflies in his stomach.

"Hey, Mac, what's up?"

"You are. You're heading out. The incident commander said to get you on the road. They'll call you en route to let you know where you'll be staging. You'll probably be on the fire line by morning."

"Got it. Thanks, Mac."

"Good luck. Stay safe out there."

"Will do."

They hung up and Troy stared at his phone,

lost in thought. This was happening, and suddenly it was all too real. Regular crew—no more babysitting. He and the other seven firefighters would be on the front lines, like the rest. A date tonight with the fire instead of one with Sienna.

Grabbing his keys from his dresser and moving toward his duffel, he thumbed to her name in his contacts and hit dial, expecting to leave a message. To his surprise, she answered on the first ring.

"Hey there," she said. "Great timing. You caught me on my break. I'm on my way back from a junk food run to the vending machine."

"Vending machine snacks? You *must* be having a tough day."

"The day hasn't been too bad. Just comfort food to get me through day six. Potato chips and really crappy hot chocolate. I would've held off, hoping for a big, special dinner, but someone won't tell me what he has planned for us tonight."

"Yeah, well about that, unfortunately nothing. I just got called out to the fire."

"Oh." Her tone sounded more worried than deflated. "So you're on your way now?"

He'd packed some extra items in his bag this morning, like his toothbrush and soap, along with a phone charging bank and a big bag of trail mix. He glanced around the room to make sure there was nothing else he needed. "Yep. On my way out the door."

"Well, if I'm not getting my special surprise tonight, then you at least have to tell me what it was."

"Fair enough. Remember when we were in Santa Fe and you mentioned that you like salsa dancing?"

"Yep. And you said you didn't even know what that was."

"I still don't. But I found out the community center gives salsa lessons. A six-week course, Thursday nights at eight. The new group was starting tonight, so I signed us up." He trotted down the steps to the main floor. "I figured if you didn't mind me stepping on your feet a few times, by the end of six weeks I might be passable enough to take out in public."

She didn't respond.

He stopped in the middle of the living room. "Was that okay? I figured I could always cancel it if it was something you didn't want to do."

"Yes, it was okay." Her voice was subdued. "It was more than okay—it was a really sweet idea. I'm sorry we won't get to go tonight. I'll tell you what. When you get back, I'll give you a private lesson to get caught up. Maybe we can start on week two."

"Sounds good to me." That private lesson thing sounded very good indeed.

He didn't want to say goodbye, and maybe she didn't either because they were both quiet for a moment before he said, "Well, I better get going…" at the same time he heard the clicks of her punching in the door lock and she said, "My break is over, so…"

"Right. I'll try to call when I can, but I'm not sure if I'll have cell service out there. Probably not. But, hey, working in dispatch you're likely to know when I'm coming back before I do."

"Maybe so. Oh, is there anything I need to do while you're gone? Like, any unfinished tasks or phone calls or shopping you might have? I do have the weekend off."

"Nope. Not a thing," he said, trying to sound reassuring for both their sakes. He could almost hear her biting her lip. "You said you trust me, remember?"

"Of course I do. I meant at the ranch, or the fire station, or whatever," she said airily, before sobering again. "Be careful out there, Troy." She paused. "I… I'll see you when you get back, okay?"

Had she been about to say something else? The thing he'd wanted to hear? The thing he wanted to say to her?

"See you when I get back," he said.

CHAPTER TWENTY-ONE

Friday, August 7th

SIENNA WOKE TO hazy sunlight. Even on her days off, she used her alarm to make sure she didn't waste her day, but last night she'd turned it off and double-checked it twice. Her first realization on waking: how glorious it felt not to get up and go to work. Her next coherent thought: Troy.

She could taste the smoke in the air, even with all the windows closed. When she opened the curtains, she found filtered sunlight drifting through what looked like high clouds. Lower down, the smoky haze obscured the horizon and even hid all but the lowest section of Blanca Peak. Going to bed last night, she'd seen an ominous orange glow to the east. She couldn't imagine what it looked like up close or how it felt to work in the mouth of that beast. Harder still was thinking of Troy there.

It had surprised her when playing backgammon the other night to find herself more concerned about him fighting wildfires than being a city firefighter. She'd been examining that reaction over the past few days. First, though she wasn't a worrier per se, someone as detail oriented as herself would always consider all the possibilities, including the negative ones. The main difference from his regular job, though, seemed to be that working in town had the illusion of being more controlled. The majority of calls they went on posed no danger, and in the rare case of a large structure fire, backup from other first responders was close and readily available. Also, a structure fire was rarely larger than the size of one building, where a wildfire could cover more than a hundred square miles.

The biggest thing, though, was that she knew so little about wildfires. A solid knowledge base and her natural inclination to logic were how she dealt with the risks inherent to all the first responders she dispatched, as well as the trauma of the citizens who called in for help. Wildfires were out of her scope and something where she had no skill set to fall back on.

She headed for the bathroom and turned on the shower. Trying to pull her thoughts away from picturing Troy on the front lines of a fire that might be fifteen thousand acres or more by now, she shifted her thoughts while she brushed her teeth to the wedding he was no longer working on.

She'd made the offer to take over for the weekend, but he'd assured her there was nothing to do. *Was that what he actually said?* She struggled for his exact words. Maybe he'd just said there'd been nothing for *her* to do. But if he hadn't finished her list already, surely he would have let her know. There'd be no reason for him not to.

Besides, she'd promised to trust him, and with him out there, putting his life on the line, it felt disrespectful to check up on him. Honestly, even if he *had* taken her up on her offer and delegated some things back to her, she didn't know how she would've managed them. She might be the queen of powering through exhaustion, but she could only do so many things at once. Sienna hadn't managed more than a few minutes at a time with her mother in days. Dan had plans to leave for Greeley, north of Denver, after work today, to visit his daughter and new grandchild for the weekend. Sienna's three days off needed to be all about taking care of her mom.

First, though, breakfast and some quality time with Tiger.

After a large cup of espresso, a homemade breakfast burrito and a rousing game of chase the laser pointer with Tiger, she gave her mom a call to let her know she was on the way.

It was a pleasant surprise when she arrived to discover that Dan had kept up surprisingly well with the everyday things at her mom's. The house was in need of a deep cleaning, but rooms were tidy, dishes were done and the rug had been vacuumed. Most importantly, it appeared that he'd taken good care of her mother—her pain management, swelling and especially her spirits. Despite herself, Sienna was warming up to the man. Still, though he'd done his best, there were things her mom would only ask of a daughter, and a dozen more that Dan probably hadn't thought of or hadn't had time to do. The shopping, chores and cleaning waiting for her would more than fill her days off.

The appointment to establish her mom with the local orthopedist and get her physical therapy scheduled wasn't until after lunch, so after a short hello, Sienna rolled up her sleeves and got started on the house.

"How are things with Troy?"

Sienna hadn't heard the knee scooter rolling up behind her.

Sponge in hand, pink latex gloves on, she froze mid-scrub on the kitchen counter. Her mother had asked about Troy each time they'd talked on the phone, but here, face-to-face, her mom would read her like a book, however much she attempted to cover it. She tried for a guarded version of the truth.

"I don't know," she said casually. "He's working that fire, and I've been at work all week."

The full truth was that things were going well. Far better than she had expected them to, but she wasn't ready to spill the beans about her feelings for Troy to anyone just yet. Okay, Kelli had ferreted it out in a hot second, but her mom was one bridge too far. She didn't need her mom's enthusiasm if she learned they were dating, and she didn't need the memories of her parents' ups and downs triggering her either. She had enough of a pro and con debate going on in her head already.

"The Raspberry Mountain fire?"

"Mmm-hmm." She moved the toaster and shoved her head under the cabinets, scrubbing harder than necessary at a corner of the counter. "He's on the Wildland Fire Team."

"Oh. When did he leave?"

"Last night."

"He called to let you know?"

Sienna involuntarily paused again. "Yeah, you know, wedding stuff and all."

At the silence, Sienna peered out from under the cabinet to catch the flash of a smile on her mom's face. A smile that said she knew exactly what "and all" meant, though her mother said only, "He seems like a nice boy."

"He's thirty, Mom. And yes, he's nice. But he's my best friend's almost brother-in-law, and that's all."

"That's too bad. But if you're not attracted to him, you're not."

Oh, but she was. She really, really was.

Her mom turned and rolled away, but not before Sienna caught that sly smile on her face again.

Rose Herrera, optimist and dreamer. What Sienna needed was logic. Sure, she might be falling for Troy, but mutual attraction didn't mean he was the right man for her, just like mutual attraction hadn't been enough for her parents. She could hope, but only time would tell.

Saturday, August 8th

ON SATURDAY, SIENNA made a massive grocery shopping run and batch-cooked for the week. She also took her mom on a couple of excursions to get her out of the house, though apparently Dan had been taking her out for dinners most nights of the week, which had probably saved her mom from going stir-crazy. Rose Herrera was not a woman to stay housebound.

By evening, the fridge was clean and filled, and she and her mom had caught up on a little quality time together. That night, Sienna devised some fun diversions, though charades nearly resulted in her mom tipping off her knee scooter while trying to pantomime *Old Yeller*, so they finished the evening by watching *Moonstruck*, a perennial favorite for them both.

At last, she headed home to bed. Lying awake, she reflected that she hadn't heard from Troy since he left on Thursday. He'd been right about the lack of cell service in the remote and mountainous area; when she'd tried calling him Friday evening, the call had gone straight to voicemail. Her mother's needs had helped to distract her from thinking about him too much during the day, but in the quiet of the night, he seemed to be all she could focus on.

Is he safe? Does he miss me? Could he really be the one?

Sunday, August 9th

AROUND LUNCHTIME ON SUNDAY, Dan called her mom to confirm he was more than halfway home and would be in Burgess in time for dinner. Her mother shooed her out of the house, insisting Sienna take some time for herself to catch up on her own life.

It felt like weeks since she'd had free time in the middle of the day, and once she had her own errands done, Sienna found herself standing in her living room, at a loss for what to do next. The sudden lack of purpose created a void, and with that void, a vacuum that sucked her concerns over Troy rushing in to fill the empty space. As someone used to having all the information about emergency situations at her fingertips, it frustrated her no end to be out of the loop. She'd adopted Troy's habit of watching the incident updates online in the mornings, but they provided little to no information about specific teams. Fed up with not knowing, she dialed the back line for dispatch.

"Hey, Lisa," she said when her supervisor answered. "Don't worry, I'm not calling in sick for tomorrow or anything. I was just wondering if you have any information on the wildfire."

"Not much. It's spreading from Costilla County into Huerfano instead of heading this way, so we're not on pre-evacuation anymore and La Veta is, but that's about all I know. If they change the evacuation status, we'll get notified, but other than that, we're on a need-to-know basis now and there's not much we need to know."

"Oh. Okay." It was all Sienna had expected, though she'd hoped for more.

"Why?" Lisa asked. "Is the smoke getting to you or something?"

"No... Well, yes...but I called because I know someone out there."

"One of our guys on the Wildland Team?"

Sienna winced, having said too much already. She'd kept quiet at work, as well, regarding Troy. At first, because she'd been convinced that nothing could ever work out with him. Later, more from a superstitious desire not to jinx it. Now she kind of wished Lisa knew so she could share her concerns with her.

"Ooh, is this the best man for the wedding you were so frustrated with?"

Why was that the one thing that stood out in everyone's memories?

"Um, yeah. He's going to be my best friend's brother-in-law. I'm sure my friend and her fiancé are concerned about him. I thought maybe I could find out how he's doing."

"Let me see what I can do. I'll say I'm calling because the fire department has to keep the wildland team's shifts covered, and we need to know if they have any updates, or something."

"Thanks, Lisa. I appreciate it."

Lisa called her back a few minutes later.

"I know one of the county supervisors," Lisa began. "She gave me a number for an incident leader at the fire. It's still increasing rapidly, but there've been no significant injuries beyond a couple of sprained ankles and one chain saw incident a couple of days ago. All he said about that was 'It wasn't as bad as it could have been.'"

The commander hadn't released a name, but Sienna felt certain it hadn't been Troy, or she would have heard from someone when he came back into cell range for medical treatment.

She thanked Lisa and decided to take a drive, hoping that getting out of town for a bit might settle some of her restlessness. Half an hour later, she found herself on the remote dirt roads leading to Forbes Park Lake and Raspberry Mountain, the area of the fire. Surprisingly, the smoke diminished the closer she got, as if she drove under the thick layer drifting up into the sky. Even in daylight, though, she could see the deep orange glow of the flames as they ran up the steep slopes and marched across the tops of the foothills.

This was ridiculous. What was she even doing here? It wasn't like she was new to the idea of first responders being sent into dangerous situations. And she certainly wasn't out here to suit up, pick up an ax and help fight the fire. Was not being familiar with wildfires really the only thing that had put her out of sorts when Troy said he might get called out? And what had led her to drive more than an hour just to see this mountain for herself? It seemed there was only one answer: *This must be what happens when you love a firefighter.*

Love. It was her first time using the word when thinking of him and it surprised her—like turning around to find someone you'd been unaware of standing right behind you. There it was, though. And now that she'd acknowledged it, there was no more calling this simply an attraction or "feelings."

Still miles from the edge of the fire, she was prevented from getting any closer by a young firefighter with his vehicle parked across both lanes of the road. Leaving her Kia on the shoulder, she sauntered toward his truck with a smile and a wave. He got out and stood by his door.

"Hey," she said, looking around at the 360-degree expanse of nothing and no one. "You get the short straw?"

"Something like that," he said with a smile.

He must have been eighteen or nineteen years old, tops.

"I work for dispatch. Just thought I'd come out and see things for myself." She didn't specify which dispatch in case he made any assumptions that might help her. "How's it going up there?"

He shrugged. "Okay. Be better if there weren't so many crews tied up in Idaho and Washington right now. We could do with about twice as many people as we have, but the other states are probably saying the same thing. Sure hoping for that rain they're talking about this week, though."

"I'll bet. Where are you from?"

"California. San Diego."

"First season with the Forest Service firefighters?" She'd seen the logo on his truck.

"Yeah. It's just for the summer. I start at SDSU in a couple of weeks. I've been up there, though." He nodded over his shoulder to indicate the mountain. "We have to take turns at the roadblocks." A burst of static squawked from the radio in the holster on his belt, followed by what must have been the kid's designation.

"I'll let you get back to it," she said. "Thanks for all you guys do."

He nodded his acknowledgment to her as he keyed his mic and answered the radio.

She returned to her car but instead of leaving, leaned on the open door, staring up the mountain. She thought of the wild animals running for their lives, so many creatures displaced or endangered. Mice and squirrels thinking themselves safe in tree boles or underground. Slow-moving porcupines and raccoons. Deer and mountain lions, bobcats and coyotes and bears. Mostly, though, she thought of the men and women out there. Breathing that smoke, working in the heat of the day, amplified by the heat of the fire, while they climbed the steep hillsides. Some people might not comprehend anyone wanting a job like this, but the adventurous side of her had to admit she could understand how this had become Troy's passion.

Glancing again at the kid whose name she hadn't gotten, something clicked so suddenly that she could almost hear the penny drop in her head. Fresh out of his San Diego high school and here he was, in the Colorado wilderness, alongside scores of other young people doing this job. On the other hand, Troy was a thirty-year-old firefighter with seven years' experience. Strong, physically in his prime, fire-academy trained—someone who'd been studying wildfire incidents with a vengeance for the past year, and who had passed the wildland fire training that many of his fellow firefighters had failed.

All the pieces that had been up in the air these past weeks—jangling her nerves with uncertainties—seemed to fall into place at once. This was so much simpler than she'd been making it. She loved Troy and was pretty sure he felt the same. With love came worry. On top of that, Troy was a first responder—a firefighter. But here was the crux of it: He was good at his job. She'd needed to understand the source of her worry and then step back from it, just like she did every day at work. With Troy, she could do that by trusting that he knew what he was doing. And as for her feelings for him…no more denial. She needed to tell him how she felt when he got back.

With a heart twice as light as it had been driving out here, she got in her car and headed back to town.

CHAPTER TWENTY-TWO

Monday, August 10th

"TYLER," TROY'S SUPERVISOR shouted to him from a few yards downhill. "Take Anderson and Mendez and extend that trench to that tree line there." He pointed upslope.

Troy raised one hand to signal that he'd heard, gestured to the other two men and slung his pickax over his shoulder.

This fourth day on the line he'd felt more at ease than his third, which had felt better than his second or first. Like the rest of his team, he'd progressively settled into the rhythm and expectations of the work. Moreover, the camaraderie with both his team and the specialists they worked with shoulder to shoulder had strengthened each time he proved himself on the assigned tasks.

His metro team had all graduated together, so the firefighter with the most years on the job in Alamosa, Joseph Gonzalez, had been appointed leader. No other hierarchy had been determined, but in four short days, Troy seemed to have bubbled to the top as Gonzalez's unofficial second-in-command.

Troy, Anderson and Mendez reached the end of the previous trench, spaced out and began swinging their pickaxes into the clay soil peppered with rocks. The physical demands had been even more strenuous out here than Troy had expected…and he'd expected a lot. He considered himself to be at a high level of physical fitness, even among his peers, but when lying in his sleeping bag at night, his aches and pains held a lively conversation across every major muscle group in his body.

He'd bushwhacked through heavy undergrowth, dug trench and cleared brush, set backfires and cut timber. He ended each day exhausted, his face black with soot, and whole-body soreness making him shift and turn on the hard ground until sleep grabbed him by the throat. Yet, despite it all, he was as happy as he'd ever been. He'd gained the respect of his peers, proven to himself he could do the job he'd dreamed of since childhood, had some measure of authority with his crew and still got to leave the final decision-making up to their supervisor, Gonzalez.

Troy planted the head of his pickax on the

ground and stretched backward before he became permanently bent double. Straightening, he paused and took in the clear view of the northwestern margin of the fire provided by this new vantage, above the leading edge that burned perhaps a mile and a half downhill. At the same time, he felt a breeze blow across his sweaty face. Studying the flames, he swiveled his head until he pinpointed the wind direction.

"Daydreaming about your girlfriend again?" Hammer Anderson asked.

"Bite me," Troy said. Apparently, he'd said Sienna's name in his sleep the other night and hadn't heard the end of it since. "At least I've got one, Hammer Toe."

When Troy first met Hammer in training, he'd assumed the nickname came from a construction hammer, but it turned out to be a hammer toe from a fracture as a kid that necessitated special work boots.

Troy hadn't divulged any specifics about Sienna—not even that she worked in dispatch—though he'd wanted to. He'd wanted to tell these guys everything about her: The way her smile lit up her face. How her hair felt like satin. How her kisses were the first thing he thought of when he woke. How smart she was. She'd even expressed interest in the technical aspects of his job, wondering how firefighter engineers controlled the water pressure on the pump truck. When he explained it to her, she'd grasped it better than he had the first time it had been explained to him.

He would've gladly told them all that—well, most of it—if not for the impression that Sienna was moving into their relationship more slowly than he was. It gave him a "fish on the line" sensation to think about it. Like she had caught him but might cut him loose at any moment. For once, he didn't want to be the one that got away.

"You guys notice how the wind has shifted?" he said instead to Anderson and Mendez. They straightened and tested the air.

"Not really," Hammer said.

"Supe!" Troy shouted down to Gonzalez. "You checked humidity or wind speed lately?"

"Next reading isn't due for another couple of hours," Gonzalez replied.

"You might want it sooner. Seems to me the wind has shifted toward us and picked up some."

Gonzalez turned his head toward the wind, then shrugged. "I don't notice much difference."

The morning briefing had emphasized that the fire was at a tipping point: If they kept control of the perimeter and were lucky with rain, they might get it contained this week. If those things didn't happen or the winds picked up again, it could flash into new areas of dense fuel and turn into a 100,000-acre monster.

Troy's brow furrowed, unsure if Gonzalez was taking his suggestion to heart. But after finishing some notations on their map, Gonzalez turned for his supply pack and pulled out the humidity instrument.

Troy made his way downhill while Joe separated and prepared the two parts of the tube, then swung the loose end for ninety seconds. By the time he finished, Troy had reached him.

"I can record it if you want," Troy offered.

Gonzalez handed him a small spiral notebook and pen from his shirt pocket. Troy made the notations while Joe radioed in to get the latest weather and wind speeds. Troy jotted down the report, then flipped the page in the notebook, planning to compare the readings to those from this morning.

"I got it," Joe said, pulling the notebook from him before he could see them. Gonzalez flipped back and forth between the two pages. "Minimal changes," he said.

The gruffness in his voice could have been from the smoke, but Troy didn't think so. Joe seemed to like bouncing ideas off Troy those first couple of days when they were all fish out of water out here. He'd assigned people to him and acted like he trusted his judgment. But today he'd been more standoffish: less conversational at breaks, asserting his leadership more during work.

Troy had watched enough people competing for status in his life to recognize the signs. The jockeying from junior high onward, stepping on one another to gain superiority in everything from peer groups to jobs. For him, lead guitar was far preferable to lead singer. Being the front-man—the one in the spotlight, the one being weighed and judged—held no appeal. He wasn't gunning for Joe's position as supervisor, but this was too important not to speak up.

"I'm not trying to tell you what to do, Joe. It's just that I felt the change in the wind from higher up on the hill there, more exposed. I've also been watching that fire line shift from east to north for the last hour or two. Being uphill from that perimeter puts us in a precarious position if the conditions worsen, so I wanted to tell you. We both know what it means if it makes a sudden uphill run this direction." He glanced up toward the summit of their foothill, five hundred feet or more above them.

"I know what it means," Gonzalez said.

Troy gave a short nod and started back up toward his men.

"Thanks, though," he heard Gonzalez say behind him. "Keep an eye on it."

Troy turned back. "Will do," he said, but he

was more than keeping an eye on it; he was worried.

An hour later, they sat scattered in a loose circle. Taking a group break, they refilled canteens from their five-gallon container and ate snack bars and trail mix to replace a few of the many calories they'd burned. The breeze had stiffened into gusts, still blowing northwesterly, when a harder than normal gust hit them. Troy and Gonzalez lifted their heads at the same time, then exchanged glances.

"Mind sharing those measurements from this morning?" Troy asked again, not concerned anymore if Joe took offense.

The others were watching the two of them closely.

Troy's knack for logic and his ability to learn had never been part of his insecurity about leadership. The arguments for sharing the numbers waited on his lips, but he also didn't want to incite a mutiny or undermine his supervisor and teammate. To his relief, Joe nodded, pulled the notebook out of his pocket and handed it to him. Troy flipped back through the readings from the past twenty-four hours, then studied the ones from an hour ago again.

"It's drying out and the wind's increasing. What's the latest from base?"

"Weather report is still winds five to fifteen

miles an hour. Gusts to twenty-five ahead of that cold front moving in, but they aren't expecting that yet. The conditions are ripe for the fire to increase, but they're still saying it's going to keep creeping east, away from us. We're to call in any changes we see."

"What about working a bit west of here to be on the safe side? If we got higher, we could start a new break on top of that small shoulder in case it does make a run." Troy pointed up and to their left.

Gonzalez's mouth tightened, his defenses back up. He glanced around at his team, then at Troy—a warning look that said this wasn't the right place or time to talk about it. For Troy, this seemed exactly the right place and time. The whole team needed to understand the situation and be ready to move at a moment's notice.

"We move if base tells us to. Otherwise, we keep working this line. If it does shift this way, they're going to need these breaks here. Base can see the whole situation, and it's why they put us where they did. If we do need to move in a hurry, we'll go up." He took the notebook back from Troy and tucked it into his pocket, buttoning the flap as he talked. "With the fire moving two or three miles per hour, we'd be way ahead of it. Once we're over the top, we'd have better extraction options. Go west and we could run into a bluff, a cliff…who knows? We haven't even scouted that direction."

If this had been Troy's team, he would have sent Berger, the youngest and fastest of them, first thing this morning to do just that. Gonzalez wasn't entirely wrong. If the fire shifted but progressed normally, they could outclimb it. But if the winds suddenly picked up—pushed by the rainstorm they all hoped was building and heading their way in the next couple of days—the fire could make a hard run. Not even Berger would outrun it up these steep slopes if the blaze hit speeds of fifteen miles per hour or more, just like the South Canyon fire had done thirty years ago in Western Colorado.

The break ended. They went back to work trenching line, if possible, even faster than before. Everybody had followed their discussion, and now the whole crew kept glancing toward the flames below them.

Troy took a big swig of water and wiped the sweat from his face. Both his supervisor and base were saying the same thing, but he couldn't help but feel uneasy. He'd been watching months and months of incident reports and fire behavior. It didn't make him an expert, but he'd learned enough to be concerned. Nobody from base was out here with them. None of the experienced Hotshots or firefighters were within a quarter mile. Teams were scattered all around the perimeter of the fire, but the incident commanders expected each team to act independently, working toward the whole.

Twenty minutes later, Troy glanced downhill again, as he'd been doing every few minutes. He knew the exact triangulation of trees and bushes marking the northwestern edge but saw now that the fire had jumped well past its last mark, coming northwest…toward them. The wind blew straight into his face as he stared at the perimeter half a mile below.

"Joe, we need to get out of here! Now," he shouted.

Joe glanced at him and then stared down at the fire, studying it for a long moment. A gust of wind hit them, the strongest yet that day.

"Grab your gear!" Joe shouted. "Uphill. Move, move, move!"

CHAPTER TWENTY-THREE

SIENNA'S COMBINATION OF studying wildfire incident briefings each day and her belief that Troy's skill and experience would keep him safe had worked wonders. Moreover, admitting to herself that she had fallen in love with him had lifted a weight from her shoulders. No more second-guessing herself on whether to commit to the relationship. She was ready to move forward and give this a try, and she planned to tell him so the next time she saw him.

With those two things resolved, only one nagging concern remained, and now that it had room to move to center stage, it dominated her thoughts: the wedding planning.

He'd kept reassuring her, but in ways that could also be seen as evasion. He could've put her mind at ease any of the times they'd been together by just letting her know what he'd done, but he hadn't, and she had no history of actually seeing him follow through on anything to bolster her confidence.

She'd already asked Kelli if she'd seen any physical evidence and didn't want to bring it up again, planting worries in Kelli's head if nothing was amiss. Sienna knew Troy better now and felt certain he wouldn't let her down—not to mention his brother and Kelli—but there was no telling when he'd get back. No way for him to let her know if she needed to pay for things or pick up anything. She'd promised both Troy and herself that she'd trust him, but under these unusual circumstances, breaking her promise could be forgiven, couldn't it? With just a phone call or two, she could assure herself that all was well. And if he'd taken care of things, it would also be proof that they could be a good match as a couple. She could throw herself into this relationship with confidence and tell him that she loved him without reservations or worry.

Fire dispatch had been slow all day. She talked herself out of checking up on him over lunch, but when things were still slow enough to take an afternoon break, she couldn't hold out any longer. It was three o'clock already and the rental place would close at four. Tomorrow she might not even have time for a break. With him out of cell range and the possibility he might not be back until late in the week, checking on things now was only logical. Besides, with a little assurance, her brain could quit spinning on this and focus where she needed it to. It was the way she was wired: Information gave her peace of mind. Troy wouldn't even know she'd checked up on him, and she could assure her best friend that her wedding plans were all set.

Wandering outside to soak in a bit of hot afternoon sunshine instead of fifty-miles-per-hour air conditioning, she called the rental store.

"All Occasion Rentals," a man answered.

"Hi, I was just calling to confirm a pickup date for some items. The person who reserved them is out of town, and I'm not certain if it's under Tyler or Hinton."

"Do you have the receipt ID or a phone number associated with the account?"

She gave them Troy's number.

"I'm sorry, I'm not seeing any reservation."

With a chill running through her veins, she tried giving him Kelli's number. When that didn't work, she scrolled through her texts until she found one from Cole the day they'd moved Kelli's large animal stuff to the ranch, then read that number to the store clerk.

"Sorry, no."

Anxiety left her lips feeling thick and numb and her fingertips tingling. "Do you have chairs that I could reserve?"

"Yes. We carry gray metal folding chairs and a few white wood-slat chairs."

"Are either of those available for this Saturday?"

"Give me a moment to pull them up on the computer." There was a pause, then, "I have seven of the white ones left."

They hadn't been the ones she was interested in any way. Probably nicer, but not as practical. "What about the metal ones?"

"Don't even have to look. All seventy-five are booked for a fiftieth wedding anniversary and a quinceanera party that day."

"Oh, I see." Devastating news, but maybe not Troy's fault. Maybe they'd been booked for weeks. Maybe Troy had found another place. "Have they been reserved for a while?"

There was a hesitation at the other end at the unusual question and then, "Um, let's see, a week ago this past Saturday and a week ago today." Troy had come home from Santa Fe days before the first reservation, Wednesday afternoon, and he'd been off work the next two days.

"Would you like the wooden chairs instead?" the clerk asked.

They needed fifty chairs at least. Seven were as useless as none. Sienna's heart sank, her hopes for the wedding and her faith in Troy both shattered.

"No. Thank you." Out of pure desperation she asked, "Can you tell me if you have *any-*

thing at all booked under Tyler? Or Hinton?" With a sudden surge of new hope, she blurted, "Maybe Herrera." She rattled off her phone number. "Anything at all. Tables, dishes and silverware. Wedding arch. Anything?"

"No, ma'am. I'm not seeing anything under any of those names."

With her stomach crawling up her throat, she hung up and did a search for florists before remembering there was only one and they were closed on Monday. Caterers, then. She'd located two in the area and had written out all their info on the list she'd given to Troy, along with the guest count, budget and possible menus. She searched for their numbers and called them both. Neither were booked for the wedding. One had another booking that day—the anniversary party again—and the other caterer had a message that she was out of town for two weeks. Next, she tried the two venues she'd suggested for the reception. Nothing.

The numb sensation spread until it covered her entire body and mind like a chilly fog. *He hadn't done anything. Not a single thing.* If not these biggest, most important items, then certainly not decorations, table gifts, a guest book. He'd taken her to dinner and told her to trust him. He'd sat in her living room, playing backgammon, and told her not to worry.

This went beyond her mother's brand of flaky, beyond untrustworthy; he was a liar. A con artist. A man she wouldn't be involved with if they were the last two people on earth.

CHAPTER TWENTY-FOUR

"MOVE!" JOE YELLED AGAIN.

After the discussion the team had witnessed at the break, each of them had packed their scattered possessions and kept their packs nearby. Grabbing them up now, Troy and the rest of the team ran.

A strong gust pushed at Troy's back like a hard shove, hitting him squarely between the shoulder blades. He glanced down to the perimeter. The flames had jumped uphill at least a couple hundred yards. Above them, in the direction Joe herded them, lay an area thick with oak brush.

A static-filled voice on the walkie-talkie conveyed a belated warning that the winds had shifted direction and asked their status. Joe pulled the radio from his belt as he scrambled up the steep slope, using his free hand for balance while answering in gasps and requesting an airdrop on the fire at their location.

Troy could overhear their base advising them

to keep moving to safety, saying they'd get help to them as soon as they could.

"We can't go this way," Troy shouted, pointing uphill. "That oak will go up like matchsticks."

"We'll be ahead of it," Gonzalez yelled back. "That summit can't be more than four hundred feet away, and there's a road at the top that'll act as a firebreak. Keep going!"

Four hundred feet might as well have been four hundred miles with the brush and a steep incline Troy guessed at around seventy or eighty degrees. The last thing he wanted was to mutiny against his team leader. Worse, what if he did and turned out to be wrong? West of here could be a cliff with no way around, like Joe had suggested, or the fire might shift again and follow them, yet every fiber of his being told him going uphill was the wrong decision. They were out of time. Debating this now could kill them all.

"We have to go west! We'll make that shoulder quicker, and the fire's pushing uphill. We can drop down that gulch and be in the clear." He said it to the team more than to Gonzalez. Without waiting for an answer, he cut across the slope to lead the way. When he saw the others hesitate and then head in his direction, he stopped and waved them onward, ahead of him.

"Don't do it, Tyler," Gonzalez yelled from the

back of the line. "We don't know what's over there."

Troy made eye contact with each teammate who passed him to make sure they were all on board. It could be fatal if the team split up or anyone hesitated out of indecision.

"Grab your shelter and drop the rest of your gear," he shouted, shrugging off his own pack and ripping the zipper open.

He counted each man as they passed him and checked to make sure Gonzalez was coming this way. He was. With their burdens decreased from nearly sixty pounds to five, the six men ahead of Troy ran for their lives. Another wind gust blasted into his left side. He heard the whoosh of flame to the east as it hit the thin patch of scrub oak just below where they'd been working minutes ago.

Once Gonzalez went by—without so much as a glance in his direction—Troy fell in behind, his long legs keeping up easily with the others. In just the few minutes they'd run west, the fire had pulled level with their old position, moving straight north, uphill. The roar of that voice unique to fire filled Troy's ears. Deeper than the wind. A churning rumble like a tornado, but charged with the constant crackle of dry fuels being endlessly consumed by a beast that could never be satiated.

They reached the shoulder of the hillside and started down the steep grade on the far side in huge, hopping jumps. The leading edge of the fire hit the scrub brush behind them and flames shot into the air. Troy stopped and watched as the arm of the blaze they'd been working to contain roared past them in a curtain of heat. He guessed the height of the flames at nearly a hundred feet, and moving perhaps twelve miles an hour now. If they'd hesitated even a moment longer before running west, they'd probably be lying in their flimsy shelters at the edge of that perimeter right now, maybe inside it, with the flames roaring over them. And if they'd followed Gonzalez's order to keep running for the top of the hill, none of them would have survived.

The freight train inferno roared up the hill, pushed by the gusts from the low-pressure system moving in and following the line of the driest fuel. They weren't entirely out of danger, but the odds of the fire coming this way or moving downhill or faster than they could run were almost nil.

Troy slowed the group to a saner and more cautious pace down the rocky shoulder, then did a second, silent head count. All accounted for.

"Joe, you want to see if you can raise base from here before we drop any lower?"

Gonzalez raised his head, and Troy met his vacant gaze.

"It's okay. We all made it. Under almost any other conditions, your plan would have been the best option."

Expressionless, Gonzalez nodded and pulled the radio from his belt. He handed it to Troy, walked to a nearby boulder and sat.

Troy debated what more he could say to the man, but Berger, the kid, headed over and squatted by their supervisor, speaking too quietly for him to hear. Troy keyed the mic and filled in the base commander on their situation and the fast uphill run the fire had made.

"Let's get down a bit lower," he said when he'd tucked the radio into his oversize jacket pocket. "Find some cover under the trees. The plane is close. It's water, not retardant, but if they overshoot this edge, it'll feel like getting hit with a fire hose at full blast."

Their team didn't end up needing extrication. The fire burned past them, hot and fast, and a few minutes later, the western edge was doused with thousands of gallons of water from the plane. They hiked up and out along the edge of the burned area by midafternoon. Even most of their packs and tools were largely undamaged, though one chain saw had exploded and melted into an orange puddle.

Joe remained quiet, so Troy led the team out with reminders to be cautious of stepping in holes created by burned tree roots, and to be extra vigilant of falling trees—a far more common cause of injury and death to wildland firefighters than fire itself. From the summit, they were transported to the base camp.

That evening, Troy received an "attaboy" from the top incident commander along with the kudos and thanks from his team.

Tuesday, August 11th

THEIR TEAM WAS ASSIGNED to a new area for the day, closer to base operations. The commander assured both Troy and Joe that it wasn't out of concern over their decision-making abilities or the inexperience of their team, but in case the rainstorm hit this area as predicted. If it did, there was a chance they'd be going back home soon.

No one criticized Joe, and throughout the day, Gonzalez slowly eased back into the routine of working the fire line alongside the rest of them, though he continued to let Troy lead. Troy hadn't wanted to be their supervisor, but now that it was done—at least temporarily—it felt like slipping on his city fire department turnouts. Something heavy, but that fit him comfortably.

The dark clouds built all morning and finally drifted over the hillside where they worked. Light rain began before lunch, mucking Troy's boots with heavy clay mud and making work with the pickax twice as hard. Once the showers turned to heavy rain, though, he and the rest of the team cheered, pumping fists and waving their shovels at the sky.

They shared lunch under a tarp they held over their heads, all squashed shoulder to shoulder and hip to hip. Shortly after, Troy received instructions for the team to meet up with a convoy and return to base. By the time they arrived, the rain had turned torrential, and more teams were congregating at the base camp.

"Gonzalez. Tyler. Over here," their area incident commander called out.

Troy followed Joe into the large tent near their van where the team had been sheltering. Maps covered the back wall—hung on the heavy canvas by clothespins—and computers, monitors and radio gear covered two folding tables.

"We've recorded one and a quarter inches of rain so far today," the commander said. "The weather forecast is calling for rain to continue through the night and heavy showers and cooler temps tomorrow." He turned one laptop so they could see the weather radar. The dark orange Doppler swept over their location, looping over and over as the predicted movement of the storm played out and reset.

"The powers that be are predicting that with this rain and the help of the air teams, we'll have the perimeter one hundred percent contained by the end of the week. In short, we're sending you back to your metro department." The commander tapped a pencil on the edge of the table. "I want you to know how much we've appreciated you boys out here. You proved yourselves, all of you." He locked eyes momentarily with Gonzalez. "You should feel proud. Your whole team should."

CHAPTER TWENTY-FIVE

Wednesday, August 12th

TEN MINUTES INTO her evening commute home, Sienna's phone rang. Anxiety tightened her throat as she stared at Troy's name in large font over an avatar of him chopping vegetables in her uncle's kitchen.

She'd heard from her supervisor this morning that the wildland team was on its way home. The fact that the near-record rainfall for this time of year had brought the fire perimeter 72 percent under control, coupled with the fact that Troy and the others were returning safely, loosed the tension that had tangled her shoulder and neck muscles the past few days.

There'd been shock and anger when she first realized he hadn't followed through on anything on the list, but once past that, she'd forced her emotions into a little box of numb denial and kept them there for the past forty-eight hours. A speck of hope shined inside that box—hope that there was a reasonable explanation. That he'd actually followed through on everything somehow. Maybe he'd gone to Colorado Springs after all. Maybe he'd handed the list to a wedding planner. Something. Anything. Because anything that redeemed him would save not only Kelli and Cole's wedding but also his very precarious relationship with her.

And she wanted so very much for it to be saved.

She reached up to the phone in its holder on her dash and touched the button to answer the call. "Hello?" she said in as neutral a voice as she could manage.

"Hey, babe. It's me."

Babe. He called her babe. The word warmed her like sunlight on snow. Only her father's lifetime of cautions and reverence for logic kept her giddiness in check. Her entire future with Troy lay in the balance.

"Are you home?"

"Yeah. We got back around midmorning, but it was noon by the time we had everything unpacked and cleaned. My regular crew is on today, but they gave us two shifts off as comp time for the fire. I figured I wouldn't reach you until your shift was over, so I went home and slept the rest of the day. Just woke up about half an hour ago."

"I can't imagine how exhausting that work must be."

"Apparently, I couldn't either. I think it was more than any of us imagined. But, you know, in a way it feels good to do a job that's harder than you expect."

"So it all went well? Nothing scary?"

She sensed a beat of hesitation, but then, "All good. I'll fill you in on the humdrum of digging trenches when I see you next. Speaking of, I was kind of hoping that could be tonight if you're not too tired. I've missed you."

Hearing that from him meant the world. She'd missed him too. So much. But she couldn't say it yet. Couldn't agree to a date tonight, no matter how much she wanted to. Her throat tightened again, as if trying to throttle down her next words.

"Troy, I have to ask you something first."

"Okay." She heard his concern in that single word, the sudden shift of his mood to match her own.

"It's about the wedding. You were out of town and out of cell range, and neither of us knew when you'd be back. I didn't want to break my promise to you, but I had to make sure that everything was done for Saturday." The silence at the other end of the line was deafening. "Troy, I couldn't track down a single thing you'd accomplished. Tell me the truth, did you contact anyone on that list?"

Again that condemning silence and then, "I thought you were going to trust me."

"I'm trying to. That's why I'm asking you now. Why I'm looking for something that explains why it looks very much like you've dropped the ball. Did you rent the chairs? Have you ordered flowers? Did you buy any supplies to decorate the wagons or the cabin? Did you reserve a place to have the reception?"

"Sienna, I know these seem like straightforward questions and you want a straightforward answer, but it's not that simple."

He spoke softly, not defending himself, just shutting down. The ice was back, filling her veins like a time-lapse of a river freezing. It crawled into her chest and headed for her heart.

"It really is, Troy. It really is that simple. I'm asking you if you followed through on even one thing on that list before you left for the fire, and it seems like the answer is no."

"Sienna, I told you right from the start that this wasn't something I was going to be any good at but I know..."

Barely conscious of her actions, she pulled over onto the shoulder of the highway and parked. The chill in her body spread to her voice. "No excuses, just straight answers. I had phone numbers to the only two caterers written down for you. Did you hire one of them?"

"No." His tone sounded equally chilly, or perhaps just despondent.

"Did you make a reservation at one of the options I had listed for the reception?"

"No."

"Did you buy any decorations at all? Anything?"

"No."

"Did you reserve chairs or buy shade cloth for the guests?"

"No."

The enormity of his laziness and his dishonesty crashed into her like a speeding car running a red light.

Trust me, he'd said. *I promise.*

At least her mother would've made some kind of attempt. Maybe her own wild take on the list or getting part of it done and then airily saying something else had come up. But this? Troy had not only let her down after a solemn oath, he'd let Kelli down too, as well as his own brother. He'd let down their families who were looking forward to this wedding, and every guest coming to celebrate the marriage of two people they knew and cared about.

"Then I have nothing more to say to you."

"Sienna, I know it isn't what you wanted, but—"

She hung up.

Sienna leaned against the driver's door, one hand across her mouth to hold back the torrent of wordless sounds bubbling up from some deep emotional well.

A gasp escaped her fingers at last, followed by a choking, shuddering sob. The first teardrops, when they came, loosed a flood of deep, racking sobs. Sitting alone on the side of the highway, her blinker clicking like a metronome, Sienna cried harder than she'd done since the day her parents announced they were getting a divorce.

CHAPTER TWENTY-SIX

Thursday, August 13th

AFTER A SLEEPLESS night followed by a light doze somewhere in the small hours of the morning, Troy lay staring at the ceiling, biding his time until dawn, hoping that he'd drift off and knowing he wouldn't. When at last his windows glowed with faint light behind the dark brown curtains, he threw off the covers and shambled to the bathroom.

A long, hot shower failed to rinse off both the malaise and the dejection he'd wallowed in since Sienna had hung up on him last night. Downstairs, he had no appetite for anything beyond a strong cup of coffee for breakfast. With his giant travel mug filled, he discovered that even the coffee depressed him. He stared lackluster at the black liquid, thinking of the coffees Sienna had made for him and the fantasies he'd had of them in the future. Imagining them drinking their coffee together in the morning before work or relaxing with a cup on a veranda on their day off, with a view of some bustling new city where they lived.

He'd blown that fantasy to smithereens. She'd been so specific about what she'd wanted when he offered to take over—things she'd dreamed about for fifteen years—and he hadn't stepped up. He'd let his worry about her expectations of him get in his way. He'd wanted things to be easier for him and convinced himself she'd be okay with it. If only he had a time machine to go back and do it over again.

He took his mug upstairs to check on the progress of the various fires and then shuffled through the rest of his morning like a zombie. He avoided Sally as much as possible, shifting from room to room ahead of her.

A little past noon, the front door banged closed. Cole's heavy tread resonated on the wooden floor downstairs. Troy was finally hungry, and Sally had just gone into his room to clean. He gave up on running away from everyone and went down to join his brother for lunch.

Cole's dog, Baxter, trotted to Troy, tail wagging, stared soulfully up while Troy petted him and then headed for his dog bed in the living room and plopped down. Cole glanced up from pulling Saran Wrap from one of the two lunch plates Sally had left on the counter, then did a double take.

"You look like something the cat dragged in."

"Thanks," Troy said. "I feel like it."

"The fire that rough?"

Troy had retreated to his room last night before Cole had come in from the fields, and definitely before Kelli had shown up to spend an evening laughing and snuggling with his brother.

"Yeah, I guess." Troy unwrapped his own plate of butcher-cut ham, Havarti cheese and fresh-sliced tomato on homemade sourdough with just the right amount of mustard and mayo. The sides of Sally's macaroni salad and home-canned pickles filled the rest of the plate. "No, not really," he amended. "I don't know, yeah, sort of."

"Well, I'm glad you cleared that up." Cole sat on the left-most of the three island barstools and took a large bite of his sandwich.

Troy sat on the right-hand one to give them both elbow room, then just stared at his plate. "It felt really good out there, Cole. Better even than I felt working that three-alarm fire a couple of years ago. Better than passing my engineer's exam."

If his brother had responded by asking about the fire, Troy would have probably buried everything he really wanted to say. But Cole had always known when to talk and when to listen. He listened now in silence, reading the room well enough to know that his brother wouldn't look like the world had crashed down around his head if everything was peachy.

"I even made a good call out there," Troy confessed. "A tough one. It meant going against my supervisor's orders, but it also meant that eight of us walked out of there, where I'm pretty convinced we wouldn't have otherwise."

Cole set his sandwich down and twisted in his chair, giving Troy his full attention.

"I guess I came to some realizations after that," Troy continued, "about decisions I want to make going forward. About not holding back just because taking initiative is scarier than coasting." He pushed a dill pickle wedge around on his plate with his fork rather than meet his brother's dark eyes. "I decided I want to look into applying for one of the Hotshot teams."

"You're going to move away?"

He turned back to Cole, one elbow on the counter, his fork still in his hand. "It's time. Time to turn the house over to you and Kelli. Give you room to grow a family of little ranchers. And it's well past time for me to try new things. The things I've always said I wanted to do and never did."

"I'm happy you've found something you want

to shoot for, Troy, but don't ever think you need to move on our account. There's plenty of room for all of us, for as long as you want to be here."

"I know. This really feels like a lot of things coming together at the right time, though. Sienna told me she'd always had a dream of moving to the LA area. And there's a Hotshot team just above Pasadena and another one farther north, near Santa Barbara. I'm thirty already. If I'm going to do this, even for a handful of years, I have to do it now. I was planning on springing it on Sienna to see what she thought."

"You *were* planning on it?"

Troy sighed. "I think I blew it with her."

"How so?"

He shrugged, reluctant to start. "We've been getting to know each other pretty well, even though it all happened kind of fast. But it felt right, you know? Not like me and Jan. Not like anyone else. I really wanted this to work out, but I tried to help her out with the wedding stuff and now she thinks I let her down."

"Did you?" His brother kept his tone neutral, even though Cole knew him well enough that he must be making some educated guesses.

"I don't know, maybe I did." He toyed with the macaroni salad but still didn't eat. "You know me, Cole. I've always hated people watching to see if I'll do everything just right." He pushed on, defining the feelings that roiled in him in more detail than he could ever remember saying out loud before. "It's always been a hurdle for me, imagining what people will think if I try to step up and then don't live up to what they want." He gave up and tossed his fork to the plate. "You were just all so good at everything. All of you, Mom and Dad, you and Lane. Now I actually want to try my best with Sienna, and I think I'm too late."

"How'd you manage to step up at the fire?"

He gave a one-shoulder shrug. "I just did it. Lives were on the line. Besides, that's firefighting. It's something I've always known I had an aptitude for. I never wanted to be the one in charge, making decisions, but now that I have, it's like it's unlocked something in me. I want more."

Like Red Adair. Like the fire captain at his school career week all those years ago. Firefighting was in his blood and now that he'd proved to himself that he could step up, it felt like the sky was the limit. If he continued to lead the Wildland Fire Team or joined the Hotshots, there could be mistakes made—hopefully never major ones or life-threatening ones—but doing your best all the time was the most anyone could do. He'd always accepted that in others, just not in himself. Until now.

"So what's different about committing to trying with Sienna?" Cole asked.

"She doesn't want me anymore."

His brother looked down in thought for a moment, then back to him. "What I saw with Jan was that anytime she was upset with you, you hung back, left it all up to her, waited for her to get over it…until one day she didn't. You remember how I nearly lost Kelli doing that? Only I was worse than you. We had a misunderstanding, and she held out an olive branch. I was too stubborn and stupid to take it. It took her getting hurt for me to wake up. What's it going to take for you?"

CHAPTER TWENTY-SEVEN

Normally Sienna enjoyed her three-day work weeks, but today she would almost have preferred to work. At least then her mind would have been occupied. Forty-eight hours till the wedding, an appointment this morning for her mother, and not enough time for her to do anything for her friend's wedding that would truly make any difference.

Once her mother finished her PT and Sienna picked up lunch for them both, her reckoning time had arrived. She needed to come clean with Kelli and see if the two of them could figure out a salvage plan together.

Kelli had her small-animal clinic hours this afternoon, so Sienna called her there.

"San Luis Valley Animal Clinic," Rikki answered.

"Hey, Rikki, it's Sienna. Does Kelli have any openings this afternoon, by chance?"

"Pat Wodell just canceled his two o'clock."

"Oh, perfect. Could you pencil me in? Tiger

missed his vaccinations a couple of weeks ago, and I haven't had a chance to make them up yet."

"Sure thing. We'll see you in about an hour."

FORTY-FIVE MINUTES LATER, Sienna headed to Kelli's house. With Tiger mewing in his carrier, she walked around back to the metal barn Kelli had converted into her clinic, thinking about all the things that had happened for her friend since she'd moved back to Burgess. Best of all, she'd fallen in love with Cole, and in two days she'd be marrying her soulmate and the love of her life. Well, at least one of them was getting a happy-ever-after.

The guilt of not being able to make Kelli's big day everything Sienna had pictured for so long tightened her chest until her breath grew shallow. Her confession burned in her throat as she approached the front door of the clinic. While she checked in with Rikki, Kelli emerged from her office behind the front desk to lead Sienna to the exam room herself.

"Well, this is one way to catch up," Kelli said. "It feels like forever since I've seen you, though I guess it's only been a little over a week."

Her friend wasn't going to be so happy when she found out what they were catching up on, Sienna thought morosely. Never one to mince words or delay the inevitable, she dived in feet-first as soon as the exam room door closed behind them.

"Kelli, I have something to tell you, and you'd better brace yourself for it."

Her friend's brows drew together in concern. "What's the matter? Are you okay?"

"Yes. Well, no, not really, but that's another story. The thing is, I promised you I'd take care of everything for your wedding, and I didn't." She set Tiger's carrier on the metal exam table, then sighed deeply and pushed on. "I'm so, *so* sorry, Kelli. I know how much you've been going through with your sister and brother-in-law, and how busy Cole's been. Your mom is at your sister's and your dad has his heart surgery coming up. And even if everybody had been doing just fine, this was something I really wanted to do for you." She shook her head. "I couldn't have failed worse at this if I'd been trying to." Her jaw clenched on the words, but she straightened her spine and faced her friend. "I didn't get a single thing done."

"You did too. You got the bridesmaids' dresses. You even sent me photos of them."

Sienna threw up both hands in exasperation. "Okay, fine. I did one small thing."

"That wasn't a small thing. And Troy got the groomsmen taken care of when you were shopping together, right?"

"All right, nobody will be up there in their underwear. Yay, me." Sienna stared at Tiger in his crate and clicked her thumbnail across the metal door wire before facing Kelli again. "I don't think I'm getting the enormity of this across very well. There is literally nothing else done. No caterer, no chairs, no nothing."

She gathered what was left of her dignity and continued. "I have the rest of this afternoon and most of tomorrow. I swear I'll move heaven and earth to do what I can. I'll stay up all night tonight and tomorrow. I'll drive wherever I need to go to get things. But I've already tried the only rental place in the county and that was a bust, so I'll need help from Cole or his wranglers or a client of yours for a trailer large enough to haul all the chairs and whatever else I can get. Slamming things together like this at the last second, it won't be anything elaborate, but I thought I'd better talk to you first and see what you want me to prioritize. I know you're working today and tomorrow because of being out of town last week, but you point and I'll do it."

"I thought the last time we got together you said Troy had taken over everything."

"Yeah, well, not so much, apparently."

Kelli gave a fake gasp, one hand to her chest. "You mean Troy pulled a Troy?" She laughed.

Sienna really didn't see the humor in this. "He

did. I never should have trusted him. I could've made phone calls from Albuquerque or during my work breaks or left messages at night to caterers and stores. I could've ordered a cake and hired someone to take care of my mom and gone to Colorado Springs. I could have checked out restaurants in the evening for the rehearsal or reception. I had to help my mom last weekend but I…"

"Stop, Sienna." Kelli wrapped both her hands around Sienna's forearm, imploring her. "Cole and I are the ones who moved the wedding date up by months. We knew we only had three weeks and that things were likely to come off a bit thrown together, and that's fine."

Kelli let go of her arm and scooted so that she sat perched on the edge of the exam table. "Your mother broke her ankle so badly she needed surgery. You had to go rescue her, and then you worked six days in a row—a seventy-two-hour week. Did you think I didn't notice? I saw Troy once or twice in the evenings and asked him if there was anything we should be doing, but he just kept saying everything would be fine. I left it at that. Who knows? Maybe he did stuff he didn't tell you about."

Sienna shook her head, sick at dashing Kelli's faint hope. "I'm sorry. He lied to you like he lied to me, and it's not going to be fine. I nailed him down yesterday when he got back. He hadn't done a thing."

Kelli shrugged, unfazed. "Then he didn't do a thing. It is what it is. But look at what we do have. I already had my dress, and Cole has his clothes. We have the rings and the paperwork, and we confirmed the new date with the preacher and the band. We have the meadow, and you and Troy took care of the wedding party's clothes." She reached out and gripped Sienna by one shoulder, making her meet her eyes. "And even none of those things matter. The only thing that matters to either of us is that we're getting married day after tomorrow in front of our friends and family, and that my dad will walk me down the aisle. That's it. That's all either Cole or I care about. Really."

"But there won't be..."

"That's *all* we care about," Kelli said again. "Sienna, I love Cole with all my heart, and by Saturday afternoon he's going to be my husband for the rest of my life." Kelli had let go of her shoulder and clasped her now by the hand. "I wish for *your* sake that you'd been able to follow through on all your lovely plans. It would have been beautiful—I know it would have. And that would have been its own kind of special. But if Cole and I married in a pigsty in a rainstorm, I'd be fine with it as long as I get to marry that man. And the best thing is, I know he feels the same way."

Sienna squeezed her friend's hand, speechless at the thought of what it must feel like to share that kind of love and devotion.

Kelli continued. "If Troy is right and everything is fine, then wonderful. If you're right and he hasn't taken care of anything for the wedding, then we'll have a quick ceremony and drive everybody back to the ranch house. The band can set up on the deck and we'll send somebody to town for iced tea and lemonade and pizza. We'll have Hostess cupcakes for our wedding cake. And Cole and I will celebrate the beginning of our marriage with everybody we love, and *that'll* be wonderful."

If the bride could accept fate so graciously, then the least Sienna could do was try. Despite tears still burning her eyes and blurring her vision, she answered with a hint of her normal spirit. "Well, if that's the case, then get ready because I'm going to throw the two of you the best anniversary party anybody on this planet has ever seen. And just wait until your fiftieth." Kelli laughed. On a serious note, Sienna added, "I hope that someday I find a fraction of the love you and Cole have for each other."

"You will, honey. I know you will. You're one of the best people I know, and there's no way the right guy isn't going to be attracted to that light inside you." Her friend sighed. "So does this mean that things are over with you and Troy?"

Sienna nodded and wiped at her eyes, but new tears brimmed in their place. She scanned the office for the box of Kleenex that every vet exam room stashed somewhere. Finding it, she grabbed two and blew her nose loudly.

"I was really starting to think he might be the one. Despite our differences, like you said at dinner the other night, there's a lot we share in common too. I ended up hoping too much that there was some explanation rather than him just being flaky and irresponsible. But nope. Flaky And Irresponsible is his middle name."

Kelli's face tightened in concentration. "I don't know, Sienna. I talked to Cole at the end of my lunch break today, and he and Troy were heading out to work cattle together…which was a surprise in itself. He said they'd wanted to continue a conversation they'd started at lunch. I don't know what they were talking about, but he told me that Troy had taken over command of his team at that fire. It sounded like he might even have saved lives out there. That doesn't fit with flaky or irresponsible. Neither does the way he grew up or the job he does for the town."

Kelli opened a cabinet and pulled out a vaccine bottle. She drew up Tiger's boosters while she continued. "Do you remember saying last week, when we had dinner together, that you had a feeling there was something more going on with him? I mentioned that to Cole, and he agreed. He said Troy's never been selfish or forgetful. Whatever it is, it's something that runs deeper. Something he doesn't talk about, not even to Cole." She set the syringe on the exam table but didn't remove Tiger from his crate. "Have you talked to Troy about this? Not about what he didn't do for the wedding, but *why* he didn't do it?"

Sienna shook her head. "I've been too mad."

"Maybe you should have a real sit-down talk with him before you decide things are over between you two. You've been seeing each other less than a month. Cole and I had a bad misunderstanding when we'd only been dating a short while. It nearly ended us, but we talked it through. Look how things worked out for us."

The image of her and Troy working things out gripped Sienna's heart with longing, but she crushed the unrealistic wish like crushing a clod of dirt to dust in her fist.

"I don't want to repair this, Kelli. You and Cole have been soulmates since you were kids. You're meant to be together, but Troy and I are just too different. I can't go down the same road my parents did. They knew they were incompatible from the start, and they let their feelings carry them away. Their divorce hurt me for a long time. I lost my father and my brothers at eleven when Mom moved away and brought me here. My dad's right about this, at least. I need to look before I leap. It isn't worth getting deeper into a relationship that's just not going to work."

Kelli nodded sadly. "You've got to do what's best for you. Just do yourself a favor and make sure this really *is* what's best, and not some knee-jerk reaction because of your parents. It seems to me that you and Troy are a lot different than your mom and dad." Kelli gave her a hard one-armed hug. "I'll support you whatever you decide, you know that, but I'll always wish the best for you."

"I know you will."

With nothing more to say, Sienna pulled Tiger out of the crate, gave him some cuddles and held him for Kelli to administer his shots.

"Gotta say, though," Kelli said, getting the last word on the subject, "I was having fun this past week imagining you married to my brother-in-law. We would have been family for real."

CHAPTER TWENTY-EIGHT

IT HAD BEEN months since Troy had cowboyed up and worked cattle—not since that illness that had run through the herd last spring. He'd agreed to go with Cole because he'd been feeling at loose ends, and he hoped the physical outlet would quiet his spinning thoughts. It had also felt good to unburden his misery over Sienna onto his brother's broad shoulders, and he wasn't quite ready to let go of that rare connection.

Once they started working, though, Troy found he enjoyed the ranch work more than he had in years: Getting out on his seldom-ridden palomino, the camaraderie with Cole, the peace that crept into his soul being out in the wide-open pastures among the cattle. The quiet and the expanse of blue sky and green grass gave his thoughts room to stretch and sort themselves out.

Ranching was yet another thing that his fear of not living up to expectations had interfered with. He wouldn't trade it for his career as a firefighter, but riding knee to knee with Cole, listening to the breeze in the grass, the creak of the saddles, the soft snorting of the horses…he made a pledge to himself to get out here more often. For Cole, for the ranch and for himself.

They spent part of the day with Dustin as well, and their foreman's soul-deep, calm confidence couldn't help but seep into Troy. Like the rest of the family, Troy had often wondered about the past Dustin never spoke of—but the lean cowboy's true hallmark had always been that nothing seemed able to ruffle him. When Troy asked him how he managed four headstrong wranglers living in one bunkhouse, he answered in his soft Oklahoma drawl, "Never let anything fester. In the dark, it'll grow into a tangled mess. Once you pull it out into the daylight, the way to untangle it becomes obvious."

The approach made sense, but Troy suspected there'd been a message in there for him as well since Dustin had heard enough to pick up on the gist of his issues with Sienna. Cole's advice and support coupled with a few hours with Dustin combined to reinforce Troy's new vow to put more *try* into things. And he planned to begin with Sienna. He might win her back or he might not, but either way, he was going to give it his all.

Leaving Cole and Dustin to finish out the day, Troy rode on his own for a bit, then headed back to the ranch house before dinner. He unsaddled his horse, brushed and fed him, then went inside to call Sienna.

On the fourth ring, worried that she'd let the call go to voicemail, he heard the shift to live airspace. A slight hesitation and then, "I'm just starting dinner for my mother. What do you need, Troy?"

"A chance to explain."

He heard her sigh. "All right. I'll call you when I get home."

"I was hoping you'd let me do it in person."

"I'll be seeing you in person at the wedding in less than forty-eight hours. I don't know if that's really where you're going to want to do this, but there you go. You know where to find me."

"How about tonight? Could you meet me here at the ranch after dinner?"

"I'm tired, Troy. Why don't I just see you on Saturday?"

"If that's what you really want. But I'll be home all evening and I'll be here tomorrow too, if you change your mind. Call first, don't call—I don't care—but I'd really like it if you could come by."

"Noted. But don't count on it. I really don't feel up to this yet. Maybe after the wedding I'll feel better. Or maybe I'll feel worse. I don't know."

"I understand, but I hope I see you sooner than

Saturday. I miss you." He hesitated, wondering if the timing was all wrong, but more afraid that he might never get another chance. If he was going to start putting himself out there, then he might as well start right now. "I love you, Sienna."

There was a long pause and then a sniffle. "I think you love me too late."

"No. I *told* you too late. I've loved you since that first evening at your house. You made enchiladas, and you laughed till you cried. You played with your kitten and told me things about yourself, and you fell asleep on my shoulder watching a movie. I fell in love with you right then. And I'm still in love with you. And whether you forgive me or you don't, it's not going to change how I feel."

She sniffled again. When she finally spoke, her voice broke. "I have to go. I'll see you Saturday."

CHAPTER TWENTY-NINE

THE ONIONS BROWNING in the skillet blurred in Sienna's vision. She set her phone on the counter and dabbed at her eyes with her sleeve.

"Oh, sweetie, was that Troy?"

Her mother had approached silently on her scooter and leaned into her now, one arm around her shoulders. Sienna tipped her head against her mom's and nodded, dark brown hair mingling with flame-red. Tears rolled down her cheeks for the third time in two days.

Her mother turned the burner off. "Come on. Let's sit."

Rose's balance had improved dramatically, and she rolled expertly into the living room and hoisted herself to the couch. She patted the seat next to her.

"Tell me everything."

And so Sienna did, her voice growing more steady as she talked.

"So all this is over what he did or didn't do for

the wedding, but you're not even certain what's been done?"

"No, I am certain. I asked him and he hadn't done anything."

"But he told you or he told Kelli that everything was going to be okay?"

"He didn't say things were actually okay, he just said, 'It'll be fine.' It's what people who don't want to step up and *do* anything say about everything. It's better that we're ending things now. There's no way I could ever be happy with someone who's irresponsible or narcissistic or terminally lazy."

"Do you really believe Troy is any of those things?"

Sienna threw her hands in the air and let them drop in her lap. "I didn't want to, but apparently hoping really, really hard just isn't enough."

"So he's irresponsible, but he's been a firefighter for seven years?"

"I don't know, maybe not irresponsible so much as the rest."

"So he's a narcissist but he came to Santa Fe with you, helped cook dinner, helped me through pre-op and chose a job as a first responder?"

"Well, maybe not a narcissist exactly, but you know what I mean."

"So just lazy, then?"

"Yeah, I guess so."

"So he went out for the Wildland Team and spent days bushwhacking in steep mountains, doing hard labor to fight a ten thousand–acre fire and he's lazy?"

"Whose side are you on, Mom?" she said sharply, annoyed that her mother was right.

"Yours, sweetheart. Always. And I don't want to see you throw away a relationship with someone who's made you happier than I've ever seen you." Her mom reached over and took her hand and squeezed it. "Sweetie, I spent two days with that man and he's none of those things. He's afraid."

"Afraid?" she said incredulously. "Afraid of what?"

"Of being judged. I may dance to my own drummer sometimes, but I know people. I like people and I talk to all different sorts, and they talk to me. Everyone is a mosaic of strengths and flaws, but I've gotten good at seeing them for who they are under all that. That boy has many strengths…and like all of us, he has a few flaws too. He likes to make people happy. And I'm going to go out on a limb and guess he has a little trouble taking emotional risks because it hurts too much if they backfire and make people unhappy with him instead."

"What? Mom, where are you getting all this? I've spent a lot more time with him and all I'm seeing is a future of him doing his own thing and saying, 'It'll be fine' all the time, and it not being fine, and me being constantly frustrated."

"I didn't 'do my own thing' at first. My living such a separate life from your father as you got older was the result of our marriage unraveling. The problem wasn't that your father was different from me. Different can work. It was that he could never let go of what he'd grown up with and learned from his own father—a man who was harshly judgmental and critical. It ran so deep and entwined with so many childhood emotions that he was never able to move past it. And his anger and criticism made me unhappy too often. So I did my own thing, and he did his, but by then it was too late. I worried about the effects of a divorce on you and your brothers, but I also worried about the effects of our unhappiness on all of us. I tried to stay positive for the three of you, but your dad and I were in a pattern of expecting the worst from each other. So I ended that cycle, even though it broke my heart when the boys decided to stay in New Mexico."

Never in her life had Sienna heard her mother speak so honestly about her marriage. Then again, she'd never asked. She'd made her own assumptions about the past. Worse, she'd made her father's assumptions.

She shifted on the couch to face her mom.

"You've lived with someone who's your opposite. What makes you think Troy and I would be any different?"

"I know you would, dear. You're fun and you enjoy people. I like to think you got that from me. You may have your father's knack for detail and organization, but that's not going to stop you from being happy with someone who has a different approach to life. Besides, people who are too alike are probably less likely to get on well than people who complement each other. And Troy is a caring and responsible man. Just the sort I always hoped you'd find." Her mom patted her hand. "And a tall drink of water, too, if I might say so."

"Mom!"

Her mother laughed, and Sienna couldn't help but laugh as well.

"But the wedding…" she said, sobering.

"This side of your phone conversation sounded like he wanted to explain something to you. And if I'm not mistaken, he said he loved you."

Sienna sighed, remembering the bittersweet lance of those words. "Yeah. He did."

"Well, maybe his explanation is something you can't accept, and maybe you still won't want to be with him, but I think you should at least hear what he has to say. There are plenty of wrong men out there. Don't throw away the right one by accident because you didn't have all the information. You tend to see things in black and white, like your father. In flowcharts or allegories or whatever they're called." She flapped one hand in the air. "Those chart thingies where there are only certain paths to the end point."

It was almost a relief to have her mom sounding like her mom again, and it made Sienna smile.

Her mom continued. "Whatever they are, that's not real life. What's that saying? 'Life isn't something you solve, it's something you experience.' Something like that, anyway. There are infinite paths if you open yourself to the unexpected. Look at me and Dan. When he picked me up on the highway that day, is that how you would have expected me to find true love?"

Sienna's jaw dropped open. "True love? Really, Mom?"

Her mother nodded and gave a little smile and wink. The shock of her mother's revelation pushed her own misery and self-pity aside with a hard shove. "Oh my gosh, I'm so happy for you. That's wonderful." And she really was. They shared a big hug and the last of her reservations about Dan fell away at her mother's certainty.

The hug ended and thoughts of Troy flooded back in like a tide. She wished her reservations about Troy would dissipate like they'd done for

Dan, but now both Kelli and her mother had told her the same thing. Maybe they were right: She needed to hear him out.

CHAPTER THIRTY

BAXTER JUMPED UP from his nap at Troy's feet and ran to the front door barking. Troy followed him from the den where he'd been numbing his raw emotions by channel surfing shows on TV. His heart thumped hard enough for him to feel his pulse in his chest.

Cole was at his city council meeting and wouldn't be back for another couple of hours, and Kelli wasn't likely to come over while he was gone. He told himself it was probably just deer crunching on the driveway gravel or coyotes howling that had excited Baxter, though he hoped he was wrong.

The late summer sun had dropped behind the mountains only a short while before, dimming the daylight just enough that headlights shone from the approaching car. They lit the driveway, then swung toward the house, brightening the windows in sequence, then the beveled glass cutout of the front door as the car parked out of sight to the left. He opened the door with sweaty palms and saw Sienna's Kia.

His eyes drank in the sight of her as she emerged from her car: Her long hair loose; her long legs in blue jeans; her turquoise blouse fluttering in the light breeze—the same blouse she'd worn three weeks ago, their first day together, when he'd taken her riding out to the cabin. She was heartbreakingly beautiful, but it was the person inside he would mourn losing if she was only here to tell him not to bother speaking to her on Saturday.

One chance. He was getting one chance to win her back tonight, and he was going to give it his all.

Sienna looked up and saw him waiting for her in the doorway. Her stride hitched for a moment, and then she strode on confidently. Baxter ran to meet her and danced around her feet. She reached down to pet him, never taking her eyes from Troy as she climbed the porch stairs to meet him.

"You asked me to come over so you could explain." She stopped well short of him on the wide porch. "Here I am."

There she was. Only a few feet from him, though it felt like a mile. Too far away physically and emotionally for him to sweep her into his arms, like he wished he could.

"I'm really glad you came." The dark wings of his old doubts and fears battered at him: He hadn't done as she'd asked and, therefore, she'd never get over her disappointment in him. He ignored the impulse to shut down emotionally and withdraw and pushed on. "Would you be willing to take a drive with me?"

"Let's just talk." She glanced at the heavy, wooden porch chairs to his right.

He looked out over the fields to the east. "Daylight's going to fade pretty quickly and there's something I'd like to show you."

"If you're thinking of taking me for another horseback ride…"

The memory of her riding Willie—swaying in the saddle and clenching at the saddle horn—brought a poignant smile to his lips. "No. No horses. We can take my truck."

She glanced again at the chairs, seeming to wage some internal war, then tossed her hands up in resignation. "Okay. Fine."

"It's unlocked if you want to go ahead and get in. I'll grab my keys." He whistled for Baxter to go inside and pulled his keys from the key ring near the coatrack. Hope tried to swim to the surface of his muddled emotions.

Instead of heading off the property, he drove toward the hay barn and then to the right down a small, rough track.

"Are we going to the cabin?"

"Mmm-hmm."

Her pursed lips said she wanted to say more but refrained. Maybe she thought he was taking her out there to the first place Cole had kissed Kelli to try and woo her back. If he thought it stood a chance, he'd try it, but he had something else in mind.

The sky shifted from pale blue to steel gray to dove gray during the short, bumpy drive.

"Sorry about the road. Wagons going across the pasture will be a little bumpy too, but this road is worse. It's why I thought the wagons would be better for most people."

She didn't answer, no doubt picturing plain, undecorated wagons headed to an empty field. He stopped trying to make conversation and endured the rest of the ten-minute drive in silence. He'd just have to wait and hope.

They came around a curve in the road and the cabin came into sight. Sienna gripped the grab bar above the window and pulled herself upright, staring at the field, her face opening in wonder. He parked by the cabin and came around to open her door for her, heartened when she took his offered hand.

"Oh, Troy," she said.

CHAPTER THIRTY-ONE

FROM THE MOMENT he'd opened the ranch house door, Sienna's emotions had been all over the map. Kelli and her mother had tipped the scales and had gotten her to come to the ranch to listen to his explanation, but she'd arrived with shields up…right until the moment he stood in front of her. And there he'd been: Handsome and brave, fun and kind. Someone who shared her need for excitement and challenge. Someone who loved her.

She'd lamented the fact they were so opposite in the way they approached goals and tasks, and then she'd wondered, really, in the face of everything else, if it mattered all that much. Standing there on the porch, seeing her own sadness and longing mirrored in his eyes, her desires and fears had shouted at each other so loudly that she'd hardly heard anything he said.

Instead of sitting on the porch, where she could keep her distance and leave when he'd said what he wanted to say, they'd driven down a rough dirt road. It hadn't taken long for her to realize he was bringing her to the cabin, to the wedding site, and she'd spent the rest of the drive trying to puzzle out why. Kelli had told her that she and Cole were okay with informal, meaning if Sienna could let go of needing everything done just so, maybe she and Troy could find their way back to a second chance. *Maybe.* Did he think he could pull something off in the next twenty-four hours that would make her forgive him for breaking his promise? And if he could, would she? She didn't know.

The drive had been excruciating. So close to him physically and so far emotionally. He'd tried to make conversation, but her thoughts had roiled too intensely to answer. *Had* she been too critical and judgmental? Should she give him another chance, or would she just be prolonging their misery?

Was her father right or was her mother?

And then the cabin had come into sight. Far from the bare field she expected, a wonder had unfolded before her. She pulled on the grab bar and sat up straighter, unable to believe what she was seeing. Troy parked, then came around to her side to help her out and still she couldn't stop staring.

The field looked gorgeous.

Hay bales had been laid end to end to form

two rows of seating with an aisle between. Thick, clean, colorful horse blankets covered the tops to make the soft grass hay even more comfortable. A huge canvas tent had been erected on the far side of the site, and she could just make out long, folding, plastic tables inside. To the side of the tent, a makeshift wooden dance floor had been hammered together.

In front of the cabin, wooden poles had been braced together to form an A-frame arch, and garlands of silk roses, ivy and baby's breath wound around them. The porch banister and doorframe of the cabin were decorated likewise. Sparkling fairy lights hung everywhere: down the door flaps of the tent and threading through all the artificial flowers. She spotted tiny battery or solar packs at the base of each strand and was amazed the lights were bright enough to shine like little stars even in the early twilight.

"I can't believe it, Troy. How did you do all this?" She turned to him in amazement. Her eyes had grown moist again, but she hoped her smile let him know they were happy tears.

Instead of mirroring her happiness, his blue eyes still held trepidation. "I didn't."

He turned to her, as open in his body language as his words. "I asked you to trust me, but I also told you this wasn't going to be my strength. There are a lot of talented people around here, though, and Kelli and Cole are deeply embedded in the community. Between the two of them, there's hardly anybody they don't know in Burgess. This was what I had in mind that day at the hospital when I offered to take over. Once I got home and started making phone calls, everybody wanted to help."

"You did this two weeks ago?" she said on a breath that came out heavy with guilt. Just like her father, she'd judged and been critical. She'd broken his trust by checking up on him. And the way she'd spoken to him...

"Well, again, I didn't exactly *do* it." He sounded like someone in a twelve-step program making certain there was no holding back or justification when they came clean. "I knew there were only a couple of weeks to get things done, so I made sure all the categories on your list were covered. By the time I left for the fire, everything was underway, but I asked Dustin to keep an eye on the progress. Folks had already run their ideas by me so that I could coordinate things and still keep as much of this as possible a surprise for Kelli. And Cole too, hopefully. The wranglers have been trying to keep him away from the cabin, and when we were working cattle today he didn't give any indication he'd been out here. When I left him this afternoon, I rode out to make sure everything looked okay before I called you."

"Why didn't you tell me about this, Troy? I tried to get updates from you, and then you left for the fire, and when you came back I was so upset with you..." She trailed off in a swirl of emotions.

"You'd planned everything so meticulously. I figured if you knew I'd delegated it all that you'd worry about what everyone was doing and would try to take it all on yourself. You had so much on your plate already that I didn't want that for you."

He was right. She would never have trusted that many unknowns, and would probably have been angry with him for not doing it the way she'd planned. And, yes, she probably would have tried to take over everything herself and wouldn't have had time. And it would never have turned out a fraction as beautiful as this.

He continued before she could say any of that.

"At first, I thought it would be fine as long as I could keep you from finding out until the wedding. I hoped if I could keep it secret, that by the time you saw what had been done, you wouldn't mind *how* it got done. I realize now that I should have just done it your way."

"Troy, no—"

"Wait. Let me show you around first. Then you can tell me what you think."

She reached out and he enveloped her hand in his, twining their fingers together. They walked hand in hand as he pointed out the various details to her. The lights sparkled brighter as twilight deepened to dusk.

"Roberta Ines has a flower garden that's won the county garden club contest like six years in a row. See those milk jugs on the porch?" She turned to look at the tall, antique, metal containers. "She's bringing fresh flowers Saturday morning to fill them and to make arrangements for the tables in the tent. And I could hardly get her to stop talking about her plans for Kelli's bouquet."

He led her to the tent and stopped near the flaps. "This is our cow-camp tent. The wranglers brought it down from the meadow up on the mountain a couple of days ago. If we get rain or wind or something, we'll just do everything inside there. The wranglers were the ones who set up the hay bales too." He gestured toward the three tables near the back. "The Spicers brought those from their bingo club. We don't have a caterer, but most of the local guests are bringing potluck dishes. Two of the ranchers practically duked it out for the honor of bringing the main beef dish, so we're getting both brisket slices and shredded barbecue. And Sally, our cook, threatened me with bodily harm if I didn't allow her to make the wedding cake." He turned to her. "You haven't met Sally yet, have you? Well, trust me, she could deliver on the threat."

Still hand in hand, he led her out of the tent. "The wagons will get decorated tomorrow morning to match the cabin, and the band will set up in one once the guests are here. They're going to play acoustic."

He turned them toward the dance floor. It had been hammered together with so many different styles of lumber that it should have looked like a hodgepodge mess. Instead, as they drew closer, she could just make out in the fading light a uniquely beautiful, well-crafted quilt pattern of inlaid wood.

"We debated dancing in the field, but there are cow patties and gopher holes and uneven ground, so Dustin smoothed the area with the tractor and ranchers have been bringing spare lumber all week. Jace Heartford, you know him…?"

Sienna shook her head, reluctant to speak out loud before he finished. Everything here felt magical, as if an enchantment had transformed this meadow. Returning to ordinary banter could break the spell, like Cinderella at midnight or Orpheus looking back at Eurydice too soon.

Troy continued, unaware of her brimming emotions of wonder, joy…and so much love for him she thought her heart might burst.

"Jace runs a construction crew in the valley, but he's a heck of a carpenter. He dropped off some lumber, saw the wranglers fighting over how to lay it out and took over the project. I know it's not a proper dance floor, but I figured Cole and Kelli would rather have the reception here at the ranch instead of some banquet hall in Alamosa." He looked up at the nearly dark sky. "What else? Oh, they said they didn't need a rehearsal. I did ask on that one, but Cole said 'What's to rehearse? We show up and we get married.'" Sienna chuckled at his imitation. "I think even if they had wanted to, they wouldn't have had time to fit it in this week."

He looked around, checking to see if he'd missed anything, then gave a humble shrug, as if still unsure if he'd done enough. "Oh yeah, and Juan Escobar's wife is a really good photographer. Juan says she could have gone professional, but she didn't want to spoil it by turning it into a business. She's going to take the photos and do the prints as their wedding gift."

He looked around a final time, then took a deep breath and blew it out. Turning to face her, he took her other hand as well, like he'd done that night on her porch—the night of their first kiss.

"I've known from the start that you've had ideas about what you wanted for Kelli's wedding for a long time. Years. And if I could turn the clock back, I'd do this all exactly as you had it on your list. You trusted me to do that for you, and I didn't, and I understand you being mad at me. I know the wedding is in less than forty-eight hours, but you tell me what needs changing, and I'll get it done. For real, this time."

She huffed a half-laugh of incredulity. His brow furrowed again, with worry she saw, and she hurried to reassure him.

"Troy, I wouldn't change a single thing. This is incredible. It's gorgeous. It's everything I could have hoped for…no, it's more than I'd hoped for. Rental chairs and reception halls wouldn't hold a candle to this. I can't imagine anything more perfect or fitting for Kelli and Cole."

"Really?" he said. "You're not just saying that? I want things to be okay between us, and they won't be if there's anything here that you'll look back on with regret."

"I really mean it. This is beyond amazing, Troy. I'm so happy I feel like I'm about to burst." She imbued the words with every ounce of sincerity she could pour into them and watched his concern slowly evaporate in the relaxation in his face and shoulders. But there was more she needed to say.

"I'm the one who needs to apologize. I'm sorry that I was so rigid that you felt you couldn't explain your plan to me. This should have all been a conversation between us, not a fight. I try so hard not to be like my dad and not to be judgmental and inflexible, but I don't succeed as often as I'd like to." She let go of one of his hands to gesture around them. "You did what I need to learn how to do—not take everything on myself and not to think there's only one way to do things. You and Kelli and Cole and my mom are teaching me to be a better person. Can you forgive me for not trusting you and for being so hard on you when you were doing all this and fighting a forest fire on top of everything else?"

"You're forgiven," he said with a wry smile. "I think maybe we're both learning to let go of some old habits that are hard to change. So, we're okay then?"

Her chest ached from expanding with so many feelings. She willed all the love she felt to shine in her eyes. "We're more than okay."

There, under the first evening stars to emerge, surrounded by twinkling fairy lights and standing under the wedding arch, she tipped her head up for a kiss.

Troy obliged.

CHAPTER THIRTY-TWO

Saturday, August 15th

"DOING OKAY?" TROY SAID, sotto voce, at Cole's side. The wedding party faced the guests—all standing now—everyone watching as Kelli's father escorted her to the wedding arch and to Cole.

"Sure am," Cole answered.

Troy hadn't needed to ask. He'd heard of brides glowing—and Kelli certainly did—but he had to admit that Cole did as well. No sign of jitters, no hint of second thoughts for either of them.

He glanced past Cole and across the gap to Sienna, looking gorgeous. The pale pink bridesmaid's dress was belted at her narrow waist with a wide band of black fabric that ended in a big, flowery bow, and her dark hair had been caught up and pinned with a real flower arrangement that matched his boutonniere. She looked like a model out of a magazine, tall and elegant. Her makeup perfect. Dark eyes shining from beneath dark lashes as she watched her friend coming up the grassy walk between the hay-bale rows. As if she felt his gaze on her, Sienna turned her head. The joy in her smile and the light in her eyes shifted from happiness for Kelli to a look meant just for him. It warmed him like sun on his skin.

Kelli joined Cole under the arch, and her father patted her hand before placing it in Cole's. The bride and groom beamed at each other, then turned to the preacher. Even Troy felt a flush of sentimentality at his little brother in his knee-length suit jacket and black hat, and Kelli in her white western dress with fringe down to her white cowboy boots. The guests sat.

The ceremony was short and went off without a hitch. Baxter, in his black bow tie, didn't run off with Kelli's ring tied to his collar when Troy retrieved it to hand it to Cole. Even Tillie, Kelli's shepherd, behaved on the leash Rikki held until Sienna removed Cole's ring and handed it to Kelli. The couple repeated the vows they'd written and then, to heartfelt applause, shared their first kiss as husband and wife. Chris and his band played lively music as the newlyweds left the arch and the crowd surged forward with congratulations.

Troy crooked his elbow and Sienna took his

arm as he escorted her away against the tide of well-wishers. Dustin escorted Rikki—still leading Tillie—and Cole's friend Derek took Rikki's young niece's hand.

Troy figured they'd congratulate his brother and Kelli later, when they could find a quiet moment together. Meanwhile, Sienna seemed content to follow him to a vacated hay bale, where she plopped down as if she'd just run to the field from the ranch house. He'd never seen her at a loss for words, but for the moment, she seemed too filled with emotion to speak.

"I missed you yesterday," he said.

She gave him a Cheshire cat smile and said, "I missed you too. Althoooough—" she waggled her eyebrows "—a mani, pedi and massage spa day at the hot springs with Kelli did kinda take the sting out of it."

"I'm so easily replaced."

"Never. And without you, none of this would have happened." She spread her hands to indicate the whole of the wedding site. "You're the reason that both Kelli and I were able to take the day off and relax together."

"Well, you earned it after what I put you through."

"Nope. I put myself through it, and I didn't need to." She scanned the field from the tent where guests piled their plates high, across the makeshift dance floor, to the fully decorated cabin. "*Perfect*," she said again. "The decorations, the ceremony. Kelli's dad walking her down the aisle..." She sighed with pleasure as she shook her head. "Just everything." She straightened as a new thought struck her. "And did you *see* that cake that Sally made?" She made "holy cow" eyes at him.

"I did," he said, even though she knew he had, since he'd spent the morning helping set up the buffet in the tent as well as myriad other details. "I knew she'd come through for them, but I wasn't expecting *that*."

Four tiers of cream-colored icing with peach-colored roses like a master pastry chef might make, with lacy edging and some tiny silver beads she'd assured him were edible. He'd broken into a cold sweat at the thought of transporting it over the bumpy ground, but they'd somehow managed to get it here intact.

"And the food." She gestured to the tent, then looked up at the light clouds filtering the hot sun and lifted both hands toward the sky. "And the weather. Kelli's bouquet. And the clothes!" She gave an elegant game-show hand flourish, first at herself and then at him. "The groomsmen looked wonderful, Troy. You were so right that day we went shopping together. The white shirts and black vests and silver embroidery with the silver bolo ties were perfect without jackets. Though I gotta say, you especially rocked the look." She gave him a wink.

"I could say the same about you. I could hardly take my eyes off you. I was afraid I was going to miss my cue to get the ring." She smiled, and if he wasn't mistaken, blushed. He shifted on the hay bale, sliding one knee up to face her better. "So, just to be clear, you are completely and totally happy with the way the wedding turned out, right?"

She looked surprised, and perhaps slightly worried, as if wondering if he still thought things weren't entirely right between them. "Completely and totally. For real."

"Not a single thing you would want different or better?"

She narrowed her dark eyes at him, starting to suspect something up his sleeve. "Not a single thing," she said with a question in her voice.

"Okay. Just making sure before I cash in on that promise."

"What promise?" she said, looking genuinely perplexed.

"The one you made to me in Albuquerque when I took over the wedding planning. The one where you promised that on our next four days off together, you'd go anywhere I picked."

Her eyes flew wide. "With everything that's

happened in the last week or so, I completely forgot about that." She straightened with mock seriousness. "I did promise that, and I always keep my promises." Relaxing again she smiled and said, "Great, what did you have in mind?"

"Did you also forget the second half of the promise was that you don't know where we're going or what we're doing? You pack a bag and we take off. No planning. Everything spontaneous."

"Not even a hint if I should bring scuba gear or ice axes and crampons?"

"Not even." He couldn't resist. "Trust me?" he said with a wink.

She laughed out loud. "Yes, Troy Tyler, I trust you. Get ready for the new me. Spontaneous Sienna."

"Pleased to meet you, Spontaneous." He held out his hand and they shook. "So, by my calculations, with my six-day coming up and the comp day you're due for overtime this next Thursday, that'll give us Thursday through Sunday off together."

"I'm in."

The band started playing a slow, country love song, George Strait's "I Cross My Heart." The wedding song. Together they watched Kelli and Cole swirl gracefully across the dance floor.

After a few bars of music, other couples began to join them.

"Shall we?" Troy asked.

"Yes, please."

He stood and held out his hand to help her up. They walked to the dance floor hand-in-hand. He could hardly believe it. They were finally together with no reservations and no worries. The world had never felt more right to him, like it had been spinning off-kilter his entire life and suddenly found its proper axis.

They stepped up onto the boards and he took her in his arms. He should have known she'd be a wonderful dancer. They moved across the floor to the love ballad like a couple who'd been dancing together for decades. He drew her closer to him and knew in that moment, that from this day forward, he'd never again want to let her go.

With his mouth close to her ear, he took one last chance. "I love you, Sienna."

She turned her head to meet his eyes and the expression in the depths of her dark eyes filled him with joy.

"I love you too, Troy."

EPILOGUE

Wednesday, August 26th

SIENNA PULLED UP to the ranch house and parked. Kelli met her at the door, and they exchanged a big hug after not seeing each other for the past week.

Sienna had only been inside the ranch house a couple of times before, always in the daytime. Now, with it being eight o'clock at night and dark outside, the house looked like something from a postcard or a country-living magazine, all lit up like a Christmas tree. Even though Sienna—along with Troy and Cole, Dustin and Billy—had helped Kelli to move in over the couple of days following the wedding, it was going to take Sienna a little time to adjust to the fact that Kelli actually lived here now. In Troy's childhood home. On one of the largest ranches in Colorado. Living the dream with *her husband*, Cole.

Once inside, though, she could see all the small touches that showed Kelli had integrated seamlessly. A vase her parents had given her years ago sat filled with flowers on a windowsill. A lovely painting of a draft horse in harness that Kelli had bought in Wyoming now hung centered over the huge, stone fireplace, and her old cast-iron pan had been added to the beautiful copper pans above the kitchen island. She and Cole were beginning to nest, and it made her ridiculously happy for her friend. It also made what she needed to say a tiny bit easier.

"I know," Kelli said, watching her take in the new setting, "it still feels like a fairy tale."

"Did you find a renter yet for your old place?"

"I did! I can hardly believe it rented so fast, but they're a nice, younger couple who work at the college and they can move in next month. They don't mind the arrangement with the small-animal clinic behind the house and clients coming and going. But really, with taking care of the cattle here and my recent increase in livestock clients, I'm going to be cutting back there, anyway."

They made their way to the couch where they both took a seat in front of the stone coffee table. The table was covered end to end with the wedding photos Kelli had wanted help going through.

"I'm so glad you texted me from the airport last week, so at least I knew you were going to LA, but I've been dying to hear about your trip. Troy was at work yesterday and then I was gone all day today, and he and Cole have been out taking care of a waterline break to one of the stock tanks since I got home. And you! You were all kinds of cagey when I called you last night." Kelli locked gazes with her. "So," she said emphatically, "tell me all about it. What did you do? How did it go?" She lifted her eyebrows meaningfully with that last question, and Sienna laughed.

"It was good. It was really good." Sienna crossed and uncrossed her legs, anxious to tell her best friend everything, but at the same time hesitant. "I didn't know where we were going until we got to the airport in Albuquerque and he finally handed me my ticket. I've always wanted to go to LA, and I guess I must've mentioned that to him at some point. When we got there, I loved it as much as I've always imagined I would." Sienna stared past Kelli a moment, out the darkened living room window, seeing palm trees and beaches.

"He didn't let me plan anything or look anything up. We drove from LA up the coast to Santa Barbara. Anything we saw that we wanted to try, we stopped and did it. We snorkeled in the ocean and went on a whale-watching boat. We found a rooftop bar and danced until closing. One of the locals there told us about a swimming hole in a canyon, so we stopped at it on our way up to Santa Barbara. We went to the biggest farmers market I've ever seen, and we took a hang-gliding lesson. We wanted to go hike in Joshua Tree, but it was a bit far away since we only had three full days there."

Kelli shook her head in wonder. "That all sounds amazing. If you like it out there that much, maybe you can plan another trip so you can hike Joshua Tree."

Sienna bit her lip. She hadn't wanted to tackle this quite yet.

"What?" Kelli said. "What's that look?"

"We're moving there."

"You're what?" Kelli practically shouted. "I… sorry, I didn't mean it to come out like that, but it seems like you've barely had time to think about this, much less make a decision that big."

"Yep. Spontaneous Sienna. That's what they call me now." She laughed. "No, I've thought about moving to California for so long that it feels like it's always been the plan, just one I never thought would actually happen. But now, with my mom and Dan getting serious, I don't feel like I have to stay here to look out for her anymore. And Troy says, at thirty, it's pretty much now or never for him if he wants to join a Hotshot crew. There's one just north of Pasadena and another by Santa Barbara, so we stopped at both and he picked up applications. The one closest to LA seemed really interested when they learned about his fire department and wildland experience. They gave him a mini interview on the spot. I got in touch with the 911 office in Pasadena, and they practically fell over themselves trying to get an application into my hands."

"Wow. So you guys are—" Kelli seemed to be struggling to take it all in "—moving in together?" She tried so hard not to sound judgmental that Sienna laughed again.

"No. Spontaneous Sienna isn't quite that spontaneous yet. And neither is Troy. We've been dating less than a month. Anyway, we found a condo building that wouldn't be a bad commute for either of us if the jobs work out, and we put in applications to rent two units there. If the condos don't work out, there are a bazillion other places. We'd probably have both ended up moving out there anyway, but doing this together is so much better. I've got to confess, though, I think this might be it. The real deal."

Her friend seemed at a loss for words. "Wow," she said finally. "I'm so, so happy for you... about all of this. I couldn't even imagine living somewhere that big. This ranch—the dark sky, the absolute quiet at night unless the coyotes are howling—this is everything I could ever want, but I could totally see you being happy in Southern California." She drew back into the cushions. "Wait, you already have applications in? When are you thinking of moving?"

Sienna chewed her lower lip. "The end of next month." Kelli made big eyes at her. "It's still a month away," she said. "Besides, you and Cole have each other, and if I know you, you're going to be twice as busy soon with little Tylers running around. I can call all the time, and Troy and I already made a pact that we're going to come back here for Christmas. That's only four months from now. Are you mad?"

"Mad? Seriously? By the sound of things, you're going to be my husband's sister-in-law in no time at all. Better than that, you sound happy. Happier than I've ever heard you. Cole and I talked a lot about you guys when you were gone…" She threw her hands up. "I know, sorry. But it's no surprise it was on our minds, right? Sienna, this is everything we'd hoped for you both."

Right on cue, the front door opened, and Troy and Cole walked in. Sienna soaked in the vision of her boyfriend in his cowboy persona, complete with mud-spattered jeans, cowboy boots and hat.

"Did you get it fixed?" Kelli asked.

"We did," Cole said, using the boot puller to

remove his muddy boots. "Dustin had the break dug up already, and Troy came up with an idea for a temporary bypass while the repair sets up."

True to his new resolutions, ever since the wedding, Troy had been helping Cole more on his days off. He must have enjoyed the work, based on how often he talked about it, but Sienna guessed it was the sense of involvement in the family ranch after all these years that made him so animated.

Stocking-footed, Troy came over and sat with her, putting an arm around her shoulders and pulling her against him.

Sienna tipped her head up to meet his eyes. "I told her."

"I told Cole while we were working."

Cole perched on the arm of Kelli's chair and took her hand.

"I'm really happy for you both," he said.

"I think you and Troy are going to be amazing together," Kelli added.

Sienna turned to Troy again. She could feel her smile shining in her eyes. He held her gaze, then bent for a quick kiss.

"So do I," Sienna said, turning back to Kelli.

And she did. She really did.

* * * * *

Don't miss the next book
in Eliza D. Collins's
A Tillacos Ranch Romance miniseries,
coming November 2026
from Harlequin Heartwarming